Praise for Mary Clearman Blew's *Jackalope Dreams*

"[*Jackalope Dreams*] gives us an example—if any is required—of why fiction is still necessary and what it uniquely offers. . . . Sentences seethe with urgent, unhurried energy, and the description of the land the author so clearly loves is in service of the story, not showing off. You come to care deeply about these people, caught between an uncapturable past and an uncertain future. *Jackalope Dreams* is a small masterpiece."—**Paul Wilner**, *Los Angeles Times Book Review*

"Engrossing. . . . Blew gets so much right, from her beautiful, clear prose to her sharp humor to her rich characterizations. . . . *Jackalope Dreams* satisfies."—**Jenny Shank, NewWest.net**

"Nothing less than stunning: a story beautifully told, characters richly conceived and developed, lessons subtly delivered. . . . It is the poetry and preciseness of Blew's writing that set *Jackalope Dreams* apart from others of its ilk. Hers is storytelling of the highest order."
—**Sherry Devlin**, *Missoulian*

"[The author has a] distinctive narrative voice and knack for description."—***Publishers Weekly***

"Blew knows how to fuse the rugged with the delicate—some readers may be reminded of *Plainsong* author Kent Haruf's no-nonsense approach."—**John Mark Eberhart**, *Kansas City Star*

"A candid exploration of values in transition, caught between a tradition that has become elegy and a future transformed by canny, self-sufficient women. Itself a 'long intense shiver,' it forces us to reconsider issues of honor, violence, technology, independence, responsibility—and love. Add Mary Blew's name triumphantly to the canon of essential novelists of the new West."—**Judith Kitchen, author of *The House on Eccles Road***

"Mary Blew has written a tough, true, and starkly beautiful novel about change and tradition in the cowboy West. Her characters are authentic, her story is gripping, and her writing is splendid."
—**Annick Smith, author of *Homestead* and *In This We Are Native***

SWEEP OUT THE ASHES

A Novel

Mary Clearman Blew

UNIVERSITY OF NEBRASKA PRESS | LINCOLN

© 2019 by the Board of Regents of the
University of Nebraska. All rights reserved. ∞

Library of Congress Cataloging-in-Publication Data
Names: Blew, Mary Clearman, 1939– author.
Title: Sweep out the ashes: a novel /
by Mary Clearman Blew.
Description: Lincoln: University of
Nebraska Press, [2019]
Identifiers: LCCN 2018055531
ISBN 9781496216427 (cloth: alk. paper)
ISBN 9781496217189 (epub)
ISBN 9781496217196 (mobi)
ISBN 9781496217202 (pdf)
Classification: LCC PS3552.L46 S94 2019
DDC 813/.54—dc23 LC record available at
https://lccn.loc.gov/2018055531

Set in Minion Pro by Mikala R. Kolander.

For the Palouse Writers—all members, past and present

SWEEP OUT THE ASHES

1

Diana Karnov stood at the classroom window, looking out over the faculty parking lot in the early twilight of Montana's northern latitude. Beyond the parking lot stretched the frostbitten brown grass of the Lawn, ringed by a glow of lights like a barrier between the campus and the open prairie. As the afternoon faded into nightfall, her own reflection emerged in the glass like a ghost of herself superimposed upon an unforgiving landscape.

When she turned, the brightly illuminated classroom seemed to float before her with its cargo of students scribbling to finish their essay tests by five o'clock and escape into their weekend. She didn't wonder at their eagerness to finish. Whose bright idea had it been to schedule the Westward Movement seminar from one until five on Friday afternoons? Her chairman, Abe Dennison's, she supposed. In a couple of weeks darkness would fall even earlier as the country went from daylight to standard time for the first time in the two years since the OPEC oil embargo of 1973 had spiked fuel prices.

"Time," said Diana with relief.

Fifteen faces lifted from their concentration, as drained as though their bluebooks contained their souls instead of their dutiful regurgitations of Diana's lectures. The spell broken, the classroom returned to the normal small sounds of chairs scraping back and textbooks gathered. Diana posted herself by the door and collected their bluebooks as the students filed out.

The black-haired girl who had been watching the clock struggled out of her seat with her coat half on and her face wet and red. She tried to walk past Diana without looking at her, but Diana caught her.

"Where's your bluebook?"

The girl would not look up, but she allowed Diana to extract the damp booklet from her hand.

Her answer to the first essay question began predictably: "Women played a greater role in the Westward Movement than is generally known—without women—" Here her pen had dwindled and balked. One word had been inked out heavily. The rest of the bluebook was empty.

"Couldn't you remember anything else?"

"I guess not." The girl's swollen face revealed only her misery.

Diana knew she shouldn't think of her as a girl. As a feminist she was trying to break herself of using the word. And even apolitically it didn't denote this poor baffled woman who must be close to Diana's own age, which was twenty-eight, and whose face at the back of the classroom for the past four weeks reflected whatever blows the world must have dealt her.

"If you don't understand the lectures, you can make an office appointment. But you're going to have to take some initiative."

"I—" the eyes fell—"couldn't get started."

Diana gave up and added the girl's bluebook to the stack in her arms. "It's your grade. Your money, for that matter."

She supposed Abe Dennison would have had a fit if he'd heard her. The faculty were supposed to be encouraging students to stay enrolled, especially the so-called mature ones. But Diana treated her students as she had been treated as an undergraduate at Seattle University and, later, as a graduate student at the University of Texas. The students were adults, after all. They were accountable for themselves, and they needed to learn to think for themselves. She was turning toward her office but paused when she saw the girl's eyes brimming over.

"Cheryl—you're Cheryl, aren't you? I really do want to help you if I can."

But Cheryl, if that was her name, dashed the tears from her eyes and glared at Diana. "What can you do? You don't know anything!"

she cried and ran for the red Exit sign at the end of the darkened corridor.

Stung by the accusation, *you don't know anything,* from a young woman who had not managed to finish a complete sentence on her midterm exam, Diana thought of all the mistakes she had made on this strange campus and wondered what she had done wrong this time. Surely an offer of help was not an insult in Versailles, Montana, where the local pronunciation was Ver-*sails* and the customs were incomprehensible. Diana sighed and continued to her office.

The corridor was dark, Abe Dennison had explained to her, because after the oil embargo crippled the country's power grid, the college administrators had turned off all nonessential lights on campus and never turned them on again. Diana's footsteps echoed ahead of her. Everyone else on the third floor must have locked up and gone home, even Nelda, the history department secretary, who usually stayed long enough after five to pour Diana a last cup of coffee when her class ended.

Diana felt her way through the warren of history offices and unlocked her office door. Turned on the light, laid down the bluebooks, and sat at her desk. It was the time of day she missed smoking the most. But she liked the quiet, when the students had scattered and her colleagues had gone home to early suppers and she could let her thoughts wander without her guard up. In the full dark of night, her uncurtained office window became a mirror where Diana's eyes met the eyes of a young woman sitting behind a desk in a gray coat and skirt who wore her red-gold hair combed back from her face and pinned in a tight knot. A professional-looking woman, surely. If only she didn't feel so insubstantial.

Why had she thought that coming to Versailles might—what— *help her find herself?* Whatever that meant. She'd had the same feeling when she left Seattle to travel to Texas for her graduate studies. At least her lingering shadow-memories—the odor of gasoline, adults singing a hymn, and herself playing with other children under a hot sun—had seemed to draw her to Texas, where she'd found nothing of herself.

Diana sighed at the irony. She'd stolen her birth certificate from her great-aunt Tatiana that past September, just before she left Seattle for Versailles. If she'd seen it three years earlier, she would have had a clue to follow in Texas.

A tap at her office door brought her back from her thoughts. Damn. She supposed her office light showed under the door. Cheryl, perhaps, returning to make amends? What could Diana say to her?

"Come in," she called, and the door opened, not on Cheryl, but on a tall blonde woman whom Diana knew by sight and who taught in the English department at the other end of the corridor.

"Dr. Karnov? I was just leaving and saw your light. We met at the faculty retreat."

Diana supposed they had, but she had been introduced to so many strangers that their names had blurred. Fortunately the woman continued.

"I'm Ramona Stillinger. I've been meaning to drop by and get acquainted with the other woman on our corridor. You're Dr. Diana Karnov."

"Yes," said Diana. The old panic was rising that she would blurt out the wrong thing. Was she supposed to address this woman as Dr. Stillinger? People at Versailles State College were touchy about their titles, and those with doctorates, like Abe Dennison, looked down on those who held mere master's degrees.

He may think he's a big fish, but he's in a small pond, Tatiana had sneered in her last letter.

Ramona Stillinger seated herself with a confidence Diana longed for. Perhaps she was a woman who could not fathom herself out of place, and she certainly was expensively dressed in a dark wool dress with a fashionably long skirt and heeled shoes and pearls. She was older than Diana, in her forties, Diana guessed.

"So how are you finding life in Versailles?"

"It takes some getting used to," Diana admitted.

"Good luck! I've lived here twenty years, and I've never gotten used to it."

Ramona Stillinger's voice had lost its light social tone, and Diana hesitated. She'd never learned to read other people's moods and nuances, but something lay beneath this woman's surface poise.

"The winters are the worst. It gets dark so early."

"It does get dark early," Diana said, sounding in her own ears as though she were prepared, if asked, to rescind her agreement.

Ramona Stillinger nodded, and they both looked at Diana's office window. Through Ramona's reflection and her own, Diana picked out the row of lights that guarded the campus and let her eyes follow the headlights of a vehicle on the street beyond the Lawn. Someone going somewhere.

"What I'd hoped," said Ramona Stillinger, and her voice was light again, "was that I could persuade you to meet me at the Stockman's for a drink this evening."

"The Stockman's?"

"It's one of the bars on Main Street. You can't miss it. It's usually quiet, and there's a decent parking lot behind it. I want to hear all about the way those crusty old guys in the history department are treating you. Who'd have thought it? A *woman* teaching in the history department? With a face and a figure like yours, they must be feeling quite the shocks to their systems."

Shocks to their systems? At this month's department meeting, the three older professors had watched her covertly while Abe Dennison openly let his eyes wander over her. And it was true that, except for the nurses in the nursing department and a woman who taught typing and shorthand in the business department, Diana and Ramona Stillinger were the only women faculty on campus. So why not get acquainted with Ramona Stillinger? Maybe she could give Diana some insight about this strange campus. And at least Diana would have an excuse not to sit alone grading test papers.

"When I began here, I had to listen to the men discussing whether a woman really was capable of teaching college-level English," said

Ramona Stillinger, smiling a little. "I hope the historians aren't wondering that about you."

Diana remembered the first day she had met her morning survey class and found, scrawled across an otherwise unblemished blackboard, *Do you think she's burned her bra yet?*

Had one of her students written it? Or one of her new colleagues? Diana had steeled herself not to react, but to lay her books and notes on the table, call roll for the first time, and distribute syllabi. She would be damned if she would reveal her embarrassment. She hadn't erased the blackboard until the class period came to an end and the students had filed out.

"So what about the Stockman's?"

"All right," Diana said, and thought she should say more. "I'd be happy to," she added. "What time were you thinking?"

"I thought seven-thirty? I can't stay too late. I've got two teenagers at home babysitting a seven-year-old."

* * *

Diana listened to Ramona Stillinger's footsteps receding down the corridor toward the stairs. She had plenty of time before—whatever it was, her wine date, she guessed—so she could make herself a grilled cheese sandwich at home and change out of her teaching clothes into jeans and a sweater.

If *home* was the word. Because the president of the college had retired and moved to Arizona, and the acting president, drawn from the administrative ranks of the college, lived in his own family home in a residential neighborhood in Versailles, the dean had arranged for Diana to live in the vacant president's mansion without paying rent or utilities, as an unofficial caretaker. A search was on for a new president, and in the meantime Diana inhabited six thousand square feet of scantily furnished space and was coming to know the small creaks of settling beams, the brush of a branch on her bedroom window, the waking of the furnace, and the faint hiss of air through the vents.

The mansion overlooked the town of Versailles from the crest of a low hill that lay directly below the flight path of the twice-daily commuter airline service, morning and evening. Diana had come to welcome the sound of the commuter plane arriving and departing, dependable as an alarm clock, as a reminder of the world continuing beyond Versailles. Also, the more distant crashes of metal that the dean explained were the sounds of coupling freight cars from the railroad roundhouse.

Coupling. What a word.

"Versailles State College? *That* Versailles State? In northern Montana?" Tatiana had shouted last summer, when Diana told her she was accepting the vacancy. "You can't do this! You belong here in Seattle!"

"It's a job," Diana tried to explain. "An unexpected death—they need someone right away. But I'll have a temporary assistant professorship, which can be renewed, and I'll be teaching basic survey classes, and they've promised me an upper-level seminar in the Westward Movement, and I can work on my book."

Tatiana was angrier than Diana ever had seen her. She had jutted her jaw and bared her teeth, as though to bite Diana's plans in the bud. "You want to *bury* yourself in that remote small town? In *northern Montana?* Do you know what the *weather* will be like? Do you have any idea what the *community* will be like? No! Just admit it, Diana! You want to go to Versailles to look for that drunken vagrant!"

Well, yes, she might have admitted to Tatiana. *When I couldn't find a trace of myself in Texas, the drunken vagrant is the only clue I've got left.*

But Diana couldn't have explained to Tatiana about the shadow-memories that perplexed her. As for Versailles in northern Montana, Tatiana could have had no idea what the weather and the community would be like, Tatiana who called Seattle stultifying and unsophisticated. Diana herself could not have imagined life under a dome of sky and low horizons, or her sense of being cut off by distance and weather from anywhere ideas were being discussed and issues argued.

True, the Milk River flowed east through town on its way to join the Missouri, and a paved highway ran east and west, paralleling the railroad tracks, into open prairie in both directions, and another paved highway angled south toward Great Falls, which could be called a city. It was even possible to drive a few miles north toward Canada on pavement before the highway turned to gravel. And even, although Diana never had driven out to it, the small airport.

Now, thinking about Tatiana's threats, Diana became aware of the faraway sound of an airplane above her. She went to her window and watched the tiny lights moving across the night sky. It wasn't the right time for the regular evening flight. Probably it was a private plane coming in for a landing.

Well. She gathered her students' bluebooks into her book bag, shrugged into her jacket, and turned off her office light. Felt her way down the dark corridor toward the red Exit sign.

2

The bitter wind of October whined at the corners of downtown roofs and blew trash down the streets. Diana's students said they could get snow any day now. Already they had had a hard freeze.

Diana turned on Main Street between clots of leaves from last night's rain and sleet. She located the Stockman's by its neon cowboy riding a bronco over its door and glanced at the couple standing under the cowboy. A black man with a white girl—woman, Diana corrected herself—a pairing rarely seen in Seattle or even on the university campus of Austin, Texas. She wondered how this couple was received in Versailles, and she hoped for the best for them, although for some reason she was reminded of the signals she had missed from the student named Cheryl. Had Cheryl's face been blotched and purpled because she had been bruised?

Diana drove around the block and pulled into the parking lot, where she turned off her headlights and locked her MG Midget. She knew locking a ragtop was futile, but still. Shivering, she picked her way around puddles in the near-dark and found the Stockman's back door. It was unexpectedly heavy, and she had to use both hands to pull it open on a warm dark space with a glitter of reflection in the mirror behind the bar, hunched backs and shoulders on bar stools, and a scattering of tables, each with a lighted candle in a brass holder. She spotted Ramona Stillinger by her hair, pale and shining above the candle's flame.

"Dr. Karnov!"

Diana had changed clothes, but Ramona Stillinger still wore the dark dress she had been wearing when she knocked on Diana's office door, and she had the same immaculate every-hair-in-place appearance. The pearls. In this room where, now that Diana's eyes had adjusted to the dim lighting, she saw paintings of cowboys and cattle vying with neon beer ads for wall space, Ramona Stillinger looked as misplaced as Diana felt.

"So! You found the place!"

The barmaid bounced out of the haze of smoke and glittering reflections around the bar—"Get you ladies something?"

Ramona tapped her empty wine glass, and Diana, after a moment's pause, asked for a vodka collins, which would come in a tall glass and which she could sip and make it last. Immediately she was stricken—had she ordered a drink too sophisticated for the Stockman's? But the barmaid just nodded, as though she filled orders for vodka collinses every day, and bounced away.

"So Dr. Karnov, where are you from?"

The title again. And she still wasn't sure how to address this woman.

"Please. I'm Diana," she said, "and I grew up in Seattle."

"Oh! A big change for you! How could you give up Seattle? When it's so vibrant! I've been reading about the waterfront restaurants, the boutiques, the Pike Place Market! I'd give anything—do your parents still live there? Are they concerned about your being here?"

"They're both deceased," said Diana. It was her standard answer, and it might well be true, for all she knew. She added unnecessarily, "I was brought up by my two great-aunts." Tatiana and Maria never had permitted her to visit the vibrant Seattle scene, and they weren't worrying about her, but furiously waiting for her to give up her dream of a life of her own and come back to the silence of the Karnov house.

The barmaid brought their drinks. "You want to start a tab, don't you, Mrs. Stillinger?"

So that was one dilemma solved. "And where are you from, Mrs. Stillinger?"

"Do call me Ramona. That campus is so formal. It might as well be the Versailles that's in France. *Ver-sigh*. It took me forever to learn to say Ver-*sails*. And forever to learn all their rules. And how the men look down on me as a lowly adjunct! At least you've got your PhD. Oh, God, I can't believe how long I've lived here. Oh—where am I from? I grew up in Los Angeles. So a huge change for me. The emptiness, the wind—the wind never stops blowing, did you know that?—country music on the radio station, and just the two TV channels—If I'd known, I'm not sure I would have married Con. And then these past two years, what with that stupid oil embargo, and lines at the gas pumps, and lights being turned off, as if it isn't dark enough! But you, Diana. How did you happen to come here? You're not married, are you?"

Diana started to answer, but the barmaid was back, setting fresh drinks before them. "These are on Chris."

A burly man wearing a navy parka and a ball cap followed the barmaid.

Grinning, he set a sweating can of Coke on Diana's and Ramona's table and took a chair without being asked.

"Mrs. S," he greeted Ramona.

"Chris," she replied.

He turned to study Diana. His eyes were like blue marbles, and what Diana at first thought was a perpetual smirk was probably a squint.

"Diana Karnov," Ramona supplied. "She's a new professor at the college. Diana, this is Chris Beaudry. He's the number one badge on the Versailles police force."

His eyes were on Diana. "You're a professor? You sure don't look like one."

"You're out of uniform tonight, Chris. Off duty?"

"We—ll. Never entirely. But I think I might swap this crap for a real drink."

He glanced back at the drinkers at the bar. Some of them, Diana thought, were students. Maybe some faculty. They all knew who Chris Beaudry was. It was written in the lines of their backs and shoulders and the stiff way they resisted turning to look at him. In campus talk she never heard his name. He was always referred to as the Number One Badge. *You wanna watch out for the Number One Badge*, she heard one student warn another.

Ramona was smiling her social smile. Chris Beaudry had thrown his arm across the back of her chair, and her eyes and mouth and hands flirted up at him. But very measured. She was Mrs. Stillinger.

"Where's Con? He said something about heading for Calgary this weekend."

"Yes," said Ramona, still with her lovely smile. "He may have a buyer for the farm in Canada."

A crash sounded as a barstool was tipped over by a kid lurching toward the men's room. Diana recognized him as a student in one of her survey classes as everyone turned to look and then shrug.

"It's that Jarvis boy. He's drunk again," said Ramona.

His name was spelled *Gervais*, Diana remembered. The first day of class she had pronounced it *Szcher-vais*, and he had corrected her. *We say Jarvis.*

"You know how to get a drunk on his feet?" Beaudry asked Diana. "No."

He reached across the table and caught her by the hand. "What you do is bend his thumb back toward his wrist, like this—"

He squeezed her thumb, and Diana winced.

"Hurts, doesn't it."

"Yes," she said, pulling away.

"I don't care how far gone he is, he can be passed out cold on the sidewalk, but you bend his thumb back like that, he'll get right up and follow you on tippy-toe. Only one problem. I showed some of the boys how to do it last summer, and goddamn if Saylor didn't go out that night and find that same kid there, Mark Jarvis—" Beaudry jerked his head toward the bar— "passed out in the alley back a here. So Saylor tries my thumb trick on Jarvis and damned if he don't break his goddamn wrist for him."

Diana rubbed her hand. Ramona Stillinger was signaling something with her eyes from across the table, but Diana couldn't read it. A warning? How had she gotten into this conversation?

"Jake!" shouted Beaudry, and a man who had just come through the front door turned and spotted them, picked up his drink from the bar, and made his way to their table.

"Hell, sit down!" Beaudry was pulling out the remaining chair for him, and the man called Jake sat, nodded to Ramona, and looked at Diana.

"Good evening, Jake," said Ramona in her social voice, and Beaudry said, "This here's Diana. She's a professor at the college."

Diana felt Jake assessing her. As a kind of afterthought he removed his hat, a black Stetson that had shadowed his face, and she saw by the light of the candle that he was dark, with black hair that had gone untrimmed for some time, a crust of beard, and a scar like a seam that ran from his left temple to his chin. She couldn't tell his age in the dim light, but she thought he had moved like a young man, although with a stiffness in one leg, not quite a limp.

He still was looking at her, and she dropped her eyes. *He's trouble,* warned a voice in the back of her head.

"Jake, has Con called you?" asked Ramona.

"No, and I don't know what he wants me to do about the Jimmy truck," said Jake.

"Jake's our diesel man," Ramona explained to Diana.

Diesel man. Jimmy truck. What were they talking about? Was there a way to escape this situation without offending Ramona?

"Actually," said Ramona, "you boys are fascinating company, but Diana and I were having girl talk."

"Oh! Hell, Mrs. S, we sure didn't mean to interrupt anything." Beaudry was on his feet and picking up his can of Coke. "Come on, Jake."

Jake was still looking at Diana. He shrugged, put his hat back on, and picked up his drink. "Nice to meet you, professor," he said, and was off with Beaudry. He glanced back at Diana once. Then he and Beaudry walked past the twitchy row of backs at the bar and out the front door. The row of backs visibly relaxed when they went out.

Ramona sighed. "Those kids at the bar are almost as afraid of Jake as they are of Chris. Where were we?"

"I don't remember."

Ramona shook her head. "Chris and Jake. What a strange pair."

"Are they close friends?"

"What passes for close friends with guys like them. Both of them are fliers, that's the connection. At least, Jake flew until his crack-up two years ago when they pulled his pilot's license. A shame, really. He was on a mercy flight. You probably noticed the scar. His face was cut up pretty badly, and he had some broken bones. Then last winter he got shot in the stomach. But after he got out of the hospital, Con hired him, and he's been a good diesel man. He's got a degree, you know."

"A degree? In what? *Diesel*?" Diana finally associated the word with a type of truck. Jake apparently serviced diesel trucks for Ramona's husband. "Versailles State College gives degrees in diesel?"

Ramona smiled. "It's a strange college. And now tell me why you're teaching at this strange college."

"It's a job."

"Aren't there jobs in less godforsaken places? I mean, I'm trapped here, because of Con and his farms, but you? When you could have Seattle?"

Diana explained, as she had tried to explain to Tatiana, about the unexpected scarcity, during the past several years, of college-level teaching positions in the arts and humanities. And the preference for male applicants that continued to linger in academe three years after the Equal Opportunities Act was passed and signed. But the history department at Versailles State had an emergency, the death of a professor, and needed a quick hire. Then too, the Versailles State administrators had been warned they risked the college's accreditation if they didn't hire at the PhD level—

"So they settled for me. I don't think the news about job scarcity has reached them yet. It will, soon enough."

If she knew Ramona better, she might tell her a little of the story she hadn't told Tatiana but Tatiana had guessed, about the drunken vagrant who once lived in Versailles, Montana, and who might—no. Diana could not articulate her quest, even for herself.

"Aren't you worried—you aren't married, you're not wearing an engagement ring—is there somebody special somewhere? Back in Seattle, maybe?"

"No."

"What about meeting someone? When you're young and so attractive?"

Diana sipped her drink to hide her reaction, her ill ease—*Why don't you like to hear it?* Annabel had asked. *When you really are very attractive?*

"I saw Jake noticed you. Although, of course he's not—you wouldn't—" Ramona didn't finish her thought. "Chris noticed you, too. Chris got divorced last year."

Jake, the dark-faced man with the scar. Trouble there, all right. Crashing an airplane, getting shot in the stomach. But Jake, with his degree in diesel, probably was as good as Versailles had to offer a single woman. And some women were drawn to trouble.

"I'm not interested in meeting someone," she said, too curtly, and saw her blunder reflected in Ramona's face. Ramona, who had tried to be kind to a newcomer, now beginning to withdraw. *What a strange woman that Diana Karnov is*, Diana had overheard one of her colleagues in the history department remark. She wondered how much of the gossip Ramona had heard.

"Look," she said. "Ramona. I'm sorry. It's just that—there are things I can't talk about."

And Ramona instantly was all sympathy—"Of course! I understand! And I'm sorry if I seemed to pry! Listen, Diana, the time, I have to run, I have a seven-year-old whose ears need scrubbing, but we'll do this again soon! Lots I want to ask you, how you're getting along with Abe Dennison and how your classes are going—maybe this time next week?"

And Diana nodded.

3

Diana lay awake in bed, gazing at the ceiling in the dark. Two a.m. glowed on her digital clock. What had wakened her? Why was she feeling so edgy? Had she been dreaming? Or was she reliving a scene in Austin two years ago?

It didn't mean anything to you?

Oh God, Annabel. How could Diana's memory have retrieved Annabel's face from all the faces she had met? Annabel with the silvery hair and pale gray eyes that brimmed with tears as her lips trembled?

"It didn't mean anything to you?" Annabel had followed Diana around their shabby graduate-student apartment from one house-plant to another.

"What should it mean?" Diana had gone on watering the ivy, but she saw its leaves were yellowing. She might as well throw it out before it died. Served her right for buying houseplants to be fashionable. She would never buy another.

Now, in the darkness of her bedroom, Diana fumbled for lighter and cigarettes on the bedside table, promised herself just one, drew her lungs full of smoke, and felt the worst of her rush subside. Another stray memory—Annabel telling her about slapping a boy's face. How had they ever gotten on that subject? Maybe they'd been talking about nineteenth century novels—or films—Annabel knew her films. She said, "It was awful. I'd never do it again."

"Why did you slap him?"

"Not a good reason. Not really. I was at a football game, and he was drunk out of his mind, and he came staggering up and kissed me, a big sloppy kiss right on my mouth. And I leaned back, just from reflex, you know, and let him have it, right across the face. It was a long time ago. We were both in high school."

Diana had been intrigued by the idea of Annabel, elegant Annabel whom she had been admiring across the seminar table all semester, as an ordinary high school girl who had gone to football games and been kissed by boys. She herself had been shielded from all fumbling, thanks to Tatiana's and Maria's tight reins and the Episcopalian girls' high school in Seattle.

"What was so awful about it?" she asked Annabel.

"The way he looked. He was so shattered I thought his face would crack."

Diana shrugged, but Annabel shook her head. "He really was shattered. He was just an ordinary boy. And he was so crushed to think he'd done something so terrible he deserved to get slapped—and of course it resounded like a shot, *crack*, and everybody turned around to look, asking *what did he do?* It was awful. I'd never do it again."

"He kissed you. He broke into your personal space."

"I didn't die of it. What did it matter? All he did was kiss me."

"What does a rape matter, always supposing you don't die of it?" Diana retorted.

Was it after that conversation that her disenchantment with Annabel had grown? Diana gradually came to perceive that Annabel was a second-rate graduate student. She took short cuts in her research and depended on her occasionally penetrating, but often facile, remarks in seminars to make up for it. During Annabel's presentations Diana saw the male graduate students exchange glances, and she cringed, feeling they were judging her by extension.

A crash at the other end of the mansion brought her upright in bed, heart pounding, before she recognized the source. Damn and damn, would she never get used to it? The sound of the garage door rumbling open and crashing into its overhead rails, activated when some small private airplane, back from a night flight and angling for the airport, used its radio and accidentally touched off the activation of the door's automatic opening system. It had been a puzzle to Diana, and unsettling—what or who was opening the garage door at night? A prowler? Finally she asked the dean, and he laughed and explained that the crashing garage door also had worried the former president, who looked into the mystery and discovered the connection between the automatic garage door and the radio frequencies of certain small airplanes.

"The mansion lies directly below the approach path," the dean reminded Diana.

And now she had to get out of bed and go downstairs and close the garage door.

She switched on her bedside light and felt her way to the stairwell. The formal rooms below were never entirely dark where, as usual, she had not bothered to close the curtains and shut out the lights of the ornamental globes on posts along the driveway. Her own reflection in the windows, pale and clad only in a white T-shirt, followed as she padded through the reception room, living room, dining room, huge kitchen. With darkness falling earlier and earlier, it seemed as though she was seeing a lot of her own reflection lately.

In the kitchen she pushed the button to close the garage door and heard it start its rumble downward. Just to be sure, she waited until she heard it thump down on concrete. And then she started at something—had she glimpsed a movement on the lawn? Surely not—what time was it? Something past two.

Closing time for the bars, she remembered.

Had to be nothing.

All the same, she checked the door between the kitchen and the garage to make sure it was locked. Conscious that she could be seen in her T-shirt through the huge windows, she checked the big double doors in the living room. Went upstairs and locked her bedroom door behind her.

She got back in bed and snapped off her light, but she knew she wouldn't sleep. Annabel. That yellowing pot of ivy.

Diana had gone through the motions, trying to learn how to *fit in*, trying to seem like one of the handful of radical female graduate students at the University of Texas–Austin who had emerged from the protest movements of the 1960s with chips on their shoulders. No more taking directions from male organizers whose calls for *chicks up front* were meant to divert the worst of the cops' batons from themselves. No! For these women, fierce independence and shaven heads. Unshaven legs, thrift-shop clothes. They stopped wearing bras, although Diana had never known anyone actually to burn her bra, despite the often-heard anti-feminist taunt.

These women had not given up entirely on national political concerns. Many had campaigned for Eugene McCarthy and faced the police in the streets of Chicago in 1968, and between their classes they glued themselves to television coverage of the Watergate investigations. They rallied in support of ratification of the Equal Rights Amendment, and last spring they had applauded Gerald Ford's announcement that American participation in the Vietnam War had come to an end. But the disappointments of the 1960s had led many to withdraw into private solutions. Houseplants, cats, liaisons with each other. Everyone smoked.

Annabel had had to teach Diana to smoke. In the beginning Diana had envied Annabel for her elegance and experience. When the envy faded, nothing was left. Had she *felt* anything for Annabel, even in the beginning? No. They had given each other finger or tongue, but Diana had been going through the motions.

She'd been born asexual, she finally decided. Attracted neither to men nor to other women. And now she was awake and jittery.

Her chairman, Abe Dennison, who liked to keep her current with the campus gossip about herself: "Everyone is saying, *There's a cold, cold woman in the history department!*"

Would that be their excuse for not renewing her contract? *She just doesn't fit in here.* Without a renewed contract, she didn't know if she could withstand Tatiana's and Maria's commands that she return to Seattle, to the silence of the Karnov house.

Get it together, Diana told herself. If you aren't going to sleep, you may as well grade test papers.

4

The next time Diana woke, she had a crick in her neck and an avalanche of bluebooks across her bedcovers. The light in her window had changed from its ordinary morning gray to a white that shone. Festive, even. Diana wondered at it for a few minutes and then rolled over and sat up in bed and saw that her students' predictions had come true. Snow had fallen during the night, pure unbroken white as far as she could see. What time was it? Nine a.m., her digital clock told her when she turned to look.

The floor felt cold under her feet when she stood and reached for last night's jeans and sweater, and she felt a bolt of panic—the furnace? If it broke down, how would she know what to do? But then she heard its familiar hum of air through the floor vents and told herself to calm down. And it was just too bad she had forgotten to buy coffee last night.

The filling station with a convenience store out on the highway would have ready-made coffee. Diana finished dressing, combed her hair back and pinned it, and found her jacket and gloves and shoulder bag. She opened the garage door with the remote button in the kitchen and saw, as the door rumbled open, a new landscape.

Under a coating of snow, Versailles seemed even more isolated than it had when she first arrived. She felt all over again the emptiness that lay beyond the city limits and the hundred miles of open prairie to Medicine Hat in Alberta, Canada. Where Abe Dennison had driven her through those tough dry hills for her interview last summer would stretch endless snowfields. Snow would bury every highway.

And yet, as Diana wheeled her MG out of the mansion's garage and turned past the ornamental lights toward the highway, she thought the town would be at its best under snow. Yesterday it had seemed on the verge of blowing away. Trash and grit lay in the streets, and the older brick buildings were so eroded by the wind that their legends were illegible and their cornices warped into grotesque shapes. Now all the downtown ugliness, even the bare branches of wind-twisted trees, would be coated and clean in glistening snow.

Thinking of the beauty of snow, Diana turned on the highway as she always did, but as she slipped into third gear and accelerated on the grade that rose from the valley to the plateau above town, she felt the MG give an odd shudder under her, as though it wanted to levitate, and when she stepped down on the gas pedal for the upward slope, the little car swept into a rapidly widening spiral across both lanes of the highway that dizzied her. She frantically braked and steered, but the MG spiraled on, oblivious of her. She couldn't breathe, couldn't focus, couldn't save herself. Around and around, sky and power poles spinning past her, billboards and open sky spinning endlessly until suddenly it stopped. The MG's rear wheels were somewhere over the verge of the highway, and Diana was looking through the windshield where the hood pointed up in front of her. She gasped to breathe again.

At least she was alive. But what now?

A black pickup truck pulled over and stopped behind the MG. A man in a black Stetson and a heavy dun coat got out and walked through thin snow to tap on Diana's window, and she willed her hand to stop shaking enough to roll it down. He had to bend almost double to look in at her, and she recognized Jake the diesel man. By daylight the scar on his face looked worse.

"You're Diana the professor, right? They said you're from Seattle. You never drove on ice before?"

She shook her head, she couldn't speak.

"Better turn your ignition off. You're damn lucky you didn't go off the other side."

She was trying to focus, trying not to think of the twenty-foot drop-off on the other side of the highway, but of what she needed to do. "Will they have a tow truck at the gas station?" she whispered, but Jake had backed off and was looking over her MG and shaking his head.

"I'll get you out," he said, and turned and walked back to his truck. Diana watched as he pulled around her and the MG and pulled over again. When he backed the truck into position, she saw that all four of its tires wore chains. He got out and lifted another chain out of the truck bed and disappeared from her view under the MG. She heard a clanking almost under her feet, and then Jake was emerging from the front of the MG and hooking the chain to the bar at the back of his truck. He came back to her window and bent down again.

"Shift it into neutral," he said, "and steer, but for godsake keep your feet off the brakes and the gas pedal."

He was back in his truck, easing off the verge and onto the highway. Diana felt the gentle tug as the chain tightened and the MG followed the black truck as obediently as a spaniel on a leash. It was an odd feeling, the silence of the MG's engine, the slow, cautious forward motion, the sense of giving over her control of pace and direction to someone else. Her loss of control in her spinout had been terrifying; this loss of control was disquieting in another way, as though she were being towed into a strange dimension of time and space. The power poles and billboards that had swirled around her now crept by. The unchanging sky. The twenty-foot drop-off. Diana shuddered.

Then the black truck was making a slow wide turn at the filling station's paved forecourt and pulling into a space beside an eighteen-wheeler. When the truck stopped, the MG rolled a foot or two and also stopped.

Jake came around to unhook his tow chain from his truck and the MG and toss it back into the truck bed before he came to her window and bent down again. "You need better tires on this—"

he paused, looking at the MG—"*car*, and you need to learn how to drive on ice."

She couldn't answer.

"Oh, hell," he said, more gently. "You're shakin all over. Let me buy you a cup of coffee."

He was opening her car door without waiting for an answer. *Pull yourself together, Diana*, she told herself. She stepped out of her car, instantly slipped on snow turned to ice, and would have fallen if Jake had not caught her arm.

"Guess you'll have to learn how to walk on it, too."

Diana gritted her teeth and walked on her own, but she was careful where she stepped. Reaching bare pavement was a relief. Jake held the door of the convenience store for her, but she felt too rattled to reprimand him—the feminist response, *I can open doors for myself, thank you!*—and the warmth inside the store was too welcoming.

"They got a few booths in back," he said. "Sit down and I'll get your coffee."

She found the booths, nothing more than a row of three or four orange Formica tables with matching Formica benches, and collapsed into the first one. Even in the warmth she was shivering. She closed her eyes and opened them again. Lined up in front of her were a metal dispenser for paper napkins, a pair of glass salt and pepper shakers, and a plastic bottle each of catsup and mustard. At least all these objects were sitting still. The world had stopped spinning. She could smell disinfectant and, farther away, stale popcorn.

Then Jake came back, carrying the lid of a cardboard box doing duty as a tray for two cups of coffee and a greasy paper bag, and Diana reached for a cup and gulped coffee.

"I got doughnuts," said Jake, opening his paper bag. "Take one. The sugar will help with the shakes."

She took the sugared doughnut he handed her and tore off a bite and another. Jake was right, the sugar was what she needed. He sat across from her, watching her eat the doughnut with nothing more on his face than mild interest. And the scar, of course.

By daylight she could see it was not one scar, but many, with tiny, almost invisible lines running into the main vertical scar like tributaries into a river.

"What happened," he said. "Last night the snow thawed a little, and then it froze and more snow fell on top of the ice. It's damn treacherous out there."

She could think of nothing to say.

"Don't spose you ever spun out before," he said. "Must have been scary."

With her mouth full, Diana nodded, and Jake handed her another doughnut and watched her while she drank coffee and ate the second doughnut.

"You buy that car in Seattle?"

"No—in Texas while I was at the university."

She'd taken driving lessons in Texas so she could drive the MG back to Seattle after she defended her dissertation in the spring. How Tatiana and Maria had scolded when they saw the MG and saw Diana driving it! *Whyever would you need a car, Diana? Wherever would you need to go?*

"Want more coffee?"

She shook her head. "I think I'm all right."

"You're looking better. A little color comin back." He drank his own coffee and smiled at her. "Hell, I was wantin to celebrate. I got my license back today, and now I'm celebratin with doughnuts."

"License?"

"My pilot's license. I've been suspended since my wreck. And I was so damned eager to go aloft after two goddamn years that I was headed out to the airport, and instead I got to watch you spin out. And I tell you, girl, I was holdin my breath you wouldn't spin over that drop, and not a damn thing I could do to stop it."

Diana closed her eyes. She was sitting in a plastic booth at the back of a convenience store with a bottle each of catsup and mustard and a man who held doors for her and called her *girl*.

A man who had rescued her. She might be a *cold, cold woman*, but she wouldn't be an ungrateful one. She opened her eyes. "You can't go out to the airport because you stopped to tow my car?"

"Oh, I'll get there today, and I'll go aloft. Once I figure out how to get you and that so-called car of yours home without another spinout. Or—" he paused. Smiled at her. "You could come with me. I'll take you aloft while I think what to do with you."

* * *

Jake had glanced at Diana and turned up the heater in his truck. Now he drove out of town on the highway and turned on a county road where gravel was exposed in patches under thin windblown snow. Versailles fell behind them under a white cloud of furnace smoke and human breath. Arched over all was a pale blue sky with a sun that stung Diana's eyes through the windshield until she shut them. What would she tell someone who asked what she was doing with a man who was thinking *what to do with her*, and why she was doing it— Ramona Stillinger, perhaps. Or Tatiana, and what Tatiana would say.

Because she was curious? Because she'd never *gone aloft*, as Jake put it, in a small plane?

Diana opened her eyes. Jake had stopped at a gate in a chain-link fence. A sign over the gate, Versailles International Airport. Beyond the fence were a small terminal, hangars, and a frozen runway, insignificant-looking for an international airport. Jake got out to open the gate, and she noticed again the slight stiffness when he walked, not quite a limp. From his wreck, she supposed. It occurred to her that she could have offered to open the gate. But Jake already was back and driving through the gate into the vast space between the hangars and the runway.

Diana blinked in the glare of sun on snow. For a moment she had seen herself and Jake from a distance, as through the wrong end of a telescope. The truck, bleached and tiny, crawling out across the frozen concrete and heading into an emptiness as vast as though she and Jake and the truck had landed on the surface of the moon.

Jake drove behind the line of chained-down airplanes and stopped. "That's it," he said.

Even at close range the red-and-white plane seemed ridiculously small. Its frail shell was like an exoskeleton poised on its tiny wheels. A manmade insect for short hops.

"She's a Cessna 172. Slower'n hell. But she's what I had enough insurance money to buy."

He climbed out of the cab and walked around the plane to look it over and unsnap the chains from the wingtips. Then he turned and grinned, waiting for her.

Diana felt an obscure reluctance to get out of the shelter of the cab. But—get it over with. She wasn't on the surface of the moon, and she wasn't going to back down. The worst that could happen was that he'd crash again and break both their necks. She wished she knew the cause of his crash.

"Get in the right seat and fasten the seatbelt. What's the matter?"

"Nothing! I'm cold."

She had to stretch to reach the high step and then duck her head awkwardly to get through the door. Once inside the shell she fitted her legs into the narrow dark space under the controls and fumbled for the seatbelt. She never had been in a plane smaller than a 737. It seemed even colder inside the shell of the cabin than out on the runway in the sun. The air was so stale and unmoving that for a moment she thought she was not breathing.

The airplane quivered as Jake settled himself into the left seat. He fastened his belt and turned several switches. Diana heard the whine and roar as the propeller awoke, filled the windshield, and vanished into a blur. She felt the plane lurch out of its mooring and bump across snow to the ploughed pavement. A sharp turn and they stopped again.

Without warning came a roar of power that shook the plane until Diana thought it would be torn from its wheels. She gritted her teeth. The charge of power subsided, and they were taxiing slowly out on the runway. Jake was speaking into his radio and scanning the sky, squinting through the windshield where the sun burst in diamonds. The power grew again, swelling into a scream, and Diana found herself hurtling down the looming runway with nothing but a strip of glass and cowling between her and the snow fence rushing from the end of the runway. A river of snow poured toward her and disappeared as the plane lifted and they were airborne.

She felt suspended, motionless, in empty air. Then she glanced down and saw the hangars and the line of orange and red planes shrinking into the endless white. Versailles, a grid of miniature streets and smoke on both sides of the icebound river, was sliding away.

Jake was pointing, yelling something—"Coyote!" and she looked down in time to see the small doglike creature fleeing under the blue cross-shaped shadow of the plane on snow.

The window tipped under her as the plane banked. She braced her feet and strained away from the snowfields that filled the glass. Jake shouted something, but she could not hear him over the roar of the plane, did not care what he was telling her. Her mouth suddenly tasted of metal. With the flood of saliva came nausea. Jake banked again. Versailles rushed at her. Diana felt, first, weightlessness, and then the full force of gravity pulling at her. Don't vomit, she screamed to herself. It'll be over, somehow it'll be over, it'll be over in a few more minutes.

The plane settled into level flight, and Diana lolled her head back and gasped for breath. She felt the sticky wet wool of her scarf around her throat and took one more gasp of thick stale air before sky and earth reversed again. Gravity dragged at her temples and cheeks and throat. *Don't vomit* while gravity seemed to be tearing her loose from her own bones; *don't vomit* and to think she had walked around under the forces of gravity all her life and only now could feel it.

The passages of her skull thickened and closed with the sensation of weightlessness as the plane descended from altitude. Shapes hurtled toward the windshield, whipped past the side windows. Then the wheels screamed through snow and slowed.

They were taxiing toward the line of planes. Diana couldn't move. Hands, feet, nothing. She never had felt so insubstantial.

The propeller blades reappeared, wavered, and stopped. Diana heard Jake unbuckle his belt and climb out. A moment later his shadow fell across her as he opened the door on her side.

"You okay?"

"Yes," she gasped. She knew she had to unbuckle herself and walk as far as the truck. Her wet face stung in the cold as she clambered down from the high seat and avoided Jake's offered hand. The snowy pavement under her feet felt so rigid that she was surprised when her knees held.

Jake snapped the tie-down chains and climbed back in the truck with her.

"Hell, I didn't mean to scare you again. Once was probly enough scare for you in one day."

"I wasn't scared!" she lied, and Jake grinned.

The sun was lower in the sky. Diana could not have said how long they had been aloft. She closed her eyes and felt the jounce of the truck over snow and gravel, through the airport gates, and down to the highway. The heater was beginning to warm the cab again. She still shivered.

"I was so damn glad to get airborne again I forgot you'd never flown," Jake said. "I shouldn't a done those barrel rolls with you."

"I want to learn to fly a plane," Diana blurted and only realized she was speaking the truth when she heard herself speak the words. She was eager to know how to do what Jake could do.

Her words seemed to light something in Jake's face, and he smiled at her and pushed his hat back. He looked—*happy* was the right word, Diana thought. How he must have longed to go aloft.

"I'll teach you to fly," he said. "But first I'm going to teach you how to drive on ice and snow."

5

On Monday morning Diana, mindful of her several hours of driving instruction from Jake, drove cautiously down from the mansion and across town to campus.

Jake had spent Sunday afternoon with her in an empty parking lot, first with himself in the driver's seat of her MG while he demonstrated how to spin out, how to get out of a spin, and how not to get into one. Then he swapped places with her, grinning as she readjusted the seat he had pushed all the way back to accommodate his legs.

Just as he predicted, Saturday's sun had melted the snow, which froze overnight and turned the parking lot into a skating rink. When Diana stepped on the accelerator, the MG immediately began to fishtail.

"No! No! Steer with it, not against it! No, don't touch the brake!"

When she panicked, he reached over and wrenched the steering wheel from her and straightened her out. "Try it again."

She instantly fishtailed.

"Try it again—no, no! Steer with it! Steer with it!

"I know it feels all wrong," he said, while she sat trembling after he straightened her out again. "It feels natural to want to steer out of a spin. That's why you have to do it over and over until steering into the spin comes automatic to you. Same way when you learn to fly, you have to practice stalls over and over until you don't have to think not to pull the stick up but push it down. You just do it."

Diana had no idea what he was talking about. Stalls. Pushing the stick down. "Who taught you to drive?" she asked.

"My grandpa."

And so the afternoon had gone, until darkness had fallen and Jake was satisfied that Diana could drive him safely back to his pickup. He laughed when he saw her face as he disentangled his legs from the MG and got out.

"Hell, you'll be all right by yourself. I'll follow you home, if it makes you feel better. And by tomorrow morning the city crews probly will have the streets sanded."

And he did follow her, all the way back to the mansion. Diana had to admit to herself how reassuring it felt to see his headlights in her rear-view mirror, and then she worried he would want to come inside with her. But when she tapped the remote and the garage door began to open, he blinked his headlights once, reversed, and drove away while she watched his rear lights out of sight.

* * *

Monday morning. Diana parked the MG behind Main Hall and locked it, entered the hall by a side door, and climbed the two flights of stairs to her corridor. Her office looked just the same as it had when she left it on Friday. Well, not quite. The custodian had stirred himself enough to empty her wastebasket.

She had half an hour to herself before she had to teach her morning survey class. But no, here was Abe Dennison, lounging in her doorway like a facsimile of the history-professor image he strove for. Rumpled tweed suit, moustache, horn-rimmed glasses that did nothing to hide his speculative gaze. Abe seemed always to turn up where he wasn't expected and always on the lookout for something. He had a way of standing too close, of making her flinch by touching her arm or shoulder. Diana wondered how his wife stood him.

"Good morning," he said, and grinned. "Have a good weekend, did you?"

"My weekend was all right."

He was enjoying himself, Diana could tell. "I heard you got acquainted with some of the local color."

"I don't know what you're talking about, Abe."

"No? Jake LeTellier?"

"Oh, him. I didn't even know his last name."

"You were seen—" Abe paused for effect—"at the Quick'n'Dip having coffee with him on Saturday."

"*I was seen!* For God's sake, Abe! What are you doing? Running a spy network out of Main Hall?"

When he grinned all the more at her reaction, she went on. "I give up! I confess! I'm not used to driving on snow, and my car slid into a ditch. Jake happened by and towed me out. Then he bought me a cup of coffee. I thought it was kind of him."

"I never said it wasn't. But you need to remember, Diana. He is an Indian."

Diana stood and gathered her textbook and notes. "You need to remember, Abe. I have a class to teach."

* * *

Abe's remark festered in the back of Diana's mind as she began her lecture in the survey class. She had covered the War of 1812 and was discussing Andrew Jackson's Indian Removal Act of 1830. The war against the Five Civilized Tribes. The Cherokee and their forced removal to what would become Oklahoma on the Trail of Tears. Most of her students dutifully took notes, although she saw a grin or two exchanged. What were they thinking? *He is an Indian.*

Was having coffee with Jake—Jake LeTellier, she now knew his full name—the equivalent of a white woman having coffee with a black man in, say, present-day Georgia, once the home of the Five Civilized Tribes? She remembered the mixed couple outside the Stockman's, the young black man and the white girl, and again wondered how they were received in Versailles.

Not many Indian students were enrolled at Versailles State. The former president was said to have discouraged them, fearing they would make the college less attractive to white students. But a couple of Indians were in Diana's survey classes, and a few more had enrolled in her Westward Movement seminar that met on Friday afternoons. She supposed they were from one of the nearby reservations. A knot of three Indian students sat on one side of the classroom while two others sat on the other side of the classroom, as far apart as possible. What was that about? Diana lost her place in her notes and had to force herself to concentrate on the resistance to Jackson's removal act by some Christian missionaries and Congressman Davy Crockett. Her students brightened at the familiar name.

Mercifully the class period came to an end and Diana could pack up her book and notes while her students scrambled to close theirs and hurry away. On her way back to her office she caught one of the older history professors—George Shultz, he taught sociology—watching her from his office door with an openly avid gaze until he saw she had noticed him. She wondered how much of her conversation with Abe Dennison he had overheard. Oh, well. With luck she had an hour to herself before her afternoon survey, where she would give her lecture a second time. Yawn. But at least she didn't teach tomorrow, and she could check out the Versailles Public Library—*admit it! You're looking for that drunken vagrant!*

Digging around the inadequate college library for sources on women in the West, Diana had come upon a battered old book, written by someone whose name was either Crystal McLeod or Mourning Dove, and she decided to read it before she tried to find more information about the writer. Now, in the lull between her survey classes, she opened the book, *Coyote Stories*, sneezed in its dust, and began reading the introduction.

She had reached the third chapter when a tap at her door interrupted, and she looked up to see Ramona Stillinger.

"Could I come in for a few minutes?"

"Of course," Diana said, although her thoughts still followed a canoe paddled by the pre-human trickster god, Coyote, and his twin brother, Fox, on their way to recapture Fox's stolen wife. How to understand a buffoon god like the Coyote, who stirred up preposterous situations for his own aggrandizement? But she laid her book aside and hoped she didn't sound reluctant to Ramona. *Pretend to be a real person* was her new mantra. But was this going to be another conversation about Jake LeTellier and the trouble that trailed him? Or that he was an Indian and she shouldn't be seen with him?

Ramona herself seemed uncertain. She wandered over to the window and gazed out. The hard light of the snowy day etched the lines around her mouth and eyes, and Diana thought she looked tired. Her husband had been in Canada, Diana remembered. Was he home by now?

"Are you all right?" she asked.

"Yes. No." Ramona drew a breath and let it out. She seemed to see for the first time the chair Diana kept for students, and she drew another breath and sat.

"Maybe you'd let me just sit here in your office for a minute?"

"Do you want me to leave you alone?"

"No!"

Diana was perplexed. What would a *real person* do? "Is there something you need to talk about?" she asked, hoping she hadn't blundered again.

"Nothing I *ought* to talk about."

Ramona lifted her face, her eyes swimming. "And I don't have one friend in this town, this damnable town, I can talk to who probably doesn't already know all about it."

"I'm sorry," Diana began, but Ramona cut her off.

"I thought you might be the one woman I could—oh, I don't want to unload all this—this *crap*—on you, but—" she trailed off. Diana waited.

Ramona took another deep breath and seemed to get her face under control. Her voice was almost steady when she spoke.

"I'm almost certain—I *am* certain—that Con, my husband, took a girl with him on his Canadian trip. And I know who she is. One of the barmaids from the Bellevue Lodge."

"I'm sorry," Diana began again. Somewhere the Coyote and Fox were trying to reclaim her attention as, in snatching back Fox's stolen wife, they instilled hatred between the Water People and the Land People. She had to force herself back into the present.

"This town. This awful town. I don't know how much I can stand."

It occurred to Diana that she had returned from the Coyote's misadventures only to wander into a soap opera. Maybe she had. Maybe if she'd ever watched a soap opera, she would know for sure. What to say to this woman on the verge of tears? Should she remind her that she wasn't helpless? That she had a job?

"What will you do?" she asked.

"I don't know," said Ramona. But she sounded better. She stood and made a little gesture with her hands, dusting them off. "But thanks. I'm glad I spat it out. It helped."

"I'm glad I could help," Diana said, wondering what she'd done that was helpful.

"You listened. And maybe we could have a drink later on? The Stockman's? Seven o'clock?"

* * *

The afternoon was darkening by the time Diana dismissed her afternoon survey class and locked her office and picked up her mail. As soon as she left Main Hall and took a breath of chill air, she realized the temperature must have dropped. When she turned her key in the MG, the motor was slow to turn over, and she shook her head in exasperation. But she drove back to the mansion without incident and parked in the garage.

Once in the mansion, she tossed her mail on the kitchen counter and picked the envelope with the familiar spiky black handwriting from a paper clutter of campus bulletins, minutes of meetings, and warnings of deadlines. She set a kettle to boil for instant chocolate and supposed she should arrange to have her personal mail delivered to the mansion instead of to her campus box. Meanwhile, here was Tatiana's unopened letter.

Tatiana, tall and gaunt with a coarse crown of white hair. Maria, smaller and rounder, but with her own aggressive crown of white hair. The spinster aunts of Diana's dead mother. There had been a time in her life before Tatiana and Maria, but Diana recalled it only in her shadow-memories. Long days of hot sunshine in a place that could not have been Seattle, and certainly not Versailles, a place where she walked barefoot through tall grass and smelled a persistent odor she associated with gasoline and road tar. Where she heard adults singing together—*so I'll cling to the old rugged cross*—in what must have been a Christian church of some denomination.

Had to be Texas.

Her kettle boiled, and she poured a cup and stirred in the instant chocolate powder and looked at the unopened envelope for a moment longer before she braced herself and ran a finger under the flap of Tatiana's letter.

6

By the time Diana, peering out for any shine of ice on the streets, pulled into the parking lot behind the Stockman's Bar, she was running a little late. When she opened the heavy back door, she saw Ramona Stillinger already had claimed a corner table and was sipping wine. As before, Ramona had not changed from the outfit she had worn to teach that day, a fitted gray wool dress with a long skirt and a wide lace collar. Diana thought she looked calmer than she had that afternoon.

"Sorry I'm late," she said. "I'm having to learn how much time to allot when I'm driving on snow."

"You haven't had any trouble, have you?" Ramona asked, and Diana wondered if she'd heard Abe's gossip. But the barmaid was at her elbow, asking her what she'd have, and Diana ordered a vodka collins.

Ramona watched the barmaid as she threaded through empty tables on her way back to the bar. "Hot pants," she said. "It figures, doesn't it. After hot pants have gone out of fashion everywhere else, the barmaids at the Stockman's in Versailles have to wear them. Elsewhere in the world, 1975 is the International Year of the Woman."

Diana had noted the barmaid's outfit—black hot pants, black fishnet hose, black high heels—and wondered what she would do if someone told her she had to dress that way for work. "It's quiet tonight," she offered.

"Monday night." Ramona sighed. "Con hasn't come home yet. I talked on the phone with Douglas Mainwaring earlier, and he may drop by later."

Douglas Mainwaring. Ramona had spoken the name as though she expected Diana to recognize it, and Diana tried to remember. It did sound familiar.

"Oh," she finally said, "he's in the English department, isn't he?"

"Yes. An assistant professor. He's up for tenure this year. And worried about it."

Diana's drink arrived, and she sipped. She hoped Douglas Mainwaring's dropping by wasn't an arrangement of Ramona's for Diana to meet someone. But no, Ramona seemed self-absorbed tonight. Maybe her mind was on Con, in Canada.

"Don't turn and look," said Ramona, her face neutral. "But Jake just walked in, and he's watching you."

Diana's back and shoulders stiffened with her effort not to react and look. "Jake," she said. "Is this his regular bar? Abe Dennison warned me against him today."

Ramona nodded. "He hangs out in the Stockman's most nights. What does Abe Dennison have against him?"

"He said Jake is an Indian, as though that means I should keep away from him."

Ramona laughed. "Abe has his own agenda. And, yes, Jake's sort of an Indian. You ought to get him to tell you about his people. You teach Western American history, don't you? You'd probably find his story interesting."

"That reminds me, I meant to ask you. I've seen a young black man with a white woman on Main Street lately. They were wearing jeans and sweatshirts like students, but I don't think they're students. Are they—well—treated well?"

Ramona shook her head. "Nobody's exactly stoned them, but short of that—and even worse, they're part of that hippie colony that's camped out at the county park. Can you imagine? Living in tents in this kind of weather? People are nervous about them. Oh, here's Douglas!"

Diana had seen the young man several times in the corridors of Main Hall, darting sidelong glances as though he expected to be apprehended. He had a frizz of brown curls over a round face with pink cheeks and a pink tip to his nose. By candlelight the pink wasn't so apparent, but he still seemed jumpy. Maybe his upcoming tenure consideration was making him nervous.

"Douglas Mainwaring," Ramona introduced him. "Douglas, I'm sure you met Diana Karnov at the faculty retreat."

"Oh, yes," he bleated. As he seated himself next to her, his hands gave an involuntary jerk. Maybe she was making him nervous, Diana thought. Or Ramona was.

But after he asked the barmaid to bring him a martini, he calmed down enough to ask Diana the usual questions, how she was adjusting to life in Versailles, what she thought of her students, was she getting acquainted with everyone. He explained to her his special area of English—the Romantic poets—and the several articles he hoped to develop from papers he had written during his graduate studies. "Although with the heavy teaching load they give you here? And nobody really expects you to publish. It's all about teaching evaluations and committee work."

Ramona asked him about someone in the English department with a name unfamiliar to Diana, and they soon were deep in conversation. Diana sipped her drink while her thoughts returned to Tatiana's angry letter. The sentence underlined so heavily that the paper had torn. *Maria never should have given you that name!*

Tomorrow was not a teaching day for Diana. After the hectic weeks of meetings and organizing classes, she finally could visit the public library and see what she could uncover about the forbidden name. And wonder—an unexpected detour of her thoughts—how anyone could be "sort of" an Indian.

"Still in Canada?" she heard Douglas ask Ramona, and Ramona's sad answer.

"With *her*."

Then the barmaid in her ridiculous black heels and black hot pants was at their table, asking if they wanted another round. Diana looked at her drink and realized she had absently finished it down to the ice cubes.

"No," she said, and stood. "I'll say good night. Nice to get acquainted, Douglas. Good to chat, Ramona."

A patter of words. Maybe she could pass herself off as a real person in Versailles, just as she'd passed herself off among the feminist graduate students in Austin and absorbed their ideas. She buttoned her jacket and rehearsed how she would put off Jake LeTellier if he—what—asked her to have a drink with him, perhaps, as she walked past him on her way to the back door. But Jake already had gone.

* * *

The old Carnegie Library on Water Street was built of dressed stone, square and compact. Diana's hands were shaking as she parked on the street and told herself not to get her hopes up. She climbed a flight of concrete steps to the front door, which opened to warmth and a bookish odor of worn paper and dust that she would have known with her eyes closed. A gray-haired woman sat reading behind the circulation desk. When Diana asked her about the microfilm collection, she directed her downstairs to the basement.

Here, apparently, was the children's collection. No children at the moment, but Diana saw a pint-sized table and chairs in primary colors and a rack of picture books. Rows of metal shelving. High basement-style windows whose sills contained a dusty collection of model ships, perhaps a donation the librarians couldn't refuse.

Water stains down the walls—Diana shook her head at signs of a leaky library.

Nothing that might be a microfilm reader.

Then she heard creaks and muffled thumps from deep in the stacks and went to investigate. Another gray-haired woman looked up from the trolley of books she was re-shelving.

"The microfilm reader?" She pointed to a complicated-looking machine in a recess behind the stacks. "What are you looking for, in particular?"

"Have you got the Versailles *Daily News* on microfilm? Back as far as 1945?"

"Let's see. I think it was called the *Morning Tribune* in those days."
The librarian opened a drawer in a cabinet and ran a finger over the
boxes of microfilms. "Here we are. I'm Margaret Elder, by the way."

"Diana Karnov."

"Ah! You're the woman professor they hired at the college!"

Mrs. Elder—she wore a too-tight chip diamond and matching band on a plump finger—led Diana to the microfilm reader
and showed her how to thread the reader and turn the handle to
advance the film. "We'd like to update the reader," she apologized,
"but seems like there's always something. Do you think you're ready
to run it now?"

Diana could hardly wait for the older woman to leave her alone
with the film and the reader. *Don't get your hopes up,* she reminded
herself, even as she felt a quickening, a shiver even, although warm
air was being blown down through a vent above her head and lifting
strands of her hair. The sounds of a furnace somewhere, of books
being shelved, of faint voices from upstairs faded as she turned
the handle of the reader and found herself reading the headlines
of New Year's Day, 1945.

German air raids on Allied bases in Belgium and elsewhere.
Southern California beating Tennessee in the Rose Bowl. Not the
kind of news she needed. And yet she had to be so close. She turned
the handle of the reader and skimmed the local news of an upcoming pancake fundraiser, a notice of live music at the Stockman's Bar
(really!) and paused on a headline: *Local man fights search warrant.*

Not the name she was searching for. But she reminded herself
that her best sources might well be police reports and vital records.
Arrests, births, marriages, deaths. Arrests in particular, perhaps,
considering Tatiana's and Maria's unconcealed venom when any
topic veered too close to the bearer of the forbidden name. If the
man the great-aunts called the drunken vagrant still was alive today,
he might be one of the shamblers past the bars on Main Street,
unshaven and stinking and glaring at passersby.

Diana turned the handle of the reader again, skimmed, and turned until the peaceful library basement faded away and she was eavesdropping on the news of January and then February of 1945. Dresden bombed by Allied planes. Iwo Jima stormed by Marines, long-ago violence that felt distant, not just in time, but through the filter of the microfilm reader. By the middle of May 1945 she had read of victory in Europe and become vaguely aware her stomach was rumbling. She reached into her bag for the sandwich and hard-boiled eggs she had brought with her and lifted food to her mouth with her left hand while she turned the handle of the reader with her right hand.

August 1945 brought victory over Japan and footsteps and whispers and muffled giggles invading the silence of the basement. Diana resurfaced from the past and leaned back in her chair far enough to see the clock on the wall. It was past four o'clock, and it appeared that a local elementary school had let out its students to invade the library. She sighed at the energy the children brought with them and sank back into the depths of 1945.

She had reached the third week of October when her hand froze on the handle of the reader. The headline. *Local boy returns from Pacific*. The name Maria had let slip. *Victor Wheeler*.

Not a police report, after all. No, of course not. He had been in the Marine Corps and posted in the Pacific during the war, and it wasn't until October of 1945 that he'd finally come home. With her heart pounding, Diana groped for her notebook and a pen and began to copy the short article. When she finished, she closed her eyes for a moment, took a deep breath, and looked down at what she had written.

So. She now had a bit of his service record, the names of his parents, and a partial address. No hint that he was married, but now that he was back in Versailles, she could—but Diana realized someone was tapping her on her shoulder, speaking to her.

"—my dear, please, it's nine o'clock, and we're closing."

It was Mrs. Elder, of course. How could it be nine o'clock? But apparently it was.

"I'm sorry," Diana said. "Could you keep these reels out for me? I can come back again on Thursday."

"I'll have them ready for you. Now, please—"

Diana gathered her belongings and walked with Mrs. Elder, who turned out lights behind them, up the basement stairs and through the main library. No one was behind the librarian's desk. Mrs. Elder locked up, leaving only a security light burning, and led the way down the steps to the sidewalk. Diana saw a car at the curb, parked a little ahead of her MG, with exhaust billowing white in the frigid air, and thought that the librarians must have gone out early to start their cars and let them warm up. The evening really was very cold. She supposed she should have started the MG earlier, but she had been lost in time.

"Good night, dear."

Diana unlocked the MG and thought she might as well be climbing into a freezer. When she turned the key in the ignition, she heard only a half-hearted *ump-wump* from the engine.

"Damn," she said and saw a white puff of her own breath. Now what. The library was locked and dark, and Mrs. Elder already had driven away.

"Well, damnation." Diana got out of the MG and locked it. A few windows of nearby residences were lighted, but she winced at the idea of knocking on a stranger's door and asking for help. Tatiana's mantra: *You must learn to depend only on yourself.* She had a long walk ahead, and she was wearing only her jacket over her sweater, but at least she had gloves to pull on, and the exercise would help against the cold.

But by the time she reached the downtown area she was shivering, and she had to clench her teeth to keep them from chattering. When she saw the neon cowboy of the Stockman's Bar several blocks down the street, she thought of going in and asking to use the telephone to call—but whom could she call? Ramona? No. She would feel like a fool for not taking better care of her car. *Learn to depend on yourself.* Better to keep walking until she reached the mansion, where she could take a hot bath and use the telephone there to discover whether Versailles had an all-night towing service that could retrieve the MG and do whatever was necessary—charge its battery, perhaps—to get it started.

She walked on into cold and colder.

7

Diana had been walking for what seemed all her life when the wind at the end of a downtown block, with no buildings to deflect it, struck her with an angry force. She struggled for balance, gritted her teeth, and concentrated on putting one foot in front of the other. Of course she could do this, of course she could walk across a street. She wasn't feeling cold so much as blank with exhaustion when she was blown backward by a vicious slap of wind. Behind its howl she heard the cackle of the trickster god, the Coyote, entertained by her predicament. But she could save herself. Lying on her back in the snow, she told herself she just needed to rest for a few minutes. Just a few minutes and then she would get back on her feet and go on. Important that she go on. Important for reasons she couldn't remember.

"You okay?"

Someone was helping her to her feet. A black face in a ruffed parka. Behind the face glowed the neon cowboy of the Stockman's Bar.

Diana opened her mouth to answer and thought what strange sounds her voice made.

"You want to go into the Stocks? Good idea. Get yourself warm. Not a place for me, though."

He was opening a door for her, holding it and pushing her to walk through it. Then he was gone, and the warmth of the bar was so painful she started to sway.

"Hey—lady, you all right?"

"No, she's not!"

Someone, a young woman dressed in scanty black clothing, had taken her arm—"Can you walk?"

"Here, I've got her."

She was being lifted off her feet, being set in a chair with a heavy coat wrapped around her, and she opened her eyes on a row of silent faces that had turned from the bar to watch.

"Mind your own business!" snapped the woman in black, and all the faces turned back to the bar.

She closed her eyes as voices continued over her head. A man's voice—"You got any coffee at the bar, Celie? With sugar?"

"Yes, I'll get it. Do you think I should call for an ambulance?"

"An ambulance will cost her. Her pulse is good, her breathing's good. We'll get her warm and I'll take her home."

"Jake, you're not going out there without your coat!"

"Hell, just to start my truck. Be right back."

The woman called Celie held a cup to Diana's lips, and Diana sipped and winced at the scalding coffee.

"Don't let her go to sleep."

His voice again. Diana opened her eyes on the dark scarred face.

"Get the door for me, will you, Celie."

He was carrying her through a door, into the shock of the cold, then laying her on the seat of a vehicle in warmth that hurt so much that she rolled herself into a ball.

A truck door slammed, another door opened and slammed— "Professor Lady, I keep fallin over you," he said. "What the hell were you doin out there?"

"W-w-walking—"

"I could see you'd been doin that," Jake said, and he put his truck in gear and pulled away. She knew she was being driven somewhere and she knew she ought to object, she had to get to the mansion and use the telephone, for some reason, but she couldn't get the words out, and she couldn't remember what she was looking for.

Still, the motion of the vehicle and the hum of its heater were soothing, and her eyes drifted shut. If she could just rest for a while— sleep—if only Jake weren't slapping her face—

"Don't go to sleep on me! Talk to me!"

"Talk?" she chattered. "Talk about what?"

"Anything. What's your name?"

Did he think she didn't know her own name? "Diana Karnov."

"How old are you?"

"Twenty-eight."

"What's your father's name?"

Suddenly she remembered the answer. "Victor Wheeler."

He gave her a curious look, but he had turned a corner and pulled up to a curb. They must have gotten wherever he was taking her, because he killed his motor and got out and picked up an extension cord and attached it somewhere at the front of his truck before he opened the door on the passenger side and lifted her out.

"My place," he said. "I can thaw you out better here than in that barn you live in. Jesus, you're still shiverin. Maybe I should a taken you to the emergency room."

"No," she whimpered, "—have to call—" But she couldn't think of the name of whomever she needed so urgently to call.

"Girl, you're a goddamn magnet for trouble."

"Trouble there," she said.

She felt herself being carried around the side of a darkened house and through a doorway into a room that first was dark and then, when he flipped a switch, filled with light that made her shut her eyes again. Then another room where he set her on a bed and pulled off one of her shoes and then the other and felt her feet—"No frostbite, for a bloody mercy," he muttered.

When he unbuttoned her jacket and took it off, she saw that it was wet from the snow she had collapsed in and which must have melted in the warm truck.

"Sorry, got to get these wet jeans off you, too."

He was unzipping her jeans, sliding them down around her hips, and she felt as though she had been carried into another time and place, like the world of microfilm, where what was happening to her couldn't be happening. Now she was in the bed, covered to her chin, and Jake clicked another switch—"Electric blanket," he said. "Now don't go to sleep on me. I'll be right back."

Something wet touched her cheek, and she turned her head and found herself gazing into the worried eyes of a shaggy black-and-white dog that had raised itself by its paws on the bed.

Then Jake was back, setting down a mug of something steaming and propping her up on pillows—"Tip, you been keeping her awake for me? You can get down now. Diana, can you hold the cup?"

"I don't think so."

He held it for her, and she sipped heavily sweetened tea.

"Take your time, but drink all of it."

When she finished, he took the cup and checked her hands and feet. "I think you're beginnin to thaw. But don't go to sleep yet. Talk to me."

She tried to think of something to say. "What kind of dog?"

"Border collie. You never saw one before?"

"No. Jake. My chairman warned me you're an Indian. And Ramona said you're sort of an Indian."

He smiled a little. "I guess *sort of* would cover it, all right. Yeah, I'm an Indian to a lotta folks. Like that bastard Dennison you work for. But no. I'm not tribally enrolled. I'm Métis."

"May-tee?"

"Métis." He spelled it for her. "It's French for mixed. As in mixed-blood. Down in Murray County where I come from, they call us breeds."

"You're a half-breed?"

"Um—it's like—all border collies are dogs, but not all dogs are border collies. All Métis are mixed-bloods, but not all mixed-bloods are Métis." He grinned at her, and she saw again how his face could light up.

Diana struggled to sit up straighter on the pillows. She did feel better, she realized. Her head was clearing.

"You teach Western American history, right?"

"How did you know that?"

"My sister's in one of your classes. So you'd know some about the people I come from? Like Louis Riel?"

"No."

"Guess it doesn't surprise me," he said. "Lotta people don't. But you're a professor, and I've got a book you ought to read."

He stood and went to a bookcase Diana now saw was crammed with books. He pulled out a book with a tattered dust jacket and handed it to her. "*Strange Empire*," he said. "Good place to start."

"You read?"

She saw from the way his face changed how she had blundered.

"Never mind," he said, and laid the book down beside the empty tea mug. He left the bedroom and came back with her jacket and jeans.

"They're dry," Diana said in surprise.

"I put em in the oven," he said without looking at her and left the room again. In a moment she heard him talking, she thought on the phone. She could make out only a few scattered phrases. ". . . from what I could get outa her . . . parked by the library . . . get it started and get her home . . ."

Diana got out of bed, switched off the electric blanket, and pulled on her jeans. When the dog, Tip, came to see what she was doing, she scratched his ears while he wagged his tail. At least she wasn't so shaky now. But what to say to Jake? Not knowing what else to do, she sat on the bed and picked up his book, *Strange Empire*, and read the couple of paragraphs on the inner flap. He was right, this was a book she needed to read, but she couldn't borrow his, not after what she'd said. She would track down her own copy.

Time passed. She read a page or two and was thankful for the company of the dog. Then voices from the next room—

"Where'd you find her?"

"Somebody picked her up in the street and helped her into the Stockman's. Celie and I pulled her back together as best we could."

Diana looked up to see a uniformed policeman in a navy parka. He looked as young as one of her students.

"Ma'am? Do you have your car keys?"

When she took the keys from her jacket pocket and handed them to him, he explained, "My partner's outside with a cruiser. We'll take you to your car and get it started, and then we'll see you home."

She needed to say goodbye to Jake and thank him, to find a way to mend what she had broken, but he was standing by a window with his back turned, and she didn't dare. The young policeman was waiting for her, and she followed him out into the shock of the cold.

"That's no kind a coat for this weather," he said, and held the door of the cruiser for her.

* * *

"Holy smokes," the young policeman said as he pulled up in front of the garage at the president's mansion. "You live here? By yourself?"

Back at the library his older, larger partner had squirted something, Diana didn't know what, under the hood of her MG and climbed in with some difficulty and started it. "No, you stay here where it's warm," the young policeman had said when Diana tried to get out of the cruiser and drive herself home. "We'll see you home." And he had driven her across town and up to the mansion in the cruiser while the other policeman followed in the MG and Diana tried to tell herself that Jake had been too touchy and wondered how he came to have the city police playing AAA at his request.

"We'll see you inside," the policeman said now. "Make sure you'll be all right. Don't you have somebody we can call to stay with you tonight?"

"I'm fine," she insisted, but they came in with her anyway and waited while she reheated coffee. They were full of questions and instructions. Stay awake for another couple of hours. Do you have a warmer coat to wear? Keep a blanket in your car. Keep your gas tank topped off. Might be a good idea to start your car again in the middle of the night, let it idle for a while. Are you sure you don't want somebody to stay with you?

"Hell, I don't like it," said the young policeman as they finished their coffee and stood to leave. "I'm going to bring Celie back from the bar to stay the night with her."

He touched Diana's shoulder. "This weather's nothing to fool with. You gotta respect it. Couple-three people freeze to death every winter around here."

To her horror, Diana felt her eyes well up. "I think I hurt Jake's feelings," she said, "and I didn't even thank him."

"Jake's a good man," the young policeman said, "and you were lucky."

He turned and followed his partner out the door, and Diana stood alone in the silent mansion.

8

Diana dragged herself through the next day. Her night had been restless. As she'd been advised, she got out of bed at one in the morning and went downstairs and started the MG and let it idle for twenty minutes. A couple hours later Celie arrived, smiling and ready to climb into bed beside Diana after ending her shift and closing the till at the bar. Again Diana tried to sleep, but her phone rang and she fumbled the receiver up before it could disturb Celie, but no one answered, not even the sound of someone breathing on the other end, and she hung up.

Her alarm clock showed she'd been asleep a couple of hours when her phone rang again, and again she answered to no responding voice.

She was up again before it was light, with Celie rousing only enough to give a sleepy wave. Celie would sleep late after her long shift at the bar, but Diana was giving herself plenty of time to fuel the MG, wondering why keeping its tank topped off was so important, before she drove to campus. At the gas station she asked the attendant about the engine heaters so many people seemed to have installed in their cars, the little plug-ins she saw dangling from under hoods, but the attendant just shrugged. She could ask her dealer, he said, but he didn't think cars like hers could be fitted with headbolt heaters. Her car was more of a summertime car, like.

On campus, she parked behind Main Hall in the lot, entered the side door, and climbed the echoing stairs to her office, where she sat with her office door closed, trying to concentrate on her lecture notes. But instead of concentrating on her notes, she was praying she wouldn't get another early morning visit from Abe. What would it be this time? *You were seen* in Jake LeTellier's bedroom, letting him take your clothes off?

He's an Indian, don't forget.

She shuddered.

In the sober morning, with her familiar books on shelves around her, *Coyote Stories* lying open on her desk, and gray daylight filling her office window, it sank in that the young policeman was right. She had been lucky last night. Strangers had helped her. The black man in a parka who lifted her up from the street. Celie. The policemen. Jake, whom she had insulted.

Almost worse was forcing herself to admit she had no idea how to go about her life, how to take care of herself, in this awful country. Her student, Cheryl—*What can you do! You don't know anything!*—had been right. Diana might have been the brightest student of her class at St. Agnes's High School in Seattle, she might have graduated from college with distinction—diplomas, awards—and she held a doctor of philosophy degree in American history from the University of Texas at Austin—but that young policeman thought she was stupid. Jake LeTellier thought she was rude and ungrateful. And stupid.

Have you had enough yet? Tatiana had written with angry jabs of her pen. *It's high time you listened to reason and came home.*

Diana's eyes brimmed and she dashed angrily at the tears. Sitting here feeling sorry for herself! Well. She might have been—yes, she *had* been thoughtlessly rude and ungrateful, but she wasn't stupid, and she'd never yet backed away from a challenge. She was damned well going to learn how to take care of herself in Versailles, Montana.

* * *

In the survey class she was unprepared for, Diana droned her way through the abolition movement and the Compromise of 1850, dismissed the students, put her coat on, and went out and started the MG. Sitting in the car, watching its exhaust billow out around her, it occurred to her that although she might have to skip lunch, she could drive down to the untidy little bookstore on Main Street as easily as she could sit here in the Main Hall parking lot waiting for the MG to warm.

The owner of the bookstore, an owlish fellow with glasses and a paunch and *Bob* on his name tag, led her to his regional collection of new and used books at the back of the store. "Howard's *Strange Empire*? Right here. And here's another one you might be interested in. Ever hear of Lucullus McWhorter? No?"

And Diana discovered she also was going to purchase a book by McWhorter, entitled *Yellow Wolf: His Own Story*.

* * *

One of the strange differences between the undergraduates Diana now taught and those of her own undergraduate days was that while she and others had been addressed by their professors as Miss Karnov or Mr. Whoever, the students at Versailles State College, apparently by some common agreement, all were called by their first names. Diana had known her classmates' last names but not their first names. Now she remembered all the first names of her students but not their last names unless she looked them up on class rolls or grade sheets.

After she dismissed her second survey class, she returned to her office and ran a finger down her class rolls, looking for a name. It wasn't until she came to her Westward Movement seminar roll that she found the name she wanted. The black-haired woman who was floundering so badly in class, who was about Diana's own age. Cheryl. Cheryl LeTellier.

* * *

Diana stopped at the gas station on her way home and had her tank topped, although the attendant gave her a strange look when her bill came to seventy-eight cents. Then she stopped at the Goodwill store next to the liquor store and walked through the familiar stale popcorn odor at the front of the store to the racks of winter coats at the back.

The selection was thin, for which she supposed she could thank the cold weather. She looked at what she thought might be an old army parka, a bright plaid coat several sizes too big for her, a yellowish woolen with a shredded lining, a couple of sad-looking grays that might as well have been sacks. At the end of the rack she found a dark brown three-quarter-length coat that at least fit her. The coat had a dark fur collar, and she wondered about the ethics of wearing it. Oh well. She shrugged. She had to have a warm coat, and probably nobody in Versailles worried about the ethics of wearing fur, one way or the other.

"What kind of fur is it?" she asked the portly woman who laid down her magazine to ring up the sale.

"Dunno. It's sure not mink."

Diana drove up to the mansion and carried in her purchases. She hung up her jacket and her new coat and made herself a cheese sandwich and started up the stairs, then had another thought and returned to the kitchen to pour herself a glass of wine.

She had finished *Coyote Stories* and left the book in her campus office. Now in her bedroom, wrapped in a comforter and curled in an armchair, with her sandwich and wine at hand, she opened the first of her new books and began to read.

    * * *

At one a.m. she laid *Strange Empire* aside and went down to start the MG and warm it. When she came back upstairs, the phone rang.

After last night's experience, she hesitated to answer. But Tatiana and Maria. Both in their eighties, after all.

"Hello?"

"Diana?" The voice was so shaky she hardly recognized it.

"Ramona? What's wrong?"

"—I can't talk—"

Diana sat on her bed and listened to soft sobs but no words. "Ramona," she said after a minute or two.

"Con's listening. Maybe tomorrow."

The line went dead.

Diana sat for a moment without replacing the receiver. She hadn't talked to Ramona today, although she had seen her slipping into someone's office. Maybe it was Douglas Mainwaring's office. Now she wondered if Ramona was being overly dramatic. Wondered what kind of education it took to understand what was happening around her. Even in her strict high school, knots of girls had gotten their heads together and giggled. Looking back, Diana wondered what they had been learning that she never learned.

Diana hung up the receiver and slid back into bed, clipped off the light and dragged her mind away from the puzzle that was life in Versailles and back to *Strange Empire*.

Why had she known none of the history it recounted, or of the mixed-blood culture that had played its part in that history? Had its account of the Riel Rebellion been scorned as mere local history by the professional historians who taught her? Or did they scorn the book because, as she had learned, the writer was not a historian himself, but a journalist? Or—a more troubling question—was it because *Strange Empire* narrated a version of Western American history that ran counter to established historical ideology?

Whatever the answer, Diana had been riveted and unable to lay down the book, an account of what was no local matter but an international incident that spilled over the border between Montana and Canada, nothing less than a rebellion against the Canadian government in an attempt to establish an independent Métis nation. Led by the man Jake LeTellier had spoken about, Louis Riel.

The Métis. Descendants of French fur trappers and Cree or Assiniboine women who preserved a unique culture with its own language and traditions. Jake's culture.

The question was, how much more didn't she know? Her blood stirred, as it had during her graduate seminars, with the lure of the hunt, the search for answers. She had two targets now. Louis Riel and Victor Wheeler.

Tomorrow, she promised herself. Thursday. She didn't teach on Thursday.

* * *

At the Carnegie Library the next morning, Diana found Mrs. Elder downstairs and toiling at her perpetual book-shelving.

"More microfilm, my dear?" She led the way back to the reader and the cabinet and took out the reels for 1945 and 1946. "I was a bit concerned about you, working so late on a weeknight and having to drive home. I hope you didn't run into any trouble on those awful streets?" Without waiting for an answer, she threaded the 1945 reel into the reader and helped Diana find her place in late October.

Left to herself, Diana scanned through the rest of 1945 without finding another mention of Victor Wheeler. How old would he have been in 1945? He might have been eighteen or even younger at the time of the attack on Pearl Harbor—Diana lost track of her mental addition and subtraction as she changed reels to 1946.

By now she had learned to skim over the national and international news to focus on the local, which contained its own oddities. The community of Broadview, twenty miles from Versailles, apparently ran its own weekly column in the *Morning Tribune*. In January of 1946 the Poole family, each mentioned by name, had visited the Voller ranch—all the Vollers mentioned by name—and stayed for supper. A dance had been held in the community hall. The Broadview quilting society, each member mentioned by name, had held its monthly meeting. Diana wondered if the quilters or the dancers or the Pooles or the Vollers paid attention to the front-page headlines of the *Tribune*, which reported that the Emperor Hirohito had announced he was not a god and that fourteen coal miners had been killed in a mine explosion in West Virginia.

Reminding herself to keep track of time in the here and now, Diana pushed on. She had reached July of 1946 when she got up, put her Goodwill coat back on, and told the librarian she would be back shortly.

At the top of the library steps, in the shimmering air, she paused to listen to the silence. Not quite silent, of course. An occasional faint snapping of leafless frozen branches. A scrape from down the block, somebody shoveling a walk. No wind today, for a wonder. No sounds of traffic, but far down the street a car door slammed.

Detour of thought—what would Seattle sound like to, say, Jake—

She cut off that thought. Listened to the sound of her own footsteps on the steps, the audible click of the key when she unlocked the MG. The purr of the motor as it woke was reassuring as she shivered in her seat and noted to herself that she needed to bring along a book on these car-warming expeditions. And keep her mind on what mattered, which at this moment was Victor Wheeler.

Back in the basement of the library she turned the handle of the microfilm reader in a motion that had become unthinking and drifted into her state of suspension between present and past. Day after day, beyond February and into March, April, May of 1946. It wasn't until June 10, 1946, that she resurfaced with a jolt.

She had struck gold.

9

Diana had promised herself she would spend the morning in the public library, searching for Victor Wheeler, and the afternoon in the college library researching Louis Riel. But the surprise of her discovery awakened her into realizing that her wrist ached from turning the handle of the reader and that she needed to warm the MG again.

She had thought herself lucky to have found that first item about Victor Wheeler and his return from the Pacific after VJ Day. Now she wondered if she had convinced herself she'd find nothing more about Wheeler in the microfilm, if she really thought her only satisfaction would be that she'd sifted through every source, that she'd dotted every *i* and crossed every *t* of her search.

Because what she felt when she turned the handle and saw that photograph in the reader screen of those faces so long wondered about, so often speculated about, had been electric. And now she had to wait for her damned motor to warm.

When she dared, she turned off the motor and locked the MG and hurried back to the basement of the library, where she saw, to her relief, that Mrs. Elder hadn't come along behind her and tidied away the microfilm reels. Diana brought the screen back to life and—yes. The headline, *Wheeler-Karnov Marriage*. The young man and the young woman in a studio pose. Her mother and father.

* * *

Before she left the University of Texas for good, Diana had seen Annabel one more time. Diana had been hurrying to her oral defense of her dissertation, which was scheduled in a room in the liberal arts building when she saw, walking along the sidewalk toward her, Annabel with her sylvan figure and her long silvery hair and a smaller, stockier woman with cropped dark hair who looked vaguely familiar. Diana thought she was one of the young MA candidates. So Annabel had moved on. Annabel and the young woman were clasping hands and laughing, with eyes for nothing but each other. Neither noticed Diana, but Diana saw their faces as they passed by her and was stirred by the emotion she saw there.

Now, with a grainy photograph of her parents before her on the microfilm reader and the memory of her last sight of Annabel surfacing from whatever depths she had buried it, Diana saw the two women as vividly as though she had passed them yesterday on the street. Their clasped hands, their rapturous faces reflecting what they felt for each other. What, Diana wondered, had Victor Wheeler and Lillia Karnov felt for each other? Were there clues she could discover in the photograph?

For that matter, what had Diana herself felt, really *felt* in her life? A nonsensical question, she knew. Of course she had a sense of touch, she was a *real person* in that respect. She could feel the handle of the microfilm reader, feel the developing ache in her wrist from having turned it for so long. When she went out to warm the MG, of course she felt the cold, the deep chill in her bones. If she struck a match and put her finger in the flame, it would burn. But feelings?

One thing she really had *felt*, and recently, was terror. Those endless moments in the MG, spinning out of her control on the icy highway, dizzying her. And her terror in Jake's airplane when he had pulled those barrel rolls with her in the skies over Versailles and she felt for the first time the force of gravity that always had grounded her.

Diana set aside the next question—what else might she feel for the first time?—and returned to her study of the photograph.

The formality of the professional photograph, the young man and the young woman standing together beside a small table that held a vase of flowers, against a bland background, was another barrier between her and her parents. She thought perhaps if she had the original photograph, not this faded newspaper reproduction, she might make out more detail. Did such a photograph still exist?

The young man's hair was dark and straight and combed back from his face in a pompadour. He wore a dark suit and tie, but his face was indistinct and it was hard to make out his features. What else? His left hand was hidden behind Diana's mother, so she couldn't tell if he wore a wedding ring. On his feet—cowboy boots? With a suit and tie?

No sign in this young man of the old vagrant stumbling from one Versailles bar to the next. Maybe she would come across him later.

Possibly because a portrait of her mother as a child had hung in the foyer of the Karnov house in Seattle, Diana thought she could recognize the young woman. Light-haired, a full head shorter than her husband even in heeled shoes. A suit in some dark fabric, a hat, gloves. She stood partly in front of her husband, but Diana could not tell whether they touched in any way. And they gazed, not at each other, but into the middle distance. Neither was smiling.

Nineteen-forties formal wedding clothes and pose, perhaps? What about the cowboy boots? Were they a clue?

Probably not, she decided. She had students, male and female, who wore cowboy boots to class. Jake LeTellier wore cowboy boots. Although would he, or one of her students, wear boots with a suit?

Frustrated, Diana fought the urge to smash the microfilm reader's screen. Those blurry faces were her mother's and father's, but she could not touch them, could not hold the photograph in her hands. When she turned the reader handle again, they would be gone.

* * *

Darkness had fallen on Friday afternoon by the time Diana wound up her seminar and dismissed her students. She had kept an eye on Cheryl LeTellier throughout the hour, noting the other woman's averted eyes and closed expression. Cheryl fiddled with her pen, only occasionally writing a line or two on the pad in front of her, and Diana wondered what, if anything, she was absorbing of the lecture. But at the end of the hour, after gathering her books and coat, Cheryl walked past Diana and cast her a glance—furtive? Stricken?

"Cheryl," Diana said, "are you all right?"

"Yes." Cheryl's voice was little more than a whisper, and her face—yes, those were bruises, surely? But she paused with her books in her arms and her eyes downcast. By now the other students were clattering down the stairs at the end of the corridor, and she and Diana were alone.

"You don't look as though you're all right. Would you like to have a cup of coffee in my office?"

Cheryl didn't answer, but she followed Diana to her office and waited while Diana, wondering at herself, unlocked the door and flipped on the light.

"I'll fetch coffee. Do you take cream or sugar?"

"Black." Another whisper.

Diana went to Nelda's office and filled two cups with the last of that day's coffee. She half-expected Cheryl would have fled while she was gone, but no, she was sitting on the students' chair and gazing around Diana's office.

"Thank you," she whispered when Diana set the coffee in front of her.

Diana studied her over the rim of her own cup. At first she could see no resemblance to Jake, but eventually she noted the shape of Cheryl's eyes and, of course, her straight black hair. Earlier in the term she had wondered if Cheryl were an Indian, although eventually she saw Cheryl never joined either of the two—the two *what*, Indian camps?—that sat as far apart as they could get from each other in the seminar room.

Diana knew she should be asking herself what she thought she was doing and why. Here she sat in her office with Cheryl LeTellier, Jake's sister, who surely had received physical punishment recently, and she had no idea how to begin.

"You sure have a lot of books," said Cheryl.

Students always remarked on the shelves of books that lined Diana's office, and she always wondered if it was because they had no books at home. Now she gave her stock answer to Cheryl—"It's what I do."

"Read?"

"Read, study, learn."

"I used to like to."

A pause. Then Cheryl raised her face and looked directly at Diana for the first time. "You're not married."

"No." Diana hesitated. "Are you?"

Cheryl's eyes dropped to her coffee cup. She gave the slightest of nods. Diana waited, but nothing more was forthcoming. In desperation, to end the silence, she asked, "Cheryl, I've been curious. Are you an Indian?"

"Sort of. We aren't enrolled members."

It was what Jake had said.

"I don't know what it means to be an enrolled member."

Cheryl looked surprised. "It means your name is on the tribal roll, like those Blackfeet boys in class, for example. You have to qualify—blood quantum, some other requirements—I'm probly more white than I am of any one tribe. Some Cree in me, probly some Chippewa, I think some Assiniboine."

"*Blood quantum?*"

"Like, what percentage of Blackfeet are you? I think to be enrolled as a Blackfeet, you have to have at least one-fourth Blackfeet blood. Not all the tribes have the same requirement. They say the Cherokees will take just about anybody, but maybe that's a joke."

"The reason I ask—I've been wondering all term. Those Indian students in the seminar—I *think* they're Indians—don't seem to like each other much. They sit apart, never look at each other, try not to walk in or out of the classroom at the same time—is there a reason?"

Cheryl looked up and smiled for the first time, lighting her face in a way that reminded Diana of Jake. "Oh, yes, there's a reason. The two tall guys are the Blackfeet I was talking about, from Browning. The other three are those damn Crow from Hardin."

"I don't understand."

"They're tribal enemies. They fought each other, stole each other's horses—and the Crow scouted for the soldiers—"

"But that was long ago!"

"It doesn't seem like that to us. My grandma speaks the Michif. Our language. Her grandmother followed the buffalo when she was a girl. And her grandmother knew Louis Riel. It still matters to us what the Canadians did to Riel. I'm not crazy about the Canadians, either."

Diana thought of her recent late-night reading of *Strange Empire*. The Canadians had hanged Louis Riel. For treason.

She paused. "Cheryl, you seem so interested—so animated—when you speak of these things. Doesn't anything we're reading in class interest you?"

Cheryl was looking at her cup again. "The whole Westward Movement does seem distant. Long ago. All those pioneers and soldiers. But—" she glanced at her watch and set her cup on the corner of Diana's desk. "I need to go. My husband probly wonders what I'm doing. He already thinks I spend too much time up here. He tells me I ought to quit and stay home. But my brother says I should tough it out and stay."

Diana stood when Cheryl did. "I agree with your brother. Maybe we can talk again? I can ask you about things I don't understand?"

"Sure." Cheryl smiled again and was gone.

10

Diana kept busy through the next week, grading mid-quarter examinations, turning in interim grades to the registrar—a tedious process that involved sitting in the registrar's office and reading the names of students and grades aloud while the registrar noted them down, then listening while the registrar read everything back to her to check for accuracy—and laying out her lectures for the second half of the quarter. Predictably, students sought her out during her office hours, wringing their hands over their grades and swearing that their grades in their other classes were much higher than the grades Diana had given them. She had to snatch hours for the public library; she hadn't even managed to get all the way through the rest of the *Morning Tribunes* for 1946.

But today, Friday, Ramona looked into Diana's office during her office hours and, over the head of the student who was explaining how his assigned paper came to be lost, mouthed, "Stockman's?"

Diana nodded, thinking Ramona certainly looked better than she had sounded on the phone that night of strange phone calls. Maybe her crisis with Con was over.

After she left Main Hall, Diana paused only to top off her gas tank. Remembering the attendant's expression at her purchase the first time she topped off, she had been choosing different filling stations on a rotating basis. This afternoon she bought eighty-three cents' worth of fuel and then made a last-minute decision to visit the bookstore on Main Street before she drove to the mansion.

* * *

The bell tinkled when Diana opened the door of the bookstore, which usually brought Bob popping up from behind the cash register with his finger marking his place in whatever he was reading. But this afternoon he was at the back of the store, deep in conversation with another customer, a tall white-haired man in a dark suit. They both looked up at the sound of the bell.

"Diana!" Bob hailed her. "Just the girl! Come back here and meet Pat! Pat, this is Diana Karnov. She teaches at the college, and she reads our kind of books."

"I'm Pat Adams," said the white-haired man as he offered Diana his hand. His face was deeply lined, and his nose was slightly off-kilter, as though it once had been broken, but Diana was struck by his blue eyes and the radiance of his smile. Not a young man. He was elderly, even, but straight and limber in his movements.

"Pat doesn't get up to Versailles very often," Bob was saying, "but we've always got a new book for him."

"I've been wanting to get my hands on this one for some time," Adams said, "and I happen to know Bob, here, got in two copies."

He was smiling at Diana, Bob was grinning, and she realized the two men were teasing her.

"If you like what Bob and I like, you ought to have that second copy," Adams said, laying more bait and enjoying it.

"Maybe," Diana said, looking from one man to the other. She thought they must be old friends. Both were old enough to have been her father, although Pat Adams must be a good twenty years older than Bob, too old to have been a veteran of the Second World War like Victor Wheeler. For all the qualms that warred with her determination to find Victor Wheeler, the old drunken vagrant, she wouldn't mind discovering a father who—how had Bob put it—read her kinds of books.

"Anyway, good to see you, Bob. Hope I don't take so long to get up here to pester you next time."

Bob laughed, and Adams turned to leave with his book under his arm. His step had the spring of a much younger man as the bell over the door tinkled behind him.

"He's an attorney from Fort Maginnis, down in Murray County," Bob explained. "Mostly retired now, but there's a state senator here in Versailles he does some work for, and he has a couple of grand-kids here that he likes to visit and check up on, and of course he always finds time to drop in and see what I've found for him to read. You're going to buy that book, aren't you, Diana? You won't regret it."

Diana read the title of the book she apparently was going to buy. *Tough Trip Through Paradise*, by Andrew Garcia. She heard the Coyote's cackle: *You'll learn something yet, Diana!*

* * *

Cheryl LeTellier had been doing better in class after their talk, which had been much on Diana's mind. How the Indian students' history seemed so close to them, was remembered so fiercely. Tribal ene-mies after all these years. Her white students tended to idealize their pioneering ancestors. Maybe some idealization all the way around?

Her own heritage? Tatiana and Maria often spoke at length about the cruelty of the male world outside the Karnov household—Tatiana's failed career in politics, Maria's rejection by every law firm in Seattle—but while Tatiana and Maria would look stormy at any mention of the tsar of Russia, they never spoke openly about their family's experiences. And Diana hadn't been interested in Karnov family history. The tsar was someone to learn about in a history lesson. Maybe the Russian blood was too thin by the time it flowed to her, or—a new thought—maybe it was another example of her lack of feelings.

She parked as usual in the garage of the mansion and entered through the kitchen, where she heated a can of soup, drank it with a glass of milk, and changed clothes for the Stockman's. She still was thinking about Cheryl LeTellier, asking herself all over again whether she should have asked Cheryl about the bruises on her face, when she was struck by a thought so stern that she found herself nodding as though in answer.

She shook herself back into the kitchen of the mansion with its faded curtains and dusty appliances and her empty glass and soup bowl. The thought that had struck her. What she needed to say to Jake LeTellier. If he ever gave her the chance.

* * *

What a strange choice of bars for Ramona Stillinger, Diana thought every time she walked into the Stockman's. Quieter, more sedate bars with restaurants were attached to motels at each end of Main Street. Abe Dennison and his wife had taken Diana to one of those restaurants for dinner and a drink during her interview trip, and the dean and his wife had entertained her at the other one. Also there was a country club with a bar and restaurant attached to the snowbound golf course west of town. But odd choice or not, Ramona was well known to the staff of the Stockman's, and when Diana walked through the back door tonight, she saw Ramona seated at her favorite table by the wall.

Ramona smiled at Diana and took a sip of her wine as a flicker of the candle's flame animated her face. "I've already ordered you a vodka collins. I hope that's all right? I did wonder if you'd rather have a hot drink on a night like this. Did you see the thermometer on the bank as you drove by? *Thirty-three below*? Too cold to breathe!"

"The vodka collins is fine," Diana said, but Ramona already was chattering about the difficulties she'd had that day, finding a parking place on campus in the morning, and then the librarian hadn't got in the book through interlibrary loan she'd requested—"Was your office cold?" she interrupted herself to ask Diana. "Mine was freezing!"

The barmaid—Celie—set Diana's drink in front of her, winked at her, and showed three surreptitious fingers to her before she teetered off in her hot pants and spike heels. So Ramona was on her third glass of wine. No wonder she was chattering. Diana sipped her own drink and hoped she looked as though she was listening. And suddenly she was listening.

"—Douglas may drop by."

"I see."

"No! Nothing like that! I hate the gossip that starts over nothing! Douglas has been a wonderful friend to me, even though he's so concerned about his tenure application, and I'm a lowly adjunct—oh, Diana, I earn a pittance! Not nearly enough to live on, let alone take care of the kids!"

"If you say so," said Diana, trying to sound sympathetic. She was turning over her new insight into Ramona's marriage with Con Stillinger and the reasons why Ramona had not left him. "Were you married young?"

"I was nineteen."

Too young to have learned how to live alone. Diana started to ask her how she'd managed to get a college education—even an M.A. in English—while raising children and probably waiting hand and foot on Con, but she was interrupted by the arrival of Douglas.

"Ladies!"

Douglas with his frizz of hair and plump face and pink-tipped nose. He took off his overcoat and draped it over the back of a chair. He gave a little bow to Ramona and smiled at her and smiled at Diana. "It is c-c-c-cold tonight!"

Diana disliked his voice, high-pitched with a tendency to crack on his affected stutter over *cold*. The truth was, she didn't really like Douglas. And now she guessed she was his designated chaperone for the evening, because Ramona was glowing.

"Lovely ladies! Ramona, may I assume the erring Con has returned to the fold?"

"Oh, he's very much returned to the fold."

Diana looked from Ramona's face, lovely in the candlelight, to Douglas's jumpy happiness and wondered what Ramona saw in him. A man who was not Con Stillinger, apparently.

"And Nicky is taking it how?" asked Douglas.

"Oh, he was overjoyed to see his dad home again! But Douglas, he's only seven, he doesn't understand, and I've tried to keep—well, keep things as normal as I can. With the older kids, I know they know it's rocky, I just hope they don't know *how* rocky—"

Diana sipped her drink. She knew there was quite an age gap between Ramona's two older children and little Nicky. Now Ramona was chattering rapidly about her children while Douglas leaned closer to her, exuding concern. Diana could make out only scattered words, which was probably just as well. The Stockman's, which had been almost empty when Diana arrived, now was filling with customers. It hit her why the Stockman's was Ramona's choice of bars. The curious glances she and Douglas were attracting weren't from people in her own circle. Of course she wouldn't drink at whichever bar—the Versailles Inn? the Bellevue Lodge?—where her husband's friend worked as a barmaid.

Diana set down her glass, wondering if there was a tactful way of intervening, of letting Ramona and Douglas know they were being noticed, but she froze with her hand on her glass, because Jake LeTellier just had walked through the back door of the Stockman's.

11

Jake paused for a moment, then walked to the bar, but Diana knew he had seen her. When he carried his drink to his usual table at the corner of the bar, she drained her own glass for what courage it could give her and stood and steeled herself to walk across the bar to him.

Jake watched her every step of the way. What she could see of his face under the brim of his Stetson was expressionless, but at least he hadn't jumped up and walked out again. Maybe he was waiting for someone. Maybe he had a date. Maybe with a woman who wouldn't care if he was trouble. Oh, well. Diana wasn't going to take up much of his time.

She reached his table and looked at him, and he looked back. Said nothing.

She could do this. She'd faced an oral examination committee for her doctorate, after all. She could face Jake. She gulped and willed herself to speak.

"Jake. I want to apologize to you. What I said to you was rude. And stupid. When you'd done so much for me." She sounded stilted in her own ears, but she stilted on.

"The policemen said you saved me from freezing. I jumped to conclusions about you, and I hate it when people jump to conclusions about me. And I'm very, very sorry, and I apologize."

She paused and added a last sentence, one she hadn't rehearsed. "And I read *Strange Empire*, and I wish I had someone to discuss it with."

Jake just looked at her. The moment stretched until she was sure he wasn't going to accept her apology, and she was about to go back and retrieve her coat—Ramona and Douglas hadn't noticed her leaving them, wouldn't miss her—and get in her car and drive back to the mansion.

But Jake pushed back his hat and smiled at her. "Oh, hell, Professor Lady. I never could stay mad long. Not long enough, anyway. Hell, sit down. Let me buy you a drink."

Weak-kneed, Diana sank into the chair opposite him. Celie the barmaid was at her elbow—"You want what you had before?"

She shook her head; the taste of collins mix was still in her mouth, cloying, but she couldn't think what else.

"Get her what I'm havin, Celie. A Square Bottle Ditch with ice."

Celie bobbed off. Diana glared at Jake. "The man makes the decisions, is that how it is?"

Jake just looked back at her with his mouth quirked. "Professor Lady, do you ever consider just relaxin when somebody's tryin to be nice to you?"

"I don't even know what a Square—what you ordered. I don't know what it is."

"A Square Bottle Ditch. Canadian Lord Calvert whiskey, because it comes in a square bottle, and it's the bar whiskey here. The Ditch part is Milk River water. With ice. You can only get a Square Bottle Ditch up here, along the Highline, where the Milk River runs."

"It sounds awful."

"The water really comes out of a faucet." His mouth was doing more than quirking now, and Diana saw he was trying hard not to laugh at her. She could feel herself blushing and hoped the lighting was too dim for him to know. For cover, she caught at another unfamiliar term.

"What is the Highline?"

"It's where you're livin now." He paused, took pity on her. "It's this long stretch a prairie across northern Montana, from the Dakota border to Browning, where it runs up against the Rockies. Got its name from old Jim Hill's railroad that runs along it. The high line."

Celie arrived with their drinks and winked at Diana. "You've got way better company here than you did over there."

Diana glanced over her shoulder, but Ramona and Douglas were deep in conversation. When she turned back to Jake, he raised his glass to her, and she raised hers because it seemed the thing to do. Then she sipped and winced at the unfamiliar bite of the bourbon and water and dropped her eyes when Jake grinned at her reaction.

"Professor Lady," he said, "you're the goddamnedest puzzle I ever run into. It's like somebody's taken out an injunction on you, to keep you from smilin. *Can* you smile?" He sipped his own drink, watching her. "What did you think of *Strange Empire*?"

Diana fought the part of her that was warning of the absurdities of sitting in a bar called the Stockman's, drinking a Square whatever and discussing a book with a—what was Jake—a diesel man. But what she really wanted was to explore the ideas that had come to her on reading Howard's book and find a way to organize those ideas into a way of understanding the history of the American West. The story of the Riel Rebellion was, in essence, a narrative that ran counter to everything she had been taught about the Westward Movement. Were there other narratives? If she were back in Austin, among the other graduate students in the Western American History sequence, she would find plenty of willing sounding boards, but she wasn't, and not a man among her new colleagues in the history department at Versailles State was likely to take an interest. They'd probably chalk it up to her feminism. Ramona's words came back to her: *I don't have one friend in this damned town I can talk to.*

But here was Jake LeTellier, diesel man or not, willing to talk and apparently interested in the topic.

"What I don't understand," she began and paused. "Jake, how many people here in Versailles would recognize the name Louis Riel? Or know about the Riel Rebellion?"

"Not many, but—" he broke off. A scuffle had begun at the bar, some shoving and shouting, and everyone at the tables turned to look. Diana saw a young man in a Stetson and fringed jacket, on his feet and nose to nose with another man in a cap and down jacket, both of them shouting incoherently and jabbing the air to emphasize whatever points they were making. She recognized the man in the fringed jacket as her student Mark Gervais—Jarvis—just as he shoved the down-jacket man, who staggered back against the fellow on the nearest barstool. A glass of beer tipped over and rolled off the bar. Now others were on their feet, shouting and encouraging the quarrel. Somebody tried to intervene and got a shove for his trouble.

Jake leaned across the table so Diana could hear him over the ruckus. "Good time to leave," he said. "It's goin to get real lively here. Celie's callin the cops."

Diana saw the bartender was guarding the cash register with a baseball bat as the uproar grew and Celie spoke rapidly into the phone. "Will she be all right?"

"She's cool. The cops will be right here. She's goin with one of em. Saylor, in fact. The kid who drove you home that night."

"I need my coat."

"I'll wait. And walk you to your car."

Diana hesitated. The fight was spreading into the tables nearest the bar. She saw an older couple get up and sidle unobtrusively toward the front door, but she straightened her back and skirted the combatants to Ramona's table, where she found her coat but no Ramona or Douglas. So they had left her without saying good-bye.

She turned with her coat over her arm, trying to decide her safest way back to Jake, and took three or four steps before somebody slammed into her shoulder, nearly knocking her off her feet before she caught herself on the nearest table. When she looked up, Jake was beside her, and Mark Gervais was stammering.

"She your girl, Jake? Hey lady, I'm real sorry. That bastard Kirby shoved me into her."

Then he blinked and recognized her. "Oh, hell. You're Dr. Karnov! I'm in your survey class. I didn't hurt you, did I? Jake, I'm real sorry. Hey, stick around and I'll buy you a drink after we get done with this."

"You have yourself a real good evening, Mark," said Jake. He guided Diana around the edge of the turmoil, keeping between her and the shouting and shoving. At the back door he held her coat for her, and Diana felt in her pocket and found her keys and her billfold where she had left them.

Once the heavy back door closed on the racket in the bar, the night seemed very still. Even with the lights over the parking lot, Diana could see the sky full of stars. Every breath of air felt freezing. She shivered in her coat, shaken by the sudden eruption of violence in the bar.

"Did he hurt you?"

"No. I don't think so. I might have a bruise tomorrow where I hit the table. He had his back to me, Jake. He didn't do it on purpose."

"Wasn't thinkin of takin out a contract on him. But Mark better simmer down and leave before the cops get there, if he doesn't want a spend the night in the county jail. Chris has had his eye on him for a while."

They had reached Diana's MG, and she unlocked it.

"We didn't get much of a conversation, did we?" said Jake.

"No."

"Maybe another time. Or maybe somewhere quieter tonight?"

"Is anywhere in Versailles quiet tonight?"

"I was thinkin my place, if—" Jake stopped, looked at her face, and laughed. "Professor Lady, do you honest to God think I'd make an attempt on your virtue? I know a keep-away-from-me look when I see one."

"No," she admitted. She straightened her back. "All right. We can talk at your place."

He grinned at her. "One thing I have learned about you, Professor Lady. Dare you to do a thing and you'll do it. Like learnin to drive on ice. I'm parked over there on the street, if you want to follow me."

12

Diana knew Jake was waiting to pull away until he saw her car had started. All the same, she fought with herself. Was she really accepting a dare when she let Jake teach her to drive on ice? Or when she went up in his airplane with him when he asked? It would serve him right if she drove back to the mansion and locked the doors instead of following him. But—it was a struggle to admit it—she didn't want to go back to the mansion alone. She had ideas she wanted to explore.

"No, Diesel Man," she muttered out loud, "I don't think you'll make an attempt on my virtue, as you so delicately put it."

She pushed aside the next question—what *was* Jake's interest in her?—as she followed Jake's truck, turning east when he signaled and turned. Once they had traveled a few blocks off Main, the streets were quiet. Bare branches arched overhead and cast shadows across the pools of light that fell from corner streetlights. A few cars were parked at curbs. When a cat shot out from under one of the cars and streaked across the street in front of her, Diana braked on reflex and took a breath to recover.

Jake had slowed when she braked for the cat, but now his red taillights were moving away, and Diana followed. She never could have found her way back to Jake's apartment on her own. Even when the policemen had driven her back to the mansion, she had been too shaken to focus on their direction. Now it seemed like a longer drive than she remembered, until it occurred to her that Jake had been speeding that night to get her to shelter and warmth, and she felt queasy with the memory, with what Jake knew about her.

What he'd said about an injunction on her not to smile. Diana turned over the idea. Who would have taken out the injunction on her? The great-aunts, she supposed. When had she seen Tatiana or Maria smile?

About eight or nine blocks east of Main Street, Jake signaled and pulled over to a curb. Diana parked behind him. She thought she remembered the shadowed silhouette of an evergreen tree in the front yard and a walk that led around the side of the house, so she hadn't been completely oblivious from the cold. *No, but you were oblivious of a lot,* her own voice spoke in her head. She watched Jake get out and bend to unkink a black extension cord from the snowy lawn, and she knew he was plugging in his headbolt heater.

Jake waited for her while she locked the MG and then walked beside her around the house to his door, which was not locked but opened to warmth, a single ceiling light burning in the kitchen, and a polite greeting from Tip, the black-and-white dog. A border collie, Diana remembered. When she stroked his head, he wagged his tail.

Jake was hanging his hat and coat from pegs by the door—"You goin to take your coat off and stay a while, Professor Lady? Have a drink with me?"

"I don't want another Square Bottle whatever."

"Didn't spose you did." He hung her coat on a peg. Took down glasses from a shelf and a corked bottle of red wine from under the sink, poured the wine and offered her a glass.

"Try this. It's chokecherry wine, my grandma's homemade. We can sit over here."

A pair of rockers were arranged in a corner near the stove. Diana looked at the rocking chair Jake was offering her and realized it was very old. Oak, she thought, with a padded and scarred leather seat. Someone had cared for this chair, kept the wood oiled and the leather polished—*lovingly* was the word that came to mind.

Jake had seen her interest. He nodded. "Thought you might like to sit in a real Métis rocker. It's seen a whole lot in its time. Belonged to my grandma's great-aunt Josie. She gave it to my grandma, and my grandma gave it to me."

Diana sat and sipped her wine, which was dry and fragrant. She gave a tentative rock in the chair and felt as though she easily could be transported to a time and place the chair knew but she was ignorant of.

"What I don't understand," she said, "is why none of what you're telling me, or what I'm reading now, is in the histories."

"Because the books are the histories of people with white skins."

A clock on a shelf ticked. Jake leaned back in the other rocker and the dog Tip curled up and slept by his feet while Diana thought about histories written by people with white skins and the historians who read and taught them. Tatiana hovered somewhere at the back of her mind, her jaw jutting as she scolded.

Diana looked up and found Jake's eyes on her.

"Professor Lady—Diana—I'm not one to talk about white skins. My grandpa is a white man. It's my grandma that's Métis. What're you readin now, since you finished *Strange Empire*?

"The man at the bookstore recommended a book called *Yellow Wolf*, so I've started it." She glanced at Jake and decided to risk a question. "Do you know it?"

"Yeah. McWhorter's book. The Old Wolf himself. You asked me how many people in Versailles would recognize the name Louis Riel? Bob at the bookstore would be one." He sipped wine, looking distant. "Me and my sister. Other'n that, not many here in town. Probly most of the elders out on the reservation, though, the Cree and Chippewa. They'll have grandfathers who fought beside Riel, and they'll remember. Younger people, maybe not so much. They don't walk the walk any more, even if they're Métis descended. I don't think any of em speak the Michif."

"You and your sister aren't old. Jake—" she hesitated and plunged. "Your sister. Cheryl. I'm sure I saw bruises on her face. But I didn't know how—I was afraid—"

She raised her eyes, but Jake had gone expressionless. "Bastard she's married to. Had to talk to him about it."

That, it was clear, was the end of that discussion. The way wife-beating was dealt with in Versailles. Jake had talked to the bastard.

"Cheryl and I aren't from here," he said after a while. "We were raised down near Fort Maginnis, on Spring Creek, where the old Métis started their colony. It's closer down there to the memories."

He seemed to ruminate for a moment. "My grandma's great-aunt Josie and her family were some of the people who came down to Spring Creek in Red River carts in 1879. Less than a hundred years ago. Josie was before my time, a course. Wish I'd known her, though."

Diana knew about the Métis colony on Spring Creek from *Strange Empire*. Closer to the memories, she repeated to herself. "Do you speak the Michif?"

"Not really. Picked up some when I was a kid. Kinda had to, after I figured out my grandma spoke it when she didn't want me and Cheryl to know what she was talkin about. Cheryl does better than me, but I can follow some of it when my grandma and her sisters and cousins get goin. But—Professor Lady, I don't think you took this teaching job in what you think is the middle of nowhere so you could learn about the Métis. Or Yellow Wolf and the Nez Perce, for that matter. What in the hell are you really doin here, Diana?"

He was looking directly at Diana now. She thought she saw real curiosity in his face, and something else she couldn't read, but which erased all thought of spinning him her line to the great-aunts and to Ramona Stillinger about the scarcity of jobs in the humanities, the chance to teach in her specialty, the book she hoped to write. She spoke the truth, knew it was the truth when she spoke it, and wondered what Jake did that seemed to elicit the truth from her.

"No. I didn't come to Versailles to learn about the Métis or the Nez Perce, although learning about them is a gift I didn't expect. I came here because I wanted to live my own life, and I wanted to know who I am, and part of that was trying to find my father."

A long pause.

"You remember tellin me your father's name?"

When she shook her head, Jake looked down at his glass and swirled his wine before he spoke. "Yeah, you were kinda out of it at the time. You said his name was Victor Wheeler?"

What she didn't remember about that night, what she wished she didn't remember. Jake was watching her gravely. Even Tip the dog, alerted by the sudden tension, had wakened and fixed his eyes on Diana.

What to say.

"I think that was his name. I was never supposed to hear it." She made a sudden surmise. "Do you know him? Where to find him?"

"Most people around here know him. Or know of him, anyway."

Jake stood, stepped over the sleeping Tip, and walked to a cabinet by the sink, where he took a slender Versailles phone book out of a drawer. Came back and handed the phone book to Diana, who saw he'd opened it to a page of *W* listings. And there it was. *Wheeler, Victor*, and what looked like a rural address.

The rows of names and numbers began to swim on the page. "So I could just call him. If I wanted to."

The flicker that crossed Jake's face might be curiosity, she couldn't be sure, but words were spilling from her.

"I was raised by my great-aunts. I hardly remember anything before I went to live with them. They hated my father. They never spoke his name, but they had plenty to say about him. And it wasn't until I applied for the job here, in Versailles, and they were so angry about it, forbade me to come here, and Maria, she's always the easier of the two—"

Diana didn't finish that sentence. "Maria let his name drop. She and Tatiana had raised my mother, too, and when my mother was eighteen, she stole money from the housekeeper's allowance and ran away. Maria—she was furious, she couldn't hold it back, she shouted the whole story out—Maria said they traced her as far as they could. She bought a train ticket in Seattle and rode as far as Versailles, in Montana, where she got off."

Another long pause, until Jake said, "How did they find out about Victor Wheeler?"

"They came to Versailles, once they were certain she was here, but it had taken them too long to locate her, and when they finally got here, she was gone again. And that time, they never found her. But they—" Diana broke off as the realization swept over her that Tatiana and Maria probably had found the same newspaper photo of Victor Wheeler and Lillia Karnov that she had found. Maybe in a real newspaper. That they had seen it before she found it felt like a betrayal of her own response to the photo. The gold she thought she had struck was tarnished by their rage.

"I think they found a record of their marriage in the local paper. And I know they had words with Victor Wheeler." She shuddered to think what those words had been like—shrieks, insults in English and Russian, demands—"but he wouldn't tell them anything. And my mother was over eighteen, so they couldn't force him to tell. But they hated him for it. They told me he was a drunken vagrant."

Diana felt a warm weight and looked down. Tip the dog had padded over to her and rested his muzzle on her knee to bring her back from the anger-filled Karnov house in Seattle to Jake's warm kitchen. She laid her cheek on Tip's head.

"Diana? What're you feelin right now?"

Feelings? She didn't have feelings. Yes, she did. They were churning through her.

"You're not lookin too good. Even Tip is worried about you. You want another glass of wine?"

Diana raised her head and found her glass inexplicably empty. "I have to drive," she said. "I have to get back to the mansion."

"Tip's worried about you, and I'm worried about you, goin back alone to that empty rattletrap of a place."

"I don't understand—" Diana struggled to go on. "Why you're being so, well, *kind* to me, when I've—"

Jake looked down, swirled the last of his wine, and studied the dregs. Looked up and smiled at her. "Professor Lady, has it crossed your mind I might like to talk about somethin besides truck parts? I took a class or two outside the diesel program while I was at the college, and I kinda miss the discussions."

Then he laughed at her expression. "And hell, I'd ask you to stay here with me tonight, cept I don't spose you want to leave your car parked behind mine where folks can see it in the morning."

"No." She tried to laugh with him. "I don't think the sexual revolution has come to Versailles yet."

"No. Folks here still try to keep it secret. Tell you what. I'll drive you back in your car, and stay with you, and you can finish the rest of that bottle, if you want to, and at least try to relax, and spill out however much more of your story you need to. You can drop me back here in the morning. Early. Unless you're still worried I'll attempt your virtue?"

She managed a real laugh. "No, Diesel Man. I don't think you'll do that."

13

Jake had given Diana the corked bottle of wine to hold while he folded his legs into the front seat of her MG and started the motor. Diana didn't feel as though she would need more wine, but more as though she had unloaded what she hadn't known was a weight inside her. Part of the weight, at least.

"If it was me, I think I'd want to hear his side of the story," Jake had said as they were leaving his apartment, and now she thought about stories and different sides of stories while Jake drove through Versailles on streets she was beginning to know. It wasn't until he turned on the highway and she realized he was driving past the last gas station that she gasped.

"No! Stop! We haven't topped the tank!"

Jake kept driving. "Why do you want to stop for gas? You're barely below the full line."

"But I always fill up now, before I go home. The policemen that brought me back last week told me to keep my tank topped off! And to get a warmer coat, and—"

"Saw you had a new coat," Jake said. "So Chris and Saylor told you to keep your tank topped off?"

"Yes, every night, last thing before I drive up to the mansion. I felt so stupid, not even knowing how to *live* here—"

"It was good advice they gave you, up to a point. But you can wait to top your tank until you're down below the three-quarters mark, Professor Lady. Maybe even below the half mark, here in town."

Jake didn't speak again until he pulled into the garage at the mansion. Then he said, "How much does it cost you to drive this rig from here to campus and back? And warm it up a couple of times between?"

"About eighty cents."

He shook his head. "One good thing about drivin this little outfit. At least you get good mileage."

* * *

Diana had lectures to prepare for next week, but she had promised Saturday in the public library to herself. As soon as the library opened on Saturday morning, she found Mrs. Elder shelving books downstairs and asked for the 1946 microfilm reel.

"Here you go, dear. It must be quite a project you're on. I'd think you'd be blind from reading all that microfilm by now. How many more years do you plan to read?"

"I'm not sure yet."

"Just let me know."

Mrs. Elder gave her a wide untroubled smile and went back to her shelving, while Diana asked herself the same question. Based on her own age and date of birth—the great-aunts always, well, *celebrated* wasn't the word, *commemorated* her birthday on March 16, which was the date on her birth certificate—the birth certificate itself wrested from Tatiana's grim custody—and her sense that she had been no more than five when she was brought to their house in Seattle, it made the year 1947 very likely, which also was on her birth certificate, although she had her doubts about its accuracy.

"You have your birth certificate?" Jake asked her last night, after she told him more of her story.

"Yes. But I had to steal it from Tatiana's file after she showed it to me. It's one of the reasons she's so angry with me."

* * *

Diana sat down at the microfilm reader and hesitated to snap on the light. Did she really want to see the photo of Victor Wheeler and Lillia Karnov again? When seeing his name in Jake LeTellier's phone book had shaken her so badly?

Straighten your shoulders. Depend on yourself to do what needs to be done. She clicked on the microfilm reader and scrolled past the wedding photo of her mother and father without stopping.

Her birthday of March 16, 1947, fell just a few days more than ten months after her parents' wedding date of June 10, 1946. It seemed reasonable that, if the date on her birth certificate was accurate, either she would find her birth noted in the *Morning Tribune*'s vital statistics during June, meaning that she had been born here in Versailles, or she wouldn't, meaning her mother had been pregnant when she fled again, and the place of birth on Diana's birth certificate—Rockdale, Texas—might be genuine. Maybe it would also explain why the line for *father* had been filled in *unknown*.

It might also be possible that the birth certificate date was inaccurate and her mother already had been pregnant at the time of her marriage.

Diana, therefore, did not scroll rapidly ahead to June of 1947, but continued slowly past the wedding photo and on into August of 1946. As before, she concentrated on police reports and community events along with vital statistics—particularly the folksy little columns from small towns near Versailles. It had occurred to her that a young married couple in a rural community might well attend a dance or be named among somebody's Sunday visitors.

But she scanned all the way through December 1946 without finding further mention of a Wheeler or a Karnov, so she looked at her watch, put on her coat and gloves, and went out to start the MG and finish reading *Yellow Wolf*, which the press of mid-quarter had forced her to neglect, while she waited for the engine to warm.

She found her place in *Yellow Wolf* and picked up the threads of his story. It made for painful reading—a first-person account, as told to Lucullus McWhorter, of the young warrior Yellow Wolf and a breakaway band of Nez Perce Indians who refused to move off their homeland in the Wallowa Mountains of southeast Oregon.

They fought the United States Army at a place called White Bird Canyon, in Idaho, and fled over the mountains into Montana, where they fought the soldiers again at the Big Hole and fled further, a starving and depleted remnant that sought help from the Montana Crow, who turned them away. Diana recalled Cheryl LeTellier's disdain for the Crow students in the Westward Movement seminar.

Now she read how Yellow Wolf and the surviving Nez Perce had turned north, toward the Milk River and Canada. But the soldiers caught up with them on the prairie near the Bear's Paw Mountains and shelled their hastily built shelters, killing women and children indiscriminately. Starving, freezing in bitter winter cold—Diana shuddered—the Nez Perce, under what seemed to be the last chief standing, a man named Joseph, whose name at least was familiar to her as the I-will-fight-no-more-forever-chief, had surrendered to be shipped by freight car to Oklahoma.

But Yellow Wolf and a few others escaped. They had been given food and clothing and ammunition by people he called the Milk River half-breeds—and Diana stopped reading and closed her eyes. After reading *Strange Empire*, she knew the Milk River half-breeds were Métis, and that a Métis band was loading Red River carts for the trek down to Spring Creek when they met the Nez Perce. Among them would have been Jake's grandmother's great-aunt Josie.

The strange way the threads of stories crossed and interwove. And so close at hand. The Battle of the Bear's Paw had taken place a handful of miles from present-day Versailles. The Milk River Métis might well have driven their Red River carts over the soil where Versailles now stood. The Nez Perce might have ridden over it.

Well. She had her own story with its threads to untangle.

* * *

Back in the warm basement of the library, Diana scrolled slowly through January and February of 1947, finding plenty of news about bad weather, road accidents, losses of livestock to the cold, along with death notices, birth notices, notices of marriages, and community events, but no mention of a Wheeler or a Karnov. She leaned back in the swivel chair, closed her eyes to rest them from the screen, and rubbed her aching wrist.

"I don't understand what's driving me," she had said to Jake last night.

He shook his head. "I don't know what it would be like, not to know who my folks were. Think I'd want a find out."

Jake built a fire in the living room fireplace, and they sat on the sofa and drank the rest of the wine. Tip, who had ridden to the mansion with them in the cramped space behind the MG's seats, slept between them while Diana felt her tension ebb and the novelty fade of having someone with her in the mansion.

"It's not just that. You've got a story. Even the students in the Westward Movement seminar have stories. How their great-grandparents homesteaded out here, how tough it was—drought, sickness, horrible accidents, and no medical care—"

"It was pretty damn tough. But folks usually helped each other out. Your students probly told you that, too."

"Oh, yes. Whole communities turning out to look for lost children. Or harvest wheat for someone who died suddenly. Or fight prairie fires."

"You ought a hear some of my grandma's stories. She's got one about a horseback ride through a prairie fire would make your hair stand on end to hear it."

"I'd like to hear her stories."

Now, in the warmth of the library basement, Diana pulled herself out of her reverie and opened her eyes on the familiar surroundings. Child-sized library tables and chairs, racks of brightly colored books, model ships shrouded in spiderwebs in the high windows, stains on the walls. She thought she could get through at least another couple of months of the *Morning Tribune* before she had to go out and start her car again. With luck she could read to the end of June before Mrs. Elder closed the library and threw her out.

Diana had made coffee and dressed for her usual Sunday morning visit to her campus office when her phone rang. It was Ramona Stillinger, breathless.

"Diana, what happened Friday night? When that brouhaha broke out, Douglas was alarmed and insisted on leaving—we argued, and finally we went down the street to the Alibi, but he felt nervous and we didn't stay long—after he left, I walked back to the Stockman's to look for you and saw the police cars and flashing lights and people being marched out on the sidewalk, some of them handcuffed. I've been trying to call you, but you don't pick up—what became of you? Are you all right?"

Diana managed a swallow of coffee while she thought how best to gloss over Friday night.

"No, I'm fine, Ramona. Really."

"Then there was trouble on Main Street with some of the hippies—one of them was beaten up. That black kid. Everyone was talking about that. I was worried for you, Diana."

"I left the Stockman's just as the fight started, so I didn't see the police, or any hippies, either. I had a drink with a friend and went home."

Which was the truth, if less than the whole truth. "And I was at the library most of yesterday."

Ramona breathed a deep wheezing breath into the receiver. "Oh, Diana! How can you stand it? All those hours in the library—whatever it is you're researching—if I didn't drag you out for a drink on Friday nights, you'd be in the library. Wouldn't you?"

"Yes, probably, but—"

"Oh, Diana." Ramona sounded faraway and despairing. "And now Con is—I don't know how to explain it. It's like he's taking his guilty conscience out on me. Suspects me of what he knows he's done. Diana, he *watches* me—I've had to pick my moments to call you. Diana, would you ever consider—"

A pause that dragged on. Diana waited.

Then a rush of words. "Diana, I think he suspects, well, Douglas and me of—and I just thought—Diana, I had an idea. If Con thought that you and Douglas were a couple, and it would be likelier, wouldn't it, than Douglas and me? Two college professors? Both single? And I have to face it, you and Douglas are more of an age than Douglas and I are. Would you, Diana? Would you consider it? We could make it a foursome—Con and me, you and Douglas. We could have dinner and drinks together, and Con would think—and I have to do something for Douglas, he's terrified of Con now, on top of his anxiety about his tenure application—"

"Ramona, that's a crazy idea!"

"Oh, Diana, don't, don't, don't think that! When you're the only friend I have in this awful town I can talk to—when I'm the only friend you have, because you're holed up in that library for hours—"

"Ramona—"

"At least say you'll think about it! I'm begging you, Diana!"

"I'll think about it," said Diana, although she could hear the Coyote's cackle at the very idea. Just the situation he would relish! "Ramona, I have to go now. I've got lectures to plan—"

"Oh, yes. Always the little scholar-professor."

"Not always," said Diana. "I've got a flying lesson this afternoon."

14

Somehow October had segued into November, sending the red lines dropping in thermometers and another round of students' papers piling on Diana's desk. Diana worked steadily in her campus office, pausing only to open her lunch sack to munch cheese sandwiches and carrot sticks while she outlined lectures and finished grading the last of the late papers. Her brain had become compartmentalized. In her campus office, it took up classroom work and screened out everything else. When she looked at her watch, she was mildly surprised that it was two thirty. Her flying lesson was at three. She gathered up her papers, locked her office, and hurried out to the MG.

The snowfields that stretched on both sides of the highway still seemed desolate to Diana, but at least a familiar desolation. She turned off the highway on the airport access road and allowed her compartmentalized brain to wander, from Ramona's crazy plan for Douglas and Diana to her claim that Diana was her only true friend in Versailles and herself Diana's only friend. Diana supposed she was right, which was the only reason for not dismissing out of hand Ramona's plan for a—what? *Double date?*

But now Diana found herself thinking about the Friday afternoon coffees she continued to have with Cheryl LeTellier. She and Cheryl weren't exactly friends, they were professor and student, and yet Diana realized their conversations were far more interesting, at least to her, than her conversations with Ramona, which had turned into Diana's listening to Ramona's lamentations. Cheryl also must enjoy her talks with Diana, or she wouldn't wait after class on Fridays, as she did, to slip into Diana's office for a little while. Yes, on some level Diana and Cheryl LeTellier were friends.

What about Cheryl's brother Jake?

Jake, who went out of his way to be kind to her despite her unthinking rudeness. Jake, quietly and only occasionally commenting while he absorbed more of her story than she had ever told anyone. They had watched the flames from Jake's fire while his dog slept between them, and he had listened for as long as she needed to unburden, and he never—she had to smile to herself at his phrase—attempted her virtue. Yes. On some level Diana didn't understand, she and the diesel man had become friends.

* * *

It turned out to be Chris Beaudry who gave her flying lessons, because Chris had his instructor's rating. Jake's had lapsed after his wreck. The last time she had flown, Chris told her to calm down.

"What's your hurry? You ain't gonna learn any faster." By then, after her lesson, they were drinking coffee in Pete the maintenance man's house trailer while Chris filled out Diana's logbook.

"You said most people can solo after seven or eight hours of dual. I've been up five times and I still can't hold the nose off when I try to land."

"I said most *men* can. Now don't jump down my throat, because women can learn to fly, and I never said they can't. My ex learned. You just ain't got the muscles in your left arm to hold that nose off is one of your problems, and your worse problem is your reflexes."

"How long did it take your ex-wife to solo?"

"I don't remember. Quit worrying about it. It's your reflexes you got to work on. You got to go over and over your stalls and your patterns and your landings until handling that plane seems like the natural thing to do, which it ain't. You're all the time fighting to keep the plane off the ground. You're scared of the ground. Ain't you?"

"No," she said. But she knew the sick feeling that came with cutting the throttle and hearing the abrupt silence of the engine while she was still a thousand feet above the airstrip and coming in downwind. Chris continually bellowed instructions—"Tab trim! Radio!

Carb heat! Give her power, you're too low! Cut your power, damn it, you're too high!"—while she scrabbled to obey. She never knew if she was too high or too low on her approach; all she knew was that the snow fence rushed to meet her when she turned on final approach, and she could not keep herself from pulling up the nose.

"What are you trying to do? Don't you know that's how you stall?" Chris screamed, until, gritting her teeth, Diana released her grip on the controls and let the plane settle over the fence and down on the south end of the runway.

But then—"Hold the nose off when you start your flare! Keep your right hand on the throttle and pull that control all the way back with your left hand! You can smash the landing gear, slapping her down the way you do!"

"Look," Chris tried to explain to her as the short afternoon darkened outside Pete's trailer. "It'll come to you. You just got to relax and let yourself do it."

Chris wore his perpetual grin, but his blue marble eyes were expressionless. Jake had told Diana that Chris could barely read, something to do with the way he saw words on the page. His ex-wife had read every word of the police manuals and the flight manuals to him and helped him memorize the answers to the questions for the police exams and the flight exams. Chris might be illiterate, but he wasn't stupid.

To be unable to read, really unable to read. What would it be like? All information filtered through other eyes and voices, or collected from broadcasts or word of mouth? Chris would know all the stories, but with a knowledge alien to hers. She knew she never would begin to know what he saw out of those curiously opaque blue eyes, but what he saw was real in a way that excluded her.

* * *

When Ramona heard about Diana's flying lessons, she told her she had gone insane. "The rumors will be flying about you and Chris," she warned. "He's a man who gets around. He had an affair with a schoolteacher last summer, and his wife took a shot at him through a screen door. That's why he's divorced. Why are you doing this?"

"Oh, I enjoy it. It takes my mind off those pitiful sophomores."

In a way this was the truth. At six or seven thousand feet, struggling and grunting against her seatbelt to pull the nose back far enough to stall the plane, she had no time to think about anything except what she was doing. After each lesson she was faintly astonished to walk back into the world outside the cockpit with its clammy metal fittings and its smell of oil and stale smoke.

"Isn't it awfully cold up there?" asked Ramona.

"Not really. It can be fifty below zero when we're at altitude, but if the sun is shining on the windshield, I wish I could take off my coat. Chris says flying is smoothest when it's coldest."

* * *

On Monday morning Diana dropped her books and lecture notes on top of the ungraded essays on her desk and sat down to her unrinsed coffee mug from Friday afternoon. Along with a handful of junk mail and college circulars was another letter, addressed to her in the familiar spiky handwriting.

"A little weary this morning, are you, Di?" drawled Abe. He was leaning against her door with his arms folded.

Diana, who had just thrust a finger under the flap of the envelope, dropped it and looked up.

"Got a paper cut?" asked Abe.

She looked at her finger and saw the single drop of blood welling from the thin red line of the paper cut and dropping on Tatiana's letter. Abe handed her a tissue.

"Nasty things, paper cuts. What is it, a love letter?"

When she said nothing, Abe folded himself into the students' chair and put his feet on her desk.

Diana stared at him. Abe always looked too thin to be as strong as she knew he was. His suit hung on him. The note in his voice would have sounded like concern, but his eyes gave him away. Reddish and deep set, they flickered over her. Abe always knew which game he was playing. In the summer he played softball. Toward the end of the season last fall he had invited her to watch him pitch, and she had seen how the reddish eyes behind the horn-rims calculated the distance of the runner from the base. The ball cannonaded off the long arm into the first baseman's glove, and the baserunner spat in disgust and trotted back to the bench. Abe knew what game he was playing now.

"I always wonder whether you really like to teach, Di. Hardly fair to yourself, is it, to spend your life doing something you dislike?"

"Why do you think I dislike teaching?" she countered.

"Oh, come off it!" Irritated, he brought the chair down hard on all four legs. "You know goddamned good and well what I mean. The way you mope around here is your business. Whether you mope around in your classes is what I worry about."

"Abe," Diana said. "Don't do this. You know the quality of my classroom teaching."

"Do I?" His lips formed a soundless whistle as he studied her.

"Damn it, you know you do!" She knew she was playing into his hands, but she saw no way but to plunge on. "You're going over the past like a historical revisionist on a petty scale—" *revisionist* had been a dirty word in the history department at the University of Texas—"and reexamining my teaching and the reasons you hired me and the directions you wanted the department to take and decide hell no, that wasn't what you meant at all? That I'm the mistake? That I *mope around?* That I'm *cold?*"

"Oh, Jesus Christ!" Abe threw up his hands. "Oh, shit. I knew it! I knew you'd blow up the minute I opened my mouth."

"You know I'm competent, Abe."

"By God, if anybody wants to hear a reason not to hire academic women, I can sure the hell give him one."

Diana did not trust her voice. If she quavered, she was lost. Her only chance was to glare him down.

Abe started all over again with elaborate patience. "Look. I swear to God. All I came in here to talk to you about is a student in your Westward Movement seminar. You know the campus committee I'm on, to study our retention of nontraditional students?"

"Yes."

"Okay. Background. A while back, a chick came to see me with a drop-add card. Chick by the name of Cheryl LeTellier. Mean anything to you?"

"I know who she is."

"She was pissed off and wanted to drop the seminar. Thought you were making fun of her. I urged her to talk to you. And I told her to give me a chance to talk to you first. But I didn't get around to it right away, because I knew I'd have to wade through every pile of the shit you carry around with you before we could talk about Cheryl."

"Go on."

"So the retention committee met last week." He waited. Diana said nothing.

"And who shows up to testify how well we're doing? Cheryl LeTellier. You want to know what she said?"

"I'm sure you're going to tell me."

"She said she'd taken my advice and talked to you. She said you'd been real interested in her family background. Asked her a lot of questions about her—what did she call it, her heritage. And now she was doing a lot better in your class."

"She is doing better."

"And I wonder why that is." Abe's eyes searched Diana. "I wonder why that is," he repeated.

Diana waited.

"You know she's Jake LeTellier's sister?"

Pieces were tumbling into place for Diana. She wanted to flinch from Abe's stare, but she locked eyes and looked steadily at him. She was Tatiana's grand-niece, after all, and she had to smile at the stray thought.

"Is that all?"

Abe didn't blink. "Di. You can call me a chauvinist or any other kind of son of a bitch you feel like, but something's wrong with you. You're going to have to get yourself straightened out."

"Let me see if I understand you, Abe." Diana found herself sitting straighter in her chair, fixing Abe with the gaze that often enough had pinned Diana herself when she stood before her great-aunt. Channeling Tatiana! An idea she would have to think about more deeply, but not now.

"You're suggesting, Abe, that Cheryl LeTellier is doing better in the Westward Movement seminar because of a—" She paused. "A relationship you *imply* I have with her brother. Are you *implying* that her brother is paying me in some way to make sure his sister passes the class? Or perhaps it's the other way around. Perhaps I'm the one who is *paying* Cheryl's brother to screw me? Is this the kink I need to *straighten out*?"

She was enjoying the expression on Abe's face and blessing the fringe benefit of an expanded vocabulary of obscenities the radical feminists in Austin had offered.

Abe's mouth opened and shut, but no words emerged. He took his feet off Diana's desk and stood.

"It must have something to do with living all by yourself in that mausoleum," he muttered.

"I'm sure that must be the ultimate reason a student has improved in my seminar."

"You're fighting yourself, Di. I'm not fighting you. But you're headed for real trouble in this town if the story gets around that you're seeing that buck Indian."

He unwound himself from his chair and affected a saunter out of her office. Diana got up and closed the door behind him. She leaned against it with her eyes shut and her fists clenched until she could feel the rush of anger subside like gravity returning to the familiar. When she opened her eyes, she saw cinder block walls painted peach and a stained ceiling and a chair and desk scarred by twenty years in the institution. A stack of essays from the afternoon survey class that she had to grade. Stacks of thermofaxed memos of the daily routine, of department meetings and catalog deadlines and student events and potlucks and changes in the health insurance plan and notices from the curriculum committee and bulletins from the dean's office, all collecting dust and fading in the unobstructed north light.

So this was the teaching career she had fought for. Her life of her own, her escape from Tatiana and Maria. Ironic, she thought. If she had Tatiana's backbone, maybe she could make a life here in Versailles. For now she reached for the trash can.

15

Tatiana would be eighty-six on her birthday this November. Diana always kept track, although birthdays held only chronological importance in that household. Too bad Diana's freshmen never had learned such penmanship. Tatiana wrote the fine legible script she had been taught as a girl with real steel pen points and real ink. The old secretary in the library in the house in Seattle had a drawer with boxes of steel pen points and bottles of dried-up ink.

The library had been Diana's favorite room. Her great-grandfather's chair stood where the thin Seattle light fell across the pages of whatever book she dug out to read—the Alcott books or *The Little Shepherd of Kingdom Come* or perhaps a volume from the complete set of Charles Dickens—when she sat with her feet under her in the cushion of old, old black leather with its myriad hairline cracks and its faint odors left over from other times and other readers. In the drawers of the secretary were pencils of all colors and lengths scarred with teeth marks, string and nails and keys that fit no locks, tablets of slick white paper ruled in fine magenta lines, and a collection of Little Orphan Annie paperbacks. The shelves held her great-grandfather's textbooks and the rows of blue bound volumes of Washington State education acts.

Nobody else used the library—Tatiana liked to sit at the dining room table, doing her mysterious work with books piled around her—but Diana had moved the horsehair chair so she could watch the elaborately carved archway that led to the shadowed hall. She always feared being taken unaware.

In truth, Diana was the intruder. She knew it when she tiptoed across the hardwood floors, when she smelled the dust that fell when she pulled a book from the shelves. Some were written in other languages, other alphabets. Strange names were written on their flyleaves. Their pages fell open of their own accord as if in other hands than hers. Sometimes she found pressed flowers, forgotten and crumbling past recognition, old envelopes addressed to her grandmother or her great-grandmother, sometimes even corroded pennies. Nothing belonged to Diana. To anyone entering from the hall, it would have seemed that the small red-haired figure crouched with her book in the armchair was the ghost, nothing more than a reflection in a darkened window tapping at the glass in this silent house where no radio played nor voice raised unless in fury.

Tatiana would not have told her if Diana had asked. But she never asked. What difference did it make whether or not her mother, Lillia, perhaps wearing a blue dress with a string of red beads, got off a train in Versailles and followed a man to Texas where he took a job in a filling station to support her. The hot sun, the high dry grass, the odor of gasoline and road tar. Because if Diana's birth certificate was authentic, Lillia for some reason had journeyed from Seattle to Versailles to Rockdale, Texas.

Diana's fantasies could always conjure an answer, just as her fantasies conjured the blue dress and the red beads. Fantasies could run to anything. Maybe Lillia in her turn got fed up with the man *and left behind that little bit of a baby*—had Diana heard someone speak those words?

What fantasy could not do was answer real questions. Why had her mother fled Versailles? Why did Texas, or a place like Texas, recur in the shadow-memories that had led Diana to the University of Texas in Austin? For the thousandth time she regretted seeing her birthday certificate only after she'd returned to Seattle, when Tatiana showed it to her to lure her off the trail of Victor Wheeler. *Rockdale, Texas. Father unknown.* If she'd seen her birth certificate while she was living in Austin she easily could have driven to Rockdale and searched its newspaper archives.

If Diana was born in Texas, how had she found her five-year-old self in Seattle?

For that matter, how had Lillia come to be buried in the Russian cemetery in Seattle? Diana had seen her grave, which the great-aunts tended meticulously.

Although she dreaded it for reasons obscure to her, Diana needed to see Victor Wheeler for herself. It was possible she looked like him. With her red hair and hazel eyes, she certainly didn't look like any of the Karnovs. Red hair was said to run in families, and it probably would look as dark as Victor Wheeler's did in the black-and-white photograph.

Well. She gathered her materials for her morning survey class. As she left her office and passed George Shultz's open door and his avid eyes, she thought of a line she could have used on Abe, even if he fired her on the spot for it.

As for how I'm paying Jake LeTellier, Abe—I'm sorry to have to tell you, Abe, but your theory is all wrong. I've never had sex—with a man, that is.

She was still smiling to herself when she entered the classroom.

* * *

"Please, Diana."

"Ramona, it's a crazy idea. No."

"Please."

* * *

"So you're originally from Seattle?" Douglas bellowed in her ear.

Diana nodded. They were sitting at a table by the dance floor in the Three Hundred Club, a rambling space in a converted ware-house with a bowling alley and bar Ramona had insisted on vis-iting. Con Stillinger had shrugged and driven the four of them in his Cadillac up a steep grade to a plateau above Versailles, known as the east Orchards, where the Three Hundred Club was featur-ing live music. A band played country-western music in front of a fortress of amplifiers, and a scream could barely be heard over the din. Diana wished Douglas would stop asking questions.

But no. "What's your father do in Seattle?"

"He's dead," she screamed back.

"What?"

She was saved by Con Stillinger, who tapped her on the shoulder and mouthed, "Dance?"

She nodded gratefully and followed Con as far as she could into the shadowy thicket of bodies thrashing and flailing to the music as though in the grip of a killing wind. Con faced her and began to gyrate. In his stockman's suit and string tie he was easily as exotic a sight on the Three Hundred Club dance floor as his wife. He grinned good-naturedly as the red and purple strobes flickered over his face.

On the raised stage Diana could see the lead singer in his rhinestone-studded cowboy shirt smirking at the crowd and pretending to pick his nose. Occasionally through the thicket of bodies she caught glimpses of Douglas and Ramona sitting side by side at the table by the dance floor. For the first time she understood how rumors floated into the air and spread. Although they never looked at each other, vulnerability shimmered around them like an odor of violets rising through whiskey fumes and farts. Douglas and Ramona vanished again and reappeared as the strobes revolved like a giant kaleidoscope of shifting fragments that revealed the dancers and the electronic cowboys and the lovers in turn. The intensity of Ramona's and Douglas's faces made Diana want to hold her breath and snatch at something she had never known she lost but which might be recovered if only she ran after it.

She caught herself. The feeling must be like a drug craving. She had read that people could become addicted to their own adrenalin, hence auto racers and mountain climbers and parachutists and probably airplane pilots turning barrel rolls. Perhaps the quest for love brought on the same physiological surge. *Even when you know it can't last, while it does it's a shot in the arm.* Annabel had said that.

Diana wondered if Annabel's affair with the master's degree student had lasted. She hoped so. They had looked so happy.

Mercifully the band took its break when the dance came to an end. The sudden silence was a vast vacant terrain until voices rose to shatter it. Con led Diana back to the table where Douglas and Ramona watched.

"You're crazy," Diana had told Ramona.

"Please!"

"Why do I let you talk me into situations against my better judgment?"

A better question was how Ramona talked Douglas into showing up. He had been jittery all evening. In his own way, he was as odd a sight in the Three Hundred Club as Con and Ramona. Students at Versailles State College thought he was effeminate. Diana had seen them mimic the way he walked. With his large blue eyes and fine brown hair that rose in an aureole under the pulsing lights, Diana thought he looked like an overweight Romantic poet.

Nobody could say Douglas wasn't doing his part to carry out the charade, however. He slid his chair toward Diana's until his back was half-turned to Ramona and Con. When the cocktail waitress came around with her tray of fresh drinks, he fussed over Diana's to make sure she had what she ordered.

"Is it okay? Is it too weak? So you went to graduate school in Texas? It's a long way from Seattle. How did you happen to pick Texas?"

Diana shrugged, but Douglas was not one to be distracted.

"Yes, but *why*? I mean *Texas*, my God!" His high laugh soared above the conversations of the crowd.

"I was curious about Texas," said Diana. It was the first answer she could think of.

"You were *curious* about *Texas?*"

Diana shook her head. She was not going to tell him about high grass and the scent of road tar and gasoline.

Ramona leaned over and laid her hand on Douglas's arm, claiming his attention. "Be careful! She's touchy!"

"I am not touchy," said Diana. Her throat felt parched and she reached for her drink. Then she paused, feeling all their eyes on her. Searching for chinks in Diana's defenses, probing for what was not there. Then the moment passed. Ramona was leaning on Douglas's shoulder and laughing, while Con, a little apart, more than a little drunk, smiled to himself. Diana had a stray thought. Like Abe Dennison, Con knew which game was being played.

"They're fixing to play again," said Con.

"We won't be able to hear ourselves think!" Ramona's eyes sparkled. "I know! Let's go down to the Palace!"

"The Palace? That's no place to go. Nobody but the ki-yis hang out in the Palace."

Ramona flared up. "You see? It doesn't matter what I want to do! This evening we were going to go out and have a good time and not worry, but no!"

"Oh hell," said Con, unwinding his long legs from under the table. "It don't make a rat's ass to me where we go. I just never knew you to want to go to the Palace before."

Diana waited to play her part with Douglas. But Ramona slipped her arm through Douglas's and led him around the jammed tables, and Diana found herself following with Con. They stumbled through the smoke and noise and emerged under floodlights on the parking lot in the bitter cold. The building pulsated behind them. Below them stretched the lights of downtown Versailles.

Con dug at his ear. "If that racket wasn't something."

"Come on," said Ramona. "I'm cold."

"Gonna get colder tonight," said Con.

"You were born here, is that right?" Douglas asked him.

"Bout ten miles north of here."

Diana got into the back seat of the Cadillac beside Douglas. She could smell his cologne and bodywash. Ramona kept twisting around to talk to them. "Have you ever been to the Palace? It has a wonderful mahogany back bar that was brought up the Missouri by steamboat before 1889—before statehood. Montana is a very young state."

The neon lights on the Three Hundred Club's marquee were left behind as Con drove down the grade from the east Orchards, turned on Main, and parked behind the Palace in the alley. Con held the door of the bar, and Diana saw shadowy walls and a soft wood floor that felt gritty under her boots. It was too dark to see much of the famous back bar. One light hung over the pool table, and another shone through the swinging doors from a cafe. A few customers at the bar looked around and turned back to contemplate their drinks.

"Seems quiet enough," said Douglas, laughing nervously.

"Too goddamn quiet," said Con.

Ramona led them to a booth, rattling, "Versailles wasn't even here before the turn of the century. There was a military fort and then a railroad camp. That explains a lot. People here still act as though they live in a frontier camp. That's why there's no cultural spirit. It's a man's town, and they've never gotten used to having women in it."

Diana knew from Cheryl LeTellier that some of the bars of Versailles were tacitly whites-only and some mostly for Indians, where whites showed up only if they were looking for a fight. The Palace was male Indian territory. Broad backs at the bar stretched out the fabric of their shirts. Two or three had long raven hair hanging over their shoulders. A light from under the bar lit the bartender's puffy face as he poured beer from a tap into clean glasses. Con leaned on the bar and waited for their order, looking completely at home in his boots and stockman's suit and Stetson.

"Look at him," said Ramona. "What am I going to do with him?"

"This is really stupid," said Diana.

"I know. I know I can't stand much more."

"Are your parents both deceased, Di?" said Douglas.

"Yes. My great-aunts raised me."

Con came back with the tray of drinks in his big weather-beaten hands. "John says they had a little fracas in here, but the police came and straightened them out," he reported. "Most of these guys are too stove up to fight."

"One of Diana's great-aunts was a lawyer and the other was—"

"Maria was the lawyer. Tatiana ran for state superintendent of schools on the Socialist ticket in about 1932. Of course she lost, and she reregistered as a Democrat and spent years building her base of support with the labor unions to no avail," Diana explained.

Diana thought Tatiana might have had her eye on the governorship at one time, but she had that bad start, and being a woman in Washington State politics at the time couldn't have helped. Tatiana had resigned herself to private life before Diana was dumped on her, as had Maria, who in her turn passed the Washington State bar examination and never practiced law. In Maria's day, law firms simply didn't hire women.

"Tatiana always sounds like such a cynic," said Ramona. She helped herself to one of Douglas's menthol cigarettes and struck a match before he could reach for his lighter.

"A realist. She's a realist."

"Do you *realize*," Douglas said, "we're the only white people in here? Except for the bartender?"

"You have to admit it," Ramona went on, exhaling smoke, "those old women kept you sheltered."

The swinging doors opened and two young men staggered out of the café with their eyes on the pool table. They selected cues, chalked up, and bent over the table. Balls clattered.

"If they get any closer," complained Douglas, "we'll all be impaled on the wrong ends of cues."

Con stood up. "You all ready for another round? John, he don't dare leave the cash register unguarded."

Diana recognized the pool players, slab-assed and skinny in their western shirts and Levi's, as students in one of her survey classes. One was an Indian whose name she remembered was Jerry Stiffarm, the other was Mark Gervais—*Jarvis*—who had been part of the fracas at the Stockman's the night Diana had gone home with Jake.

The game was beginning again. Jerry Stiffarm racked the balls and stepped back, laughing. When he bent to take his shot, his black hair fell almost to the green baize table cover. Diana tried to imagine him as a warrior and could not.

His cue cracked.

Mark took his turn at a shot and whooped. "You see that? Old nine went in the pocket like he had eyes!"

"Ah, take your shot and shut the fuck up."

They both were drunk and unsteady on their feet. Jerry swaggered around the table with his can of beer in one hand and his cue in the other, picking his shot. He bent down and sighted along his cue, making a production of lining up his shot. It was not a difficult one. Diana, who once took a class in pool-playing for physical education credit, thought if he sheared the ball a trifle, it should roll straight into the side pocket.

Con came up behind Jerry just as he rammed the cue and caught the ball off-center. As if it too were drunk, the ball wobbled across the baize, poised on the rim of the pocket, and toppled.

"Did you see that? Did you see that fuckin' shot—whoa!"

Jerry was jerked backward so suddenly that his neck popped out of his shirt collar.

"You hear me? No goddamn way to talk in front of ladies!"

Con had Jerry by his hair, forcing him into an awkward backbend. His cue clattered to the floor.

"No!" wailed Ramona.

"Hey, man!"

Mark was coming around the pool table, raising his own cue. In the petrified moment Diana saw John the bartender standing in front of the cash register with his arms folded. He glanced at the telephone, but apparently decided against picking it up. Not with Con Stillinger in the mix.

Con dropped Jerry in a heap of flailing arms and legs and turned to greet Mark with a cackle of laughter. One big hand met the cue as it descended, then Con had the cue and Mark was backing around the table. Cackling, Con raised the cue. As it cracked on bone, Mark folded onto the floor.

Con took a step backward. Then, looking surprised, he sat down on the floor. Jerry had crawled up behind him and wrapped his arms around Con's legs. Together they thrashed into a table and upset it.

The men at the bar turned to watch, but no one moved to intervene.

Con writhed and got one leg free. He steadied himself on the back of a chair and pulled himself up. His string tie was up around his ear and his hat was gone, but he took time to straighten his jacket. Jerry still was locked around one of Con's legs. Con hopped about on that leg, jerking Jerry up and down while he took aim with his other foot and kicked. Jerry catapulted backward, crawled behind the overturned table, and retched while Mark sat up, looking dazed.

Con came back to their booth, grinning. Blood streamed from his nose.

Ramona's face was frozen.

"Hell, Maw," Con said. He smirked at her. "You wanted to come to the Palace. You got what you wanted."

16

As Ramona got back her voice and launched a verbal artillery round on Con, Douglas leaned toward Diana and spoke in her ear. "Maybe a good time to leave?"

"Yes."

Douglas held Diana's coat for her and they slipped away under the cover of Ramona's fury. Cold air hit them outside the Palace in an equally furious blast. The thermometer over the bank had dropped to thirty degrees below zero. Diana pointed to a full plastic drinks cup someone had set on the trunk of a parked car and forgotten, and Douglas shuddered. The contents were frozen solid.

"I need another drink to settle me," said Douglas. "Maybe we could check out the Alibi?"

"I've never been there."

"Sometimes they have real music."

Douglas held the door for Diana on a dark and overheated room. Candles flickered from tables, backlighting glittered on the rows of bottles behind the bar. Even with a full crowd, the Alibi was quiet in comparison with either the Three Hundred Club or the Palace. The bandstand was lighted but the band must have been on break.

"Maybe here?" Douglas found a table, held Diana's coat for her, and pulled out her chair. He drew a deep breath and let it out. "What a town. If it weren't for my classes—I just hope—" his voice trailed off as a barmaid teetered over in high heels and a short skirt and took their orders.

"You like to teach?" Diana asked.

It wasn't quite a question. Diana knew from the way Douglas talked about his preparations and his students that he was deeply involved in his classes. If he weren't in class, he was in his office and talking with students. Diana heard his high voice and cackle every time she walked past the English department at the other end of the corridor. His care for his students was to his credit. She knew she didn't give Douglas enough credit.

"I love it. It's what I do!" His voice cracked as it edged higher, and he gave an embarrassed giggle. "I taught for several years in a high school in North Dakota. Teaching at Versailles State is paradise by comparison, even the freshman composition classes, which everyone complains about. If only—" he interrupted himself. "Oh, look! We *are* going to have music."

A middle-aged woman had seated herself at the piano on the lighted bandstand, and now she nodded to a girl at the microphone, a beautiful young girl with an oval face and a cloud of dark hair. Douglas was staring at her.

"Oh, good," he said. "That's Rosalie Pence. She hangs out sometimes with Ramona's daughter. Ramona says her voice is out of this world. I've been wanting to hear her."

"They let her sing in a bar? She looks like she's about fifteen."

Douglas shrugged. "Yes, but that's her mother at the piano. They have an arrangement with the manager, and Rosalie's never allowed down on the floor. Ramona says they need the money, so—" he broke off as the pianist struck an opening chord and the girl at the microphone tipped back her head and sang to a suddenly silent crowd. Even Diana, who was not musical, realized what she was hearing was extraordinary as the tender lyrics of the Carpenters' hit "Only Yesterday" rose and reverberated through a barroom of rapt listeners.

The song came to an end. The girl stepped back from the microphone, acknowledging the applause.

"A voice like a bell," sighed Douglas.

But the woman at the piano stood and pointed a finger at the bartender, who was picking up a phone, and Diana stiffened. "Douglas, something's wrong!"

The young man from the Palace fight, Mark Gervais, had lurched into the barroom. His face was purpled from the battering Con had given him, but his eyes were fixed on the girl at the microphone, and Diana felt the same intensity that had passed between Douglas and Ramona. Then the pianist had placed her hand on the girl's shoulder and two hefty men from behind the bar took Mark by his arms and escorted him to the door.

Diana and Douglas looked at each other.

"What an evening," said Douglas. "I don't suppose she's going to sing again."

He sighed heavily. Diana wondered if he was regretting the interruption of the vocalist or if he had gone back to fretting about his upcoming tenure review.

But no.

"Ramona is so unhappy here. And I'm so torn."

"Torn?" she prompted. If he would tell his story, they could drink their gin and tonics, and she could go home and go back to reading *Tough Trip through Paradise* where she left off.

"I'm a Catholic," Douglas said. "I did my undergraduate work at the University of Portland—it's affiliated with the Congregation of the Holy Cross—and now I'm so torn, Diana, and I've prayed about it, and it doesn't help."

Diana began to get a sense of what he was struggling to tell her. "I'm not a Catholic," she said, "but I've been under the impression that the Catholics have lightened up since Vatican II. No more masses in Latin? Women given more voices in the Church? The Jews no longer held any more responsible than Christians for the death of Christ?"

Douglas was nodding. "I *loved* the Latin masses. But the Church hasn't lightened up, as you put it, in fundamentals."

Diana sipped her drink. She could see Douglas's dilemma, theologically speaking, but what she could not see was a reason to speak it aloud, which would only tell Douglas what he already knew. But she remembered the glimpse she'd had of the lovers' intensity that she had, well, envied. The shot in the arm. The odor of violets.

"Douglas, while I was dancing with Con at the Three Hundred Club? I saw your face and Ramona's face, and the way you were looking at each other."

He raised stricken eyes to hers. "My mother wanted me to be a priest. I considered it."

"But you didn't."

"No, I—couldn't."

"Where did you do your graduate studies?"

"At the University of Oregon. And that's another thing—I don't have a PhD. I have what they call a doctor of arts degree."

Diana had never heard of it, so he explained.

"You don't write a dissertation in a doctor of arts program. It's a degree that was developed when nobody anticipated what was about to happen to academic teaching jobs in the liberal arts. Now, with all the competition for jobs—and I'd have to compete against people with PhDs—that's if I don't get tenure—or if I—"

"Oh, Douglas. Surely you'll get tenure. With your teaching record—"

"I try so hard."

"What does Ramona want you to do?"

He swallowed. "To take her and Nicky and run away. She thinks her other children are old enough to stay with their father."

"What *are* you going to do?"

"Keep trying to pray. I guess."

Diana patted his hand, and he squeezed hers. He had long, manicured fingers. Ramona said he played the piano beautifully. "Thanks, Diana."

"Douglas, we went Dutch tonight, didn't we?" Diana laid some bills on the table to pay for her drink and thought Douglas looked relieved. She suspected he had been benefitting from Ramona's bar tab. "Good night."

* * *

From the Alibi Diana walked to the Stockman's where she started this fiasco of an evening by parking her MG in the lighted lot. She felt haunted by the glimpse she'd had of Ramona's face and Douglas's face. Her glimpse of Mark Gervais's face. What Diana had never felt. And wasn't there a religious association with the odor of violets?

She walked as fast as she could to the MG while she tried to remember what the odor of violets signified to Catholics. Then she looked up and stopped in alarm because a dark figure stood in the shadows by the door of the MG.

"Hey, Professor Lady."

"Jake!" she said. "You startled me!"

"How was your date?"

"It wasn't a date—" she began, but she stopped when she saw his teeth flash white.

"I know that. Celie filled me in."

Not much would circulate through the Stockman's that Celie didn't observe. Meanwhile Diana was glad to see Jake, who seemed matter-of-fact and solid after all she had seen tonight.

"Where's your truck?"

"Home. Chris and I'd been coyote-hunting. He dropped me off here. When I spotted your car, I sposed you'd be back for it and you'd give me a ride."

Diana's teeth were chattering. She unlocked the MG and opened the door and looked back at Jake. He was standing very close to her. She could see his breath in the frozen air and feel it on her face. What he was waiting for, a ride back to his apartment, she supposed. Then she gasped when he lifted her chin with a finger and kissed her on her lips.

She stared up at him, speechless. Somewhere on the next block, a car's horn started honking in rhythm, honk-honk-honk, and somebody swore, and the horn abruptly stopped honking.

"Professor Lady," said Jake. "I thought maybe you'd take me home with you." He grinned down at her. "Your virtue is just as safe as you want it to be."

Diana had no words. Annabel, telling her about the boy who had kissed her at a football game. The boy whose face she'd slapped. Diana's own words to Annabel: *He violated your personal space!* It seemed to Diana that her own personal space was becoming very fluid. It expanded and contracted around her like an image in a funhouse mirror. Ramona. Douglas. Celie, even. And Abe. *Damn* Abe. And now Jake LeTellier. Kissing her. Meanwhile, she was freezing.

She got into the MG and closed the door and sat behind the wheel with her teeth chattering. She heard the crunch of his boots on the crust of snow as he walked around her car to the passenger side and got in. When she reached for the ignition with her key, her hand started to shake, and Jake took her hand and folded her fingers around the key.

"Diana, are you all right to drive?"

"I—don't think I want to."

He took the key from her and got out and walked around to the driver's side and took her arm to coax her out. "You're more than cold," he said. "You're flinchin like a colt that's never felt a human hand."

When he had her stowed in the passenger seat and himself behind the wheel, he started the motor and turned to her. Although the instrument panel glowed and diffused light fell through the windshield from the security light above the parking lot, Diana could see only the outline of Jake's face under the shadow of his hat.

"Didn't mean to scare you. Seems like I make a habit a scarin you when I don't mean to."

"You surprised me, is all. Jake—" she didn't know how to go on. "I know you wouldn't hurt me."

"No," he said. He reversed out of the parking slot and drove out of the lot into the street before he added, "I wouldn't."

"Are you a horse-breaker?"

"Done some a that."

She wondered what they were talking about, something between the lines of the words they spoke. "Where's Tip?"

"He's good. He's home with food and water. I'll let him out when you take me back tomorrow." He glanced at her. "Early."

* * *

The MG was warm by the time Jake drove into the garage at the mansion. He cut the headlights but made no motion to get out of the car, and neither did Diana. They sat in silence while the motor idled and the heater hummed and the garage door gaped wide open behind them, guarded only by the palisade of pointed evergreens and the ornamental lighting that edged the circular driveway and shone like stars in the rear-view mirror. Diana knew she was trembling, not from cold, but from the tension that vibrated inside the little car until it wanted to float.

It hadn't even been a passionate kiss, like the kisses Annabel tried for. More of a—a gentle touching of lips—but she could go no further. When had anyone but Annabel ever kissed her? Certainly neither of the great-aunts.

"Why did you kiss me?"

"Wanted to."

"*Why?*"

A pause. "Maybe because I like puzzles, and you're sure as hell a puzzle? Maybe because you're brave? I've sure the hell never seen you back down from anything."

His face was shadowed. "How many reasons do I need? Maybe because you're Diana? And you're beautiful?"

He added, "You could drive me back to my place if you want to. So you can come back home alone."

Diana thought about it. He had said she was beautiful, and she wasn't cringing in embarrassment. If she wanted to drop him off and come home alone, she supposed she would have blurted it out.

"Let's go in," she said, and Jake turned the motor off.

17

In the living room, Jake lit a fire, as he had the night she had been so shaken by reading Victor Wheeler's name in the Versailles phone book, and came to sit beside Diana on the sofa.

"Got a bottle of red in my coat pocket. You want some?"

"No."

She missed the comforting presence of Tip between them. No, she didn't want to be alone, but what did she want? The tension that had filled the MG now threatened to swell the living room. To see if it eased, she laid her hand on Jake's knee.

What happened was Jake's hand coming to rest on her hand. His hand so much darker than her hand. She was afraid to look to see if he was looking at her, but sat petrified as he began to stroke her fingers.

"Diana, you said you knew I'd never hurt you. What are you so scared of, then? Is it because I'm Métis?"

"No!" She couldn't go on, because her breath seemed to have left her and her body was betraying her. Her nipples had clenched on their own, and a pulse throbbed between her legs where no one but Annabel had ever touched, and she was afraid.

"I didn't think I had feelings," she began again, stammering it out. "I didn't think I could feel anything."

Then she did look at Jake and found his eyes steady on hers.

"Everybody has feelings, Professor Lady. Unless you're a—what do they call it, a sociopath? From what I can remember from a class I took, sociopaths don't have feelins, they just pretend they do, so they can take advantage of other folks. Are you tellin me you're the opposite? That you have feelings and pretend you don't?"

"No!" But she had to smile a little at the idea. Her nipples stopped tingling as the tension between them eased, and Jake reached over with his free hand and stroked the line of her mouth, and she didn't flinch at his touch.

"You *can* smile. I don't think those old ladies who raised you did you many favors."

"I'm beginning to remember things."

That first year in Seattle. The great-aunts had had her hair cut almost at once. The wild curls from the home permanent Sister Holman—there had been a Sister Holman!—had given her for her trip to Seattle fell in clusters to the floor of the barbershop while in the mirror Diana's startled young eyes watched her own skull emerge through the closely trimmed cap she had worn until she left Seattle and started her graduate program in Texas, where she allowed her hair to grow enough to pin back into a knot.

Jake had gone back to stroking her wrist. "My grandpa and grandma raised Cheryl and me," he said.

Diana suddenly was alert. Jake had told her plenty about the Métis and the Nez Perce, but very little directly about himself. What she did know were scraps of Ramona's or Abe's that she pieced together.

"The grandma who gave you the rocking chair?"

"Yeah."

He was quiet for a time, rhythmically stroking her wrist while he watched the flames that danced on a log.

"Our folks were killed in a car wreck," he said. "They were drunk. I was ten and Cheryl was six. Grandpa and Grandma came and got us—we were home by ourselves, middle of the goddamn night—and took us back to the ranch."

Diana asked the safest question she could think of to keep him talking. "So you grew up on a ranch?"

"Yeah. Down in Murray County. But what I meant to tell you, when I started this story, is that my grandpa and grandma were great. Still are. We had horses, and dogs—Tip comes from a litter born at the ranch—and a whole pack a cousins on Grandma's side, and we all learned to cowboy, which kinda runs in the blood."

"You had aunts and uncles?"

"No. Would a had an uncle but he got killed in the Pacific. Cousins are like second, third. We don't keep count."

Jake paused and went on. "We had an old Tri-Pacer. A tail-dragger. We graded out a stretch a sagebrush to use as a runway, and Cheryl and I would take off and land in a hay meadow to visit some cousins. A wonder we didn't kill ourselves."

He stroked her wrist and watched the fire. "What I wanted to tell you. Losin your mom and dad doesn't have to be all bad. My grandpa and grandma loved us. And they were folks who laughed a lot."

"But you left the ranch and moved up here?"

"Yeah. See—we don't own the ranch, my grandpa's the longtime manager, and I wanted to learn somethin practical, which I did. But I also—hell, I always liked to read. And I ran into a couple good professors, down at the college."

Diana hadn't thought she could sleep at all tonight, but some combination of the fire and Jake's voice and his stroking of her wrist was relaxing her, making her drowsy. If she could do what she wanted, she would put her head down on his shoulder and fade away. But he might think—she supposed what she wanted was to have him close, but not too close.

"When a foal's newborn, you want a stroke every bit of him. Stroke his back and his belly and his flanks. The vet calls it imprinting, but my grandpa showed me before we knew the word for it. You get your fingers inside his ears, inside his mouth. So he'll know human touch from his very first breath. So he'll grow up to be the gentlest horse, the steadiest horse. So he won't flinch when he feels your hand on him."

Crackling of the fire.

"Don't spose you ever touched a fawn?"

"No."

"Had a pet deer once. Grandma raised him with a bottle. He hung around the ranch buildings for a long time, stealin the milk cow's grain and playin with the dogs, and he was used to all of us. But he'd never let any of us touch him. And if some smart-ass kid like me did find a way to lay a hand on him, he'd flinch like the touch was pure pain. I won't ever forget the feel of his muscles cringin under his hide."

Warmth of the fire, warmth of his hand on her wrist, the gentle roughness of calluses on his fingers. He worked for a living with his hands, after all.

"Diana, can I kiss you again?"

She stiffened, and she knew he felt it. But she had told him what she knew was true, that she knew he wouldn't hurt her, and she willed her head to turn to face him.

The dark eyes, the scar. The flickering firelight. His hand behind her head, drawing toward him. A deeper kiss. His mouth. His teeth and tongue asking her teeth and tongue to answer. Her eyes had closed without being told, and she didn't know how to breathe.

Then her eyes opened on their own, because he was drawing away.

"Professor Lady," he said, and his voice was unsteady. "There's no hurry. Most folks don't learn everything they want to know in ten minutes."

She couldn't speak.

"But I'll sleep beside you tonight," he said, "if you'd like that."

＊ ＊ ＊

After five weeks of lessons Diana still could not pull the plane back into a stall.

"Quit worrying. You'll get it," Chris Beaudry kept saying, but Diana thought he had begun to sound skeptical. He watched her strain back on the controls and shook his head. "Never seen any-body come so close as you do and still not go over the edge."

Finally, after she had been braced against the seat belt and grunt-ing and fighting the airplane for what seemed like the length of her life with the stall warning shrieking doom in her ear and the plane balanced on its tail, on what seemed like the verge, just within her fingertips of toppling over into the stall, Chris said, "Okay. Try once with both hands."

She hesitated. She had had it drilled into her to keep her right hand on the throttle, and it seemed unnatural to let go.

"Go ahead. I'll watch the throttle. At least you'll find out how close you been coming."

Diana clamped her lips shut and grasped the control with both hands. The stall warning reverberated through her bones. She hated its ear-splitting howl more than any sound she had ever heard. Sometimes she thought, more than the sense of courting danger, of approaching the forbidden, it was the screech of the stall warning that kept her from going over the edge.

Now, lying on her back with the plane on its tail with its nose pointed into the thin gray overcast, she drew back on the control with both hands and found that it easily came back a good six inches beyond the point she ever had drawn it before. The engine gasped and died, and the airplane lurched helplessly, just as it had done for Chris. Blood pounded in her ears. Her right hand flew to the throttle, but Chris's hand was there before hers to add power and send the engine roaring back to life and gaining altitude.

"See? That's why you can't never take your hand off the throttle. Okay, let's go in."

Numbly Diana hastened to obey. Tears had started at the anger in Chris's voice. Now as he sat looking out the window with his arms folded implacably across his chest and his huge body in his nylon parka filling the right side of the cockpit, she could only concentrate on flying the airplane as desolation overtook her.

Her hands automatically went through the prelanding check. At least she had learned something. She cut the power and reached for the radio to call in her position. As she turned on her final approach, she leaned over to scan the area for other aircraft, as she had been taught.

It seemed normal now to keep her eyes on the end of the runway and to forget the snow fence rushing toward her. As the plane settled over the pavement, she drew the nose back farther and farther, reawakening the ache in her left arm. The stall warning screamed briefly as the rear wheels touched down. Then she was losing speed, letting the nose down gently, and adding throttle to taxi off on the access strip. She braked at Pete the maintenance man's gate and shut off the magnetos.

The wind was blowing fingers of snow across the ploughed runway, and the sock in the infield stood out stiffly from its pole. Diana could feel the little airplane tremble around her.

"I never seen anything like it," Chris said. "You pulled the nose all the way back with one arm just now when you weren't thinking about it. Why can't you do it in the air?"

"I don't know," she whispered.

"Them stalls ain't going to kill you. It's not knowing what to do in a stall that kills you."

"I know, you told me."

"Then why don't you pay attention? There ain't nothing to a stall. There ain't nothing keeping you from it."

He unsnapped his safety belt and climbed down from the cockpit, slamming the door. Diana silently followed into the trailer.

Outside the wind howled across the flat stretch of runways and lashed the frost-covered windows with frozen snow and grit, but Pete had his furnace running full blast, and the red eye on the coffeemaker glowed. He and Jake LeTellier looked up from their coyote-hunting stories as Chris took down Diana's book to log her hour.

"The coyote story I like best," said Chris, taking up where he had left off when he went out with Diana for her lesson, "is about this dumb son of a bitch over in North Dakota."

"Yeah?"

"This old boy's been trapping coyotes. One day he goes out and finds a coyote with a leg in one of his traps, and the damn thing's still alive. Hardly hurt at all. He's growling and snarling and on the fight. But the old boy's forgot his rifle."

Diana's and Jake's eyes met, and Jake grinned.

"He wonders how the hell he's gonna kill the bastard. Wintertime out there on the prairie, and he can't find a rock or even a stick big enough for a club. But at last he remembers he's got a stick of dynamite in the back of his truck."

"They carry dynamite with them all the time, in North Dakota?"

"How the hell do I know? Anyway, the old boy gets this bright idea. He'll tie the dynamite to the coyote's tail, and then he'll spring the trap and watch him take off for his den. No more coyote, no more den."

"Oh shit," said Pete, who was drinking coffee out of a Styrofoam cup as he listened. "How's he gonna salvage his hide?"

"Never mind. That's just what he does. He ties his stick of dynamite to the coyote's tail, knots it down good and tight so it won't work loose, and then he lights the fuse and springs the coyote."

"Hmph," said Pete.

Chris went on. "Coyote, he takes off, all right, but where does he go? He streaks right under the old boy's brand-new truck and squats there."

Jake laughed, but Pete was offended. "What kind of dumb son of a bitch would go check his traps without a rifle?"

"It really happened."

The Coyote, the trickster god, had roused himself to listen to Chris's story. The Coyote, the dynamite, the trapper's new truck—just his kind of trick! And of course the dynamite wouldn't really kill the Coyote, Diana remembered, because his twin brother, Fox, would gather up his fragments and bring him back to life.

"How'd you do today?" Jake interrupted Diana's drifting contemplation. Chris heard him.

"She landed in this crosswind as good as anybody," he said.

Diana opened her eyes in the present, feeling better. She had landed in a crosswind, and Chris had logged her hour. She felt a little closer to the male circle.

"Flying's the greatest thing there is," Pete told her. He winked at her. "Just don't let these damn fools take you chasing coyotes."

"Don't listen to Pete," said Chris. "He don't know nothing."

"Listen, you smart son of a bitch. I'd logged three thousand flying hours before you was ever thought of, and I'm telling you, one of these days you'll fly under another power line on a sidehill and you'll break your worthless neck."

"Hell, I'm gonna live forever," said Chris.

"It ain't funny," said Pete. "Jake knows. He ain't the same man he was."

"You're gonna scare off my pupil," said Chris, still making a joke of it.

Pete looked at Diana, concerned. "I don't mean to scare you, honey. Hell, flying's safer than driving out to the airport. You just can't make no mistakes, that's all. Chris, he's a good flight instructor, and he ain't gonna take chances with you."

He winked at Diana. "He's makes a helluva lot better instructor than he does a customs officer."

Everyone laughed, even Chris. Versailles International Airport, so named because it accommodated occasional flights to and from Canada, employed Chris on a sometime basis as a customs officer. Last week six Canadians had landed but had to wait all day in their plane, in the cold, before being cleared for customs because Chris had been out coyote-hunting with Jake and couldn't be reached.

Diana felt far removed from worry. Abe, who was going to fire her, her ungraded papers, Douglas and Ramona, even her dread of the stall warning faded against the uncompromising demands of the airplane. She didn't feel like going back to campus. She wanted to sit here in the cramped overheated trailer and drink coffee and listen to the men swap more stories. She knew she couldn't, of course. They would only get embarrassed and polite.

Chris set down his cup and stood, zipping his parka. "Gotta go. The boys plan to burn the hippies out tonight."

18

"Did your plane wreck change you?" Diana asked Jake, who glanced at her in surprise.

"What gave you that idea? Pete talkin when he should a been listenin?"

He eased his truck over a patch of ice on the highway where a curved bank insulated the pavement from sunlight and took the turn for the mansion. The afternoon already was darkening.

"Might have settled me down, some," he said. "Guess I might a been a little cockier before then. Pete probly thinks so. Between that and—anyway. Leg still gives me trouble. One thing to go aloft with your doors shut and the sun on the windscreen. Colder'n hell with the passenger door taken off, and my damn leg starts to ache."

"You go coyote-hunting from the air with the *door* off your side of the plane?"

"Wouldn't want to put a shotgun shell through the door of a Citabria. Wouldn't want to think about the results." He added, "Safety belt's always buckled."

The idea of riding in the passenger seat of a banking airplane without a door between oneself and empty air gave Diana the horrors. Chris piloting the Citabria—Jake and Pete said Chris could set the Citabria down or take off on a handkerchief in a frozen wheat field or pasture—Chris banking at a steep angle, thirty feet above the fleeing coyote so Jake, the shotgun man, could aim and fire. She shuddered. "I don't think I wanted to know that," she said.

"You asked." He grinned at her, and she collected herself to see he had parked in front of the mansion's garage with his truck running. "Got your key?"

"Yes."

He leaned over and kissed her, quickly, which she was getting used to, at least enough not to flinch. "Somethin I have to do. I'll give you a call, maybe round ten, eleven."

* * *

Cheryl LeTellier had come by Diana's office a few weeks ago—"I want to run something by you."

Diana sipped coffee and waited. Cheryl was doing much better in class, and she was looking better, Diana thought. Maybe she was working something out with the man she was married to, and he wasn't crowding her so hard about the time she spent on class work. She hadn't come to class with bruises on her face again.

"I was thinking about our final research paper for the quarter. You said we should develop our own topics, and I wondered—what if I were to write a paper on Métis culture?"

"Where would you find your sources?"

"There's plenty written about the rebellion, and there's *Strange Empire*, of course, and a pretty bad book or two about Riel. But what I want to write about is how everybody lived in the old days. What it was like. Some of the old people wrote down what they remembered, or told it to somebody else to write down, and some of that's been collected in a book about the Spring Creek Métis. But what I really want to do, because there's still some folks, like my grandma, who remember a lot that hasn't been written down, and I thought—"

"You'd do an oral history project?"

"Is that what it's called?"

"You interview people, and you evaluate what they tell you—do their memories seem reliable, for example? Do they seem to you to exaggerate? Do their details correspond with details that others remember? Then you try to draw conclusions from the interviews."

"Could I do that?"

Diana thought about it. "The only objection I would have—some historians don't value oral histories." She thought of the scathing words she had heard from historians in Austin about unreliability and oversimplification. "They draw their conclusions from written sources."

"But why—" Cheryl looked baffled. "Where do written sources come from in the first place?"

"Good point. But remember, the senior seminar students are required to make oral reports to the department as a whole, and everyone in the department will read your papers. I won't be the only one to judge your work."

"I'd still like to do it. If I can get my brother to fly me down to Fort Maginnis this weekend, I can start with my grandma and some of her cousins."

"Good luck with it, then."

After Cheryl left her office, Diana wondered about the seldom-mentioned husband and whatever crabbed him about Cheryl's college classes, but all she could do was listen and hope Cheryl trusted her enough to talk to her.

Ramona and Cheryl, a pair of opposites, one of them spilling words like cast-off scraps and the other hoarding them like gold.

✳ ✳ ✳

Diana was thinking about Cheryl and hoping her interviews went well and that Abe wouldn't raise objections to an oral history, although it would be just like him, when her phone rang at eleven.

"Got room for me and Tip on your couch?"

"Yes."

"Bout ten minutes."

Jake sounded tired, and Diana hoped nothing bad had happened to the hippies.

✳ ✳ ✳

She heard his truck rumbling into the garage, where she had left the door up for him, and then the sounds of the door coming down and the thud when it reached concrete. She had uncorked the wine he left the night before and was pouring when he came through the kitchen door, exuding cold. Tip was happy to see Diana and tried to push past Jake, but Jake stepped around the dog and embraced her without a word.

Diana felt the rough canvas of his coat against her face and the fierceness of his grip, and she smelled something foreign about him that might have been wood smoke. The night must have been bad. She waited with an anxious Tip bobbing around their legs until he relaxed his hold and spoke into her hair.

"Goddam fucking mess out there. They got little kids out there."

Then he let her go—"Sorry—" and hung his hat and coat on kitchen pegs that were meant to hold coffee mugs.

"Wine?" Diana said.

"Later." He took a pint bottle out of his coat pocket and poured two fingers of whiskey into a glass and shot it down. Poured himself another finger and turned to her with exhaustion and anger in his eyes.

"Didn't hurt you, did I? Didn't mean to. God."

Diana poured herself a glass of wine and followed him into the living room, where he went to sweeping the ashes from the fireplace and laying fresh logs. Tip, in anticipation, had jumped up on the middle of the sofa, and Diana sat beside him.

Jake got his kindling blazing and stood and startled Diana by singing, "*We'll sweep out the ashes in the morning,*" in a sweet baritone.

"Song I like," he explained, and then he grinned, more like Jake as she knew him. "Has to be the whiskey."

He sat and roughed Tip's ears, but he did not speak. Diana sipped her wine and watched the flames devour their crumpled newspapers and kindling and lick around the logs before she said, "I hope no one got hurt?"

"Nothin serious. That jerk Mark Gervais did somethin to his ankle, tryin to outrun a deputy in the dark, and some of their outfit took a few thumps when they tried to resist, but no. The sheriff had rounded up a bunch a deputies, and Chris and Saylor and I went with em to the park ahead a time. Sheriff had a spotlight with him, and when the drunks showed up, all set for a good time hammerin on hippies, he turned his spotlight on em and they froze like a herd a deer in the headlights."

So that wasn't what had disturbed him so badly.

"Mark Gervais from the fight at the Stockman's?"

"Him and every other goddamn barfly in town. Worst that happened, the hippies got scared out a whatever wits they might a started with in the first place."

He looked into his glass, sipped a little whiskey, and made a face.

"Why does everyone seem to hate the hippies?" asked Diana.

"Afraid of em. That cannibal hippie case, few years back in Park County, it touched off a regular panic. Story's gone around the bars, and not just the bars, that our hippies are camped in the park to prepare for an invasion of Versailles."

"A cannibal hippie?"

"Newspapers called him that. He wasn't a hippie, he was a scruffy guy with a beard. Killed him a fisherman, cut him up and threw his body parts in the river. Claimed he ate the fisherman's heart, raw."

"Was he crazy?"

"Think that's what the judge and jury decided on."

He sipped a little more whiskey, and then he reached for Diana's hand, crowding the reproachful Tip, and began his rhythmic stroking of her wrist.

"They had little kids out there. In tents. None of em with an idea how to live rough. That black kid that got bloodied up a week ago is from Philadelphia! What does he know? They got a couple a boards in the woods for a latrine. They were runnin out a wood. Sheriff had a couple axes in the county truck, and we cut em a big stack of deadfall. I probly smell of pine needles and smoke. Little kids! What ails folks?"

Diana let Jake's wrist-stroking do its work of lulling her while she thought more about the desire to be fashionable than she did about what might ail the hippies. These people probably had a Whole Earth catalog out there in one of the tents. Nothing wrong with that, although she hoped they were keeping the children warm. It was a poor radical feminist who didn't have a copy of Shulamith Firestone's or Ti-Grace Atkinson's books around her pad. Nothing necessarily wrong with Firestone's or Atkinson's philosophies, either, and certainly Diana herself had tried hard to fit in with the campus feminists in Texas. But she didn't despise Jake for being polite.

What made people afraid was another question. The hippie scare was a kind of contagion, spiked with enjoyment. A bunch of drunks like Mark Gervais got to think they were big tough men, going out to beat hell out of the hippies, until they came up against the sheriff's spotlight.

Diana thought her fears were unlikely to infect anyone else. She feared the stall warning, and she feared the ground, even though she told Chris she didn't. She feared pulling the plane over the edge. She didn't fear Jake, but she did fear going over his edge, and she was too drowsy to untangle what that meant.

"Diana," said Jake, as if he heard her thoughts, "I'd kiss you if Tip would get out of the way."

"Stay, Tip."

"Whose side are you on? His or mine?"

"His."

Jake laughed and pushed the startled Tip off the sofa and slid over where he'd been sleeping. Diana woke up enough to understand what Jake's edge was offering. She might be inexperienced, but she knew well enough what his long game was. Maybe if he kept his game slow enough, she would let down her guard and crash and burn before she knew it.

His arm around her shoulders, the soft brush of his flannel sleeve on the back of her neck. Denim whispering against denim as his thigh touched hers. His finger under her chin, turning her face to his.

"Diana," he whispered. "Can you make me feel better after what I saw tonight?"

"Will you sleep beside me again tonight?"

"Yeah."

19

Ramona dropped by Diana's office on Monday with her coffee to discuss Operation Hippie, as the *Daily News* had called it that morning. Not a surprise to learn that Ramona knew about the black kid from Philadelphia.

"The girl is local. You'd think she'd know better than move into a tent in the middle of the winter. Not to speak of hooking up with the black guy. Her parents are beside themselves."

Diana decided against trying to work out whether the girl's parents were beside themselves because she was living in a tent in the middle of winter or because she was hooked up with a black guy.

The newspaper also reported that social services were visiting the children at the hippie camp. But here in Main Hall the afternoon was one of white light and frosted windows, a quiet world away from tents in the woods and hungry children. November was coming to its chill conclusion, and the fall quarter was nearly over. Only this week and another of classes remained before finals week. The Westward Movement students would be giving their oral reports on their term papers in lieu of finals. Diana just hoped all of them were keeping their heads down and working at their research.

"What a term," Ramona sighed, having shaken her head over the Hippie Cannibal and exhausted her information about the local hippies. "I get so sick of freshmen. Do you have Christmas plans?"

"Not really."

A terse letter from Tatiana had demanded her presence in Seattle. Diana hadn't answered it yet. Between keeping ahead of her classes and the unexpected complications of her life—winter driving, flying lessons, the Ramona-and-Douglas saga, and well, yes, her friendship with the diesel man—she had put Tatiana and Maria out of her thoughts until the bombardment of phone calls.

She also had put Victor Wheeler out of her thoughts. The stinking old barfly would have to stagger along without her. The Christmas break offered three weeks with no students and time to prepare syllabi for her classes for the winter quarter and try to further her reading and her thoughts about parallel narratives. She could put off thinking about Victor Wheeler until the winter quarter began in January.

"I don't know what we'll be doing. Con seems to want to mend things, but I'm almost certain he's still seeing *her*—"

The door behind Ramona burst open, and both women jumped as Abe Dennison, red-faced, strode into Diana's office.

He was oblivious of Ramona, sitting startled in the students' chair with her coffee slopping out of her cup. He leaned on the points of his fingers over Diana's desk and rounded on her.

"Are you out of your mind?"

Diana stared at him. Then stared down at his fingers, rigid on her desk. Fingers she had seen gripping a deadly softball. Fingers with little black hairs that sprouted between the joints.

"What are you thinking? Letting that LeTellier chick get away with an oral history project? *Oral history!*" Abe was so angry that spittle fell from the corner of his mouth. "Do you have any idea how that looks? Considering your *connection* with her brother?"

Ramona sat open-mouthed behind Abe with her coffee cup shaking in her hand until she noticed it and set the cup on the corner of Diana's desk. Diana had feared Abe would disapprove of Cheryl's project, but she hadn't expected him to throw a tantrum over it in front of an audience. Channeling Tatiana seemed her best option. She straightened her back.

"What connection is that, Abe?"

He took a step back and gobbled for words. "Do you know what people will say about you and that buck Indian? *Are* saying about you?"

"No, Abe," said Diana, projecting as much interest in the topic as she could. "What are they saying?"

"Don't play games with me, Diana! You know what I'm talking about."

"Hmm. If it's what I think you're implying, Abe—" It was time for her rehearsed line. "You have no reason to be concerned. I've never had sex—with a man, that is."

Ramona had reached for her coffee cup but knocked it off Diana's desk instead. It clattered on the tile floor and broke in half, and Abe seemed to remember Ramona was there. He turned and scowled at her, closed his deadly fingers on a book from Diana's desk—it was Mourning Dove's novel, *Cogewea, The Half-Blood*—and slammed it on the floor before he strode out of her office, hurling the door back so hard that pencils jumped on her desk and loose papers floated up in the draft.

Ramona looked at Diana, and Diana looked at Ramona.

"What in the *world*?" Ramona said at last.

"How long have you got to listen?"

Ramona glanced at her watch as though taking the question literally while Diana tried to think of a starting point. The aversion of many senior historians, Abe Dennison for one, for oral histories. The student in Diana's Westward Movement seminar who seemed disengaged and unhappy with the class until Diana drew her out. How the student's conversations with Diana about Diana's new interest in individual narratives and the student's own cultural heritage had led to her improved performance in class and her idea of doing an oral history project based on interviews with her elderly relatives.

A student who happened to be the sister of Ramona's and Con's diesel man.

Ramona listened as though spellbound. When Diana finished, she nodded. "It all makes sense."

"It does?"

"Diana. You are so—oblivious. Don't you know why Abe is so angry?"

"I knew he might object to the oral history project, and I was worried for Cheryl, but this reaction of his seems all out of proportion."

"Diana. Abe has been—well, to put it crudely—trying to get into your pants ever since you came to Versailles. Haven't you noticed? How he invited you to watch him pitch softball games last fall, how he invites you to concerts with him, when he doesn't even like music? How he drops by your office for no real reason? I'll bet he finds reasons to take your arm. Or touch your shoulder. Or stand close to you. And now that he's—well, not getting anywhere with you, he's starting to needle you."

Diana stared.

"He's got a reputation, you know. With students. And there was a woman in the music department who left the college because of him. And surely you've noticed? Nelda never leaves her work-study student alone in her office when Abe's there."

Ramona paused and smiled. "The men on this corridor are enjoying the situation, you know. Haven't you seen all the open office doors? The looks you're getting? It wouldn't surprise me if they're laying bets. They get to watch Abe Dennison lay on his obnoxious charm while you don't even notice—you're *indifferent* to Abe. Of course he's angry."

Diana let out a breath she didn't know she was holding. She had plenty of time later to feel angry about Abe's intentions. "What does any of this have to do with Cheryl LeTellier?"

Ramona threw up her hands. "First he deviled you about her failing grades to make you feel bad about your teaching, so he could make it all better for you and get you another contract, and you'd be grateful and succumb. When he found out her work has improved, he deviled you about Jake because he hasn't gotten anywhere with you and he's afraid Jake has. Cheryl's oral history project is just his last straw."

Diana sighed. "The scary part is what he might do to Cheryl. Everyone in the department assigns a grade to those senior seminar papers, and the grades are averaged."

Ramona pondered. Then she looked down and noticed her broken cup. She picked up the two halves and turned them in her hands, trying to fit them together.

"What you should do is talk to Dean Maki. He was a professor in the history department before he was a dean, and he's entitled to attend the oral reports and assign grades. And he knows all about Abe and his ways."

"You think the dean would—"

"Oh, yes." Ramona smiled to herself. "We know Dean Maki and his wife very well, Diana. We're having dinner at the club with them tomorrow. It's her birthday. I may just drop a word."

Ramona stood. "I'll fetch some paper towels and mop up this coffee. I'm afraid the cover of your book got wet. But Diana—anyone who has eyes in their heads, unlike oblivious you, can see how Jake looks at you from across a room."

She paused for a long moment. "Diana, what you told Abe. Was it the truth?"

20

That was Monday. On Wednesday Dean Maki tapped on Diana's office door. He was a tall man with a narrow chiseled face and a thick white thatch of hair. Although Diana had had dinner with him and his wife at the time of her interview, and she had gone to him for an answer to the opening-garage-door mystery, she'd not seen much of him during the term.

"Dr. Karnov," he said, taking the students' chair. "I've been meaning to drop by and see how you're doing at Versailles State, but there always seems to be something critical to deal with first. How's your year going for you?"

"Pretty well," she said, wondering if Ramona had dropped her word. "The winter weather takes some getting used to."

"I had a chance to visit with one of your senior seminar students today, Cheryl LeTellier, and she told me about her final paper. I was impressed by the quality of the material she'd pulled together."

Diana didn't know how to respond. Was this a promising development or a potentially dangerous one? It was the dean speaking to her, after all.

Dean Maki smiled at her. "She's a bright young woman. One of the reasons I was so interested in her research—it dovetails in some ways with a class I taught several years ago in cultural history."

Diana was surprised. "Cultural history?"

"Well—" he looked embarrassed. "It was one of the last history classes I taught as a professor here, and I indulged myself by working out some ideas I'd come across in recent cross-disciplinary writing. Work being done in anthropology, even in literary theory. English departments and anthropology departments, even these new Native

American studies departments, have been well ahead of us historians in many ways, and I don't believe the class has been taught here again, although it went very well. Cheryl's brother, Jake, was a student in that class. I always wished he'd majored in history."

Diana could not think what to say, but he continued.

"Cheryl is drawing some interesting inferences from her interviews. She told me that you and she have been meeting after class and discussing some of them?"

Diana nodded, thankful to be talking about Cheryl and not Cheryl's brother. "It started because I was worried about her lack of interest in the Westward Movement seminar. Worried about *her*, really. But I'd been thinking a great deal about the nature of narrative—stories, really—and I was fascinated by Cheryl's story— her cultural story, I suppose you'd say—and I learned more from her than she did from me."

"My own story is one of the reasons I suppose I'm drawn to her work," said the dean. "My grandfather emigrated from Finland to file on a homestead north of Versailles. Built him a sauna. And neighbored with the old Stillingers."

"I see," said Diana, wondering how many more loose threads were going to be pulled out of the weave of her Versailles experience. "Since I came here, I've been seeing everything I once read and studied in a different light. Dean Maki, I know you're very busy, but I can't help wishing I could talk to you further."

The dean smiled at her and stood. "We'll find some time. And can I assume you're going to ask me to read the senior seminar papers and assign grades?"

"Yes."

He chuckled and left her office.

＊ ＊ ＊

Put him out of her mind? Diana had looked up Victor Wheeler's phone number in the Versailles phone book so many times she knew it by heart, but she couldn't bring herself to dial it. Then it occurred to her that if Tatiana's old barfly, stinking and unshaven and shabby, were alive and living near Versailles, she might be able to learn more about him from newspaper archives more recent than the 1940s. The final papers for either the senior seminar or the survey classes hadn't been turned in yet, so on Thursday with a clear conscience she bundled up and drove along Main Street in brilliant sunlight to turn on Water Street for the Carnegie Library. When she passed the bank, she saw its thermometer was registering thirty-two degrees below zero, and she glanced at her fuel gage, although she knew her gas tank was full.

"I don't think they've put the 1970s on microfilm yet, dear," said Mrs. Elder when Diana asked, "But I think the *Daily News* will have the paper files."

She directed Diana to the *Daily News* office, a block off lower Main Street, and wished her good luck.

* * *

Diana parked across the street from the newspaper office, which was a brick front wedged between a jewelry store and a title company. A bell tinkled when she pulled open the door of the newspaper office, and a young man sitting on a stool behind a long counter looked up from jotting notes on a pad of paper.

"Help you?"

Diana loosened the collar of her coat in the warmth of the office and explained her quest for recent newspaper archives.

"Last five years, maybe? I can show you what we got."

He slid off his stool and opened a swinging half-door in the counter. "The files are back here."

Under the counter were rows of long narrow drawers which, when pulled out, revealed stacks of pristine-looking newspapers with a papery odor overlaid by the sharper smell of printer's ink.

"Lessee—yeah, these are from 1970. We'll be gettin ready to put em on microfilm. You wanna start with these?" He laid the drawer on the counter, pulled up another stool for her, and went back to his notes.

Diana checked the hand-lettered label on the front of the drawer and found that newspaper issues from July 1 to July 31, 1970, were in front of her.

She laid her notepad and pen beside the drawer and lifted out the July 1 edition of the Versailles *Daily News*.

By now she knew not to waste time letting her attention be drawn by national and international news on the front page and to turn past the headlines and the sports sections to the state and local news and police reports that she would find deeper into the paper. Still she hesitated. After hours of slowly turning a handle and staring into a microfilm reader, the act of holding real paper in her hands, touching the actual substance instead of straining to read its facsimile, felt almost sensual.

She turned over a sheet of newspaper and scanned it, turned over another and another. She was getting a strange feeling. Police reports and community events, when read on microfilm, seemed like fiction, or perhaps a film about shark attacks, say, projected on a screen. But even police reports from five years ago, on the paper they had been printed on, were awakening a new and disturbing awareness in Diana. *Yes, these assaults and arrests for public drunkenness really happened!*

She took a breath and contemplated the plaster wall above the counter. Mottled green paint, a calendar with a picture of two cartoon cowboys sitting on a fence rail, a bulletin board pinned with dusty notes, a clock with a slow second hand. A few feet behind her, the young man writing whatever he was writing. The drunken vagrant was not a man of legend propagated by Tatiana. He was not an inhabitant of Diana's own head, like the young woman in the blue dress with the red beads she saw so often. He was a real man, and she was on the verge of finding him, *and then what?*

She shut her eyes. All this time she had imagined the search for the drunken vagrant as a search for herself, for the real Diana. What she was likely to find were complications beyond complications.

Well. She'd come this far. Jake's words—*I've never seen you back down*. She wouldn't back down now. Diana opened her eyes and found she was reading the front page of the *Daily News* for July 4, 1970.

Race riots in New Jersey. Rioting in Northern Ireland as the British Army searched for the IRA's hidden weapons. Diana turned the page. Scanned the local vital statistics, happened to glance at a photo of a local politician.

She gasped, audibly enough that the young man looked up and said, "Are you okay?"

"Yes, I just saw—something that surprised me."

The photograph. The headline. *State Senator Wheeler Considers U.S. Congressional Bid.*

Diana sped through the short column under the photo and the headline. It was a predictable piece of journalistic prose. *Versailles-area rancher Victor Wheeler . . . first elected to the Montana Senate as a Republican . . . won't rule out plans to run for congressional seat vacated by . . . deep Montana roots . . . WWII veteran . . . educated at Versailles State College and Montana State College . . .*

Tatiana's drunken old vagrant, the unshaven barfly, bowed to Diana and vanished as she studied the photograph. Clearly its purpose was political. The head and shoulders of a smiling man in his fifties wearing a suit and tie. Silver-haired, clean-shaven. She thought his face was a little fuller than it had been in the microfilm photo of him and her mother. His eyes looked dark in the black-and-white photo, although it was hard to be certain.

She skimmed the column again. No mention of a family. Then she looked up, feeling the eyes of the counter man on her. He had noticed what she was reading.

"You interested in Senator Wheeler?"

"Do you know him?"

"Shook his hand at a barbecue once. You're not from around here, are you? Are you a reporter? No, wait a minute." His momentary suspicion seemed to fade. "I know who you are. You're that lady they hired at the college!"

Diana sighed, but she had long given up any attempt to excise the word *lady* from the vocabularies of the people of Versailles. "Yes, I'm a history professor at the college. Do you still have copies of today's paper here?"

"Sure. I'll give you a free copy if you'll subscribe to us."

"Deal."

Diana filled out the form he gave her, paid him for the subscription, buttoned her coat closely, and walked back out into the cold. Getting the *Daily News* regularly, she reflected, was not a bad idea, given how many months she had been living in Versailles without knowing Victor Wheeler was a local bigwig. No wonder Jake had given her a strange look the night he asked her father's name and she answered.

A big frog in a very small pond! hissed Tatiana from somewhere, and Diana answered, "A very big frog in this pond," and realized she had spoken aloud when a passerby in a parka gave her a strange look.

But she was relieved she'd never had the courage to dial the man's phone number. A state senator hearing a strange woman claiming to be his daughter—what would he have thought?

Maybe he heard many strange claims. Or maybe he had staff to take care of strange claims. A state senator wouldn't answer his own telephone, would he?

Maybe—but Diana jumped as a horn honked. She had been so absorbed in her speculations that she hadn't realized she had stopped walking in the middle of the street. She hastily stepped back and let the car rumble past her, along with a glare from its heavily bundled driver.

She was back in the MG before she allowed herself to return to the thought that had stopped her in the street. What if the state senator had seen a short item in the *Daily News*—he probably paid closer attention to recent local news than she had—and noted that a Dr. Diana Karnov had been hired at Versailles State College? Would he have remembered the name? When he had been married to a woman named Lillia Karnov? When *Diana* was the Anglicized version of the Russian *Tatiana*?

Maybe Victor Wheeler, all along, had known more about Diana than she about him. And he hadn't gotten in touch.

Diana sighed and told herself to keep her mind on her driving as she shifted gears and pulled out into the street.

21

Chris Beaudry had told Diana he would be tied up over the weekend, flying on Fish and Wildlife business, but he could give her an hour of flight instruction on Thursday afternoon if she wanted to drive out to the airport, so after her session in the newspaper office Diana ate a trail bar and drank a glass of milk, got back into the MG, and headed west.

She found Chris, Pete, and Jake drinking coffee as usual and swapping stories in Pete's warm trailer. Nobody but Chris had much work to do. Pete had retired and only tinkered around with maintenance work at the airport because he'd gotten into the habit of doing it. Farm work had gone dormant in the depths of winter, but Con Stillinger kept his fleet of trucks and farm equipment in a heated implement building, and Jake's only task was to have everything serviced and repaired and ready by spring planting.

There was Jake's and Chris's coyote-hunting, of course, to give them something to do. Diana knew they were accumulating the prime winter pelts and flying them up to sell in Canada for the European market, which she supposed she should disapprove of more vocally than she did.

But in comparison with the pressures and frantic schedule-cramming of graduate school, or even teaching, where she constantly fell behind in grading papers and planning lessons, let alone in keeping up with her research, it seemed to Diana that all three men led relaxed and contented lives. Even Chris, freelance pilot and Number One Badge of the Versailles Police Department, seemed to structure his hours to suit himself.

Chris followed Diana out to the line of airplanes and watched as she unchained the training Cessna and did her walk-around, and he climbed in and rode right-seat with her while she taxied out to the runway to step on the disc brakes, give the plane full throttle, and run her instrument checks.

Diana always hated the way the plane quivered against the opposing forces of brakes and throttle, and even though she knew worse was coming once they were aloft, she was thankful when she could ease off on the throttle, give her position into the mike of the radio, identify her aircraft, and taxi slowly out on the runway. She glanced at the windsock—another crosswind, she'd need to crab to land.

"Take her up to seven thousand feet."

Farm buildings, vehicles moving on the highway, all becoming miniaturized beneath her.

"Where's your right hand have to be?"

"Throttle."

"Do it."

Every muscle of her body, from her scalp down, was tense. *She would do it.* Trying to make herself believe she was coming in for a landing, Diana pulled back on the stick until the training plane seemed to balance on its tail, and she gritted her teeth and gave the stick every ounce she had, and the plane gave a helpless flop as its nose fell and it swooped into a sickening race for the ground.

"Throttle?"

"Yep."

Full throttle, and the heart-relief of the engine coming to life and the plane rising until she could reduce throttle into level flight.

"By god, you did it. You finally did it."

Diana glanced at Chris, who shook his head.

"I was beginnin to wonder. But one thing I have to say for you, lady. When you set out to do somethin, you don't quit."

Diana let out her breath.

"Take her back up to seven thousand feet and do it again."

* * *

Back in Pete's trailer, Chris poured coffee for himself and Diana and pulled down Diana's logbook to enter her hour, seeming intent on his task until he looked up into an expectant silence.

"Yup," he said, and took a swig of coffee.

"She stalled?"

"Buncha times. And crabbed down in this crosswind. You boys'll get to cut off her shirttail before long."

Jake and Pete were grinning at her.

"I ain't too old to chase you around the trailer with a pair a scissors," Pete teased her. He had a corkboard pegged full of first-time soloists' shirttails.

"Bet I beat you to it," said Jake.

Chris took another long gulp of coffee, belched, and started talking about the weather, which morphed into another of his stories. "Folks talk about the wind up here on the Highline like it's somethin outa hell. I tell em, at least we got good water. That water over east, it's so alkali they can't drink it."

He started to laugh. "My old man told me a story once, about meetin a sheepherder comin across one a them alkali flats with his band. Old herder had got the runs so bad from drinkin alkali water, he got tired of takin down his pants and pullin them up again, so he was hikin along behind his sheep, bare-butt, carryin his overalls over his shoulder. Country was so goddamn empty, he had nobody to see him but sheep."

Diana could tell that Pete and Jake wanted to laugh but were embarrassed in front of her. She made herself as unobtrusive as possible, and finally Pete said, "Hell, I got a better story than that about wind."

"Yeah?"

"Think we got wind over here, you oughta live over in Browning a while. They got wind like a—" he glanced at Diana and substituted the simile he'd had in mind for another—"that'd blow the hat off your head and take your scalp with it. This old boy, pilot I know, he'd went up one day with his wife. Think he flew her over to Great Falls for some reason. They left Browning in the wind, hell, wind blows hard every day over there. But comin back, they see the windsock hangin limp from its pole. Old boy's just gettin ready to land when his wife, she yells, *No! Don't land! The Indians are tryin to kill us! They've put rocks in the windsock!*"

Chris laughed, slopped his coffee, and hunted around for a hunk of paper towel. "It's your story, Pete, and you can tell it any damn way you want to."

That, Diana thought, said a lot about stories.

She sensed Jake was watching her. He had a way of reading her reactions, to his coyote-hunting, for example, and now, to Pete's story, which might or might not be racist, depending on the way you heard it or who was telling it. Browning, home of Diana's two Blackfeet students, was a reservation town with, she supposed, its own insider stories and ways of telling them. The stories Chris and Pete told, she'd come to understand, had a common thread in their certainty that the best of all places on earth to live was the Montana Highline.

For Jake, she suspected, the best place on earth lay farther south, on Spring Creek in Murray County.

"You don't have to be so smug!" she once flared at him. "Laughing about all the things I don't know, like topping off my gas tank. How do you think you'd get along, living in Seattle?"

"Lived there for a year after I got out of the Navy. Got along all right."

That stopped her. It was the first she'd realized he was a Vietnam vet. Of course. "Why did you come back?" she asked.

"Liked it better here."

Now she stirred herself, finished her coffee, and paid Chris for her lessons to date. Another lesson next weekend, they agreed, and she put on her coat and went to the door. Jake followed her— "Walk you to your car?"

They stood for a moment by the MG in the arctic blast from the northeast.

"The radio weather report said seventy below, counting wind chill factor," Diana said through stiff lips.

"When I was a kid we didn't talk about wind chill factor. Doesn't make it any better to make it sound worse."

A pause.

"Did it feel good?"

"The stalls?" she said, and wondered when she would stop blurting the wrong thing when he grinned at her.

"Yes," she said. "It felt good after it stopped being terrifying."

"Buy you dinner tonight? To celebrate?"

When she nodded, he kissed her, cold lips to cold lips, opened the door of the MG for her, and turned back to George's trailer.

* * *

She knew in her bones what was going to happen. The question was, as Tatiana might have asked, as Ramona did in fact ask, why she wanted to take flying lessons. Well, a parallel question, at least, and the only answer she had to either question was because she wanted to.

At the mansion she showered and changed into clean blue jeans and boots and a sweater. She combed and repinned her hair, changed her mind and brushed out her hair and let it fall to her shoulders. She hung the new down jacket she'd splurged on from the dowel post, ready to pull on, but with an hour before her, well, *date* was the word for it, she supposed. She was being taken on a dinner date.

To give her mind something else to think about, she poured herself half a glass of wine and sat on the living room sofa, staring at the cold fireplace and thinking of ways she could get a glimpse of Senator Victor Wheeler in person. Maybe he held political rallies, for example, and she could—but surely this hadn't been an election year, surely she would have noticed radio ads and posters around town. Even if it were an election year, November was over. Elections would have been held and results announced.

She supposed Senator Wheeler would have an office in the capitol in Helena. She could find out when the state senate would be in session, and almost certainly find a directory in the capitol by which she could find his office. And then—

And then what? Locate which office was his and stake out his corridor?

A stakeout, indeed. What a ludicrous idea. The quest for Victor Wheeler was ludicrous. The quest for a man who turned out to be a conservative politician had eaten into her spare time this fall and kept her from doing serious work. No more unfolding consequences. She would put the senator out of her mind, right along with the drunken vagrant Tatiana had conjured for her.

Something else she would put out of her mind was any thought of spending Christmas in Seattle. It wasn't as though Tatiana and Maria could lock her in her room to keep her from coming back to Versailles after Christmas, but it would be a battle to get away from them, and she really, really didn't want to have to fight a battle, not just now, when she was feeling so vulnerable—*vulnerable?* She was feeling vulnerable? Why?

She glanced down at her wine glass, thinking to blame the wine, but she'd hardly sipped it.

Jake's truck rumbled on the circular drive; brief flash of his headlights in the big windows as he approached the mansion. Diana reached for her jacket and gloves and shoulder bag. Patted her pocket for her keys. Went to meet him at the front door.

22

Jake drove east on a narrow highway that left the lights of Versailles behind and wound past a small settlement that looked abandoned. No lights, only the silhouettes of a few roofs against the night sky. His headlights picked out a stop sign ahead, where the highway met another highway, and he braked and slowed and turned left. Then Diana saw a huddle of lighted buildings, and Jake turned into a parking lot with an overhead light and what appeared to be two houses clapped together, with a shadowy sign on the roof that Diana could barely make out. Broadview Steakhouse.

Jake held the door of his truck for her and the door of the steakhouse for her. Diana was past objecting. It was what men did in this strange country, and Jake was behaving by his best lights. She smelled the soap from his recent shower and then, as she blinked in the lighted dining room, the odor of frying fat.

A woman met them at a podium—"Jake! Good to see you! Been a while. Table for two?"

"Hey, Dixie."

She looked at Diana with open curiosity as she led them to a table in a dim corner and gave them menus. "How's Cheryl? She still with Ritchie?"

"Yeah. But she's good. She's back in school. How's your house cab?"

"Merlot's better. Two?"

"One. Beer for me. Whatever you got on tap."

The woman was gone, and Diana looked up and found Jake's eyes intent on her, and she couldn't look away. His dark eyes, his scar, the lines of his mouth and crust of beard, which gradually had become so familiar to her that she stopped seeing anything in his features but *Jake*, now frightened her with the presence of the dark male.

"Jake," she said, to call back the familiar. "You had your hair trimmed."

She sounded inane to herself, but Jake ran a hand through his hair and grinned at her. "I was gettin a bit shaggy."

"They know you here."

"Cheryl used to wait tables for em."

She could think of nothing else to say, but the waitress brought her wine and a glass of beer just then, and when Jake raised his glass, she raised hers.

A silence continued between them. Diana heard the rumble of the furnace and muted voices from the handful of other diners on a slow Thursday night.

"What're you readin these days?"

She sighed. "I finished *Cogewea*. I have to start on senior seminar papers tomorrow."

"What are the seniors writing about?"

Cheryl's oral history project Diana didn't mention. She was keeping her fingers crossed about that one. "I try to get them to choose independently, but I've got at least five who are writing about the fur trade, and I worry they'll get in the way of each other's research materials in the library. One on frontier education. One has his great-grandfather's surveying notes he's examining. Another has some family diaries. A couple are writing about Custer's Last Stand, and one of the Blackfeet boys is writing about something called the Marias River Massacre."

From the quirk of his mouth, Diana was sure Jake knew more about the Marias River Massacre than she did, but all he said was, "That'll be a pair a contrasts. General Custer and Major Baker."

At least their conversation, if a bit stilted, sounded more like one between Jake and Diana. "I was talking with Dean Maki about a class he taught several years ago. It sounded—"

The waitress was back and interrupting for their orders. That settled, Jake said,

"Yeah. I was in that class. Think it was what woke me back up."

"Woke you up from what?"

"Hell-raisin."

She remembered her reaction the first time she met him—*he's trouble*. The stall warning shrieked, and she fought down panic. What did she know about this man? He'd told her about his grandparents and growing up on the ranch with cousins, but that was the most he'd ever said about himself. Now the hell-raising. The farthest from her experience—what had she done in her life that counted as hell-raising?

"Was it—fun? The hell-raising?"

"Fun?" He gave a bark of a laugh. "I spose I thought it was at the time. Lookin back, what I hate is how I made my grandpa and grandma worry about me. They were afraid I'd go the same way as my mom and dad."

His grandparents had come to get him and Cheryl in the middle of the night, Diana remembered. Jake and Cheryl had been little kids, left home alone while their parents went out drinking.

Their food arrived, steaks sizzling on steel platters, heaps of french fries, and meager servings of coleslaw in plastic cups. Diana shook her head at the repast in front of her, about three times the amount of food she ate in a day. And the pitiful coleslaw—a line from somewhere in Shakespeare, about a disproportion of bread to sack, was trying to get her to remember it.

"Hell, you don't have to eat it all. You can take some of it home for tomorrow. Or you can give it to me."

He reached across the table and bumped her knuckles with his. "You did fine today. You stalled even though you were scared to do it. You stalled a bunch a times and recovered, and you landed in a crosswind, and you lived to walk away from the plane."

But his eyes held hers, and his breathing quickened, and Diana felt a strange spasm in her lower region. She was afraid this dinner would never end, and then she was afraid it would.

The moment passed. Jake cut himself a bite of steak. Diana took her own fork and serrated knife and cut into her steak and took a bite and found it surprisingly sweet and good.

* * *

Jake pulled up in the shadow of the darkened mansion and waited with the motor running. In the warm cab, illuminated only by the lighted dashboard, Diana felt suspended in the strange sense of motionlessness she experienced when flying at altitude. She played with the fantasy of Jake flying left seat, herself in the right seat as co-pilot, seeming to make no forward progress over a night landscape until Jake reduced altitude and she could see lights below them, and they were landing, perhaps in a hay meadow at Jake's grandfather's ranch.

"You want me to stay, you need to open the garage door for me."

The illusion broken, Diana stepped out of the cab to solid footing on concrete, dug her house key out of her jacket pocket, and fumbled in the dark to unlock the front door. Vowing to leave a light on the next time she left the mansion, she felt her way through living room and kitchen to push the remote button in the garage and see the big door start its upward rumble and Jake's headlights fill the opening space.

He caught up with her in the kitchen before she could take her jacket off, held her by her shoulders, and kissed her quickly and then more deeply as space and substance blurred and confused her. How had they gotten to the sofa in the living room? What had become of her jacket and sweater? Her jeans were around her ankles.

His whisper—"Do I have to undress myself?"

She fumbled for his shirt buttons, belt buckle, zipper, as his hand reached down to help her. He was having to show her how. His hand pushing her legs apart to touch her core as Annabel had, except that a spasm made her arch her back and gasp, except that he was turning from her to tear open a small packet and unpeel—a condom, she guessed, and had she ever seen one? He was between her legs now, pushing her knees up until she understood to wrap her legs around him, and he was guiding himself inside her, and she hadn't known what to expect, but not this relentless thrusting that sent electric spasms through her until she cried out aloud, because she had fallen over his edge.

A few more rapid thrusts until he cried out and collapsed on her. His weight on her.

His whisper. "Am I too heavy?"

"No."

Nothing then but the peace of holding and being held, until he raised his head and shoulders, and she gasped as he spoke the last words she could have imagined him speaking.

"Will you marry me?"

"I can't marry you!" Diana blurted and instantly felt stricken, because although she couldn't see Jake's face distinctly in the dark, she knew it had changed. After a breath he reared back and pulled out of her, stepped off the sofa, and picked up his clothes. She heard the kitchen door close behind him and saw a line of light come on at the bottom of the door, and she understood what she had ruined for him.

"Jake!" she cried, and ran after him.

His face was rigid as he glanced at her, turned away, finished dressing, and zipped his Levi's. Diana caught at his arm as he shrugged into his coat, but he shoved her away and pushed past her to the garage. Stunned, she heard the rumble of the heavy door opening and saw Jake's headlights sweep past the kitchen window as he backed out of the garage, turned, and drove away.

Nude and bereft, Diana watched his headlights out of sight. Now nothing but the creak of an old house settling down for the night. To fill the kitchen with something beside her emptiness, Diana clenched her fists and screamed at the refrigerator from the bottom of her lungs.

She stopped screaming when she ran out of breath. Her throat hurt. Everything in the kitchen remained unmoved, refrigerator and stove, sink and electric clock, whose second hand was beginning another slow sweep.

When the second hand began its next slow and inexorable sweep, Diana heard herself sob. She turned off the kitchen light so she didn't have to see the clock and the indifferent appliances and fumbled her way to the sofa in the living room, where she lay down on leather that still held the warmth of her naked body and Jake's. She pulled her jacket and an old afghan over herself, and then she cried.

23

Morning, of course, came. Shivering, Diana sat up on the leather sofa and pulled her jacket closer around her bare shoulders. Her eyes felt swollen and her mouth tasted sour. Now what. Whatever time it was.

Friday. Office hours to face, and the Westward Movement seminar. Final papers to collect and read. She heaved herself off the sofa, feeling as sore as though she had been beaten, and headed upstairs to the shower.

A little later, dressed for campus in her white blouse and gray suit, she crept back down to the kitchen, started coffee, and gazed out the window at the snowbound circle of driveway and snow-capped ornamental lights. Circle. She repeated the word to herself, for the sound of it.

She had lain awake off and on for most of the night, knowing when she had been sleeping only because she'd been dreaming. Details replayed themselves over and over in her head. Jake's shoulders loomed over her. His muscled arms, the texture of his chest hair and belly hair, the smell and taste of his skin. His mouth, his hands, his—*cock* was the word, and she made herself say it, until at some hour she sat up on the sofa, letting jacket and afghan drop to the floor, and screamed at the walls to let her stop remembering.

She must have slept again, because she woke to the faraway crash from the railroad yards of freight cars coupling in the near-daylight of northern winter. She pulled the afghan around her and made coffee in the presence of electrical appliances and the electric clock with its unrelenting hands. Poured herself coffee, willed herself to focus on the day ahead, and prayed her MG would start.

* * *

By five o'clock, when Diana collected the stack of final papers from the Westward Movement students and returned to her office, darkness had fallen again and the window in her office was a black mirror that she turned her back on. Instead she contemplated the stack of papers on her desk.

The stack was a good foot high, she thought. Maybe she'd take the ruler from her drawer and measure, to be certain. Maybe she wouldn't.

Had she managed a credible seminar? Except for Cheryl, the students had seemed much the same as usual. Cheryl had spoken minimally during discussion, and after class she slipped out of the room without making eye contact with Diana and disappeared. Diana supposed Jake had talked to her.

A tap at her door, and Diana looked up as Ramona let herself in. Ramona was rattling about something, about getting through another week, about Douglas becoming downright paranoid about Con, about the Stockman's and meeting tonight for a drink, before she interrupted herself—"Diana! What's the matter?"

It was a last straw. Diana had bathed her face with cold water before the Westward Movement seminar and after, but she knew she looked awful, her face colorless, her eyes swollen. And now hearing Ramona's sympathy. She laid her head down on her desk and cried.

In a parallel universe she heard Ramona close her office door and snap it locked, heard Ramona drag the students' chair around to Diana's side of the desk, felt Ramona take her hand.

"Can you tell me about it?" asked Ramona after a time.

"No. Maybe."

They both froze at the sound of footsteps in the corridor. The footsteps paused, then passed by.

"I've got to get you out of here, with that slimeball oozing his way around the halls."

"Not the Stockman's!"

"No," said Ramona. She thought for a minute. "Too many kids at my house. Too many people. What if I follow you back to the mansion? Do you think you're all right to drive?"

"Y-yes."

"I've got to fetch my coat and bag from my office. You wait here and keep your door locked. I'll tap twice, wait a beat, and tap once more so you'll know it's me. I'll walk you to your car and see you off before I leave."

In another lifetime Diana would have found Ramona's cloak-and-dagger planning ridiculous. Now she just nodded and locked the door behind Ramona as she was told.

Alone again, Diana sat drained. She had cried more in the last day and a half than in the whole of her life. For now she couldn't think of the next two weeks. The last week of classes, the finals week. Then the long Christmas break alone in the mansion.

Time to relearn how to depend on herself.

Two taps on her door, a pause, a third tap.

* * *

Ramona arrived at the mansion about fifteen minutes after Diana and found her huddled in her coat in front of the cold fireplace.

"Sorry," Ramona said. She was carrying a narrow paper bag. "I made a wine stop. It's the weekend, after all, and I called home about Nicky, so I can stay. But brrr, it's cold in here. Your furnace didn't go out, did it?"

She glanced at the fireplace, which contained the ashes of Jake's fire. "No."

"Well. This house is like a barn to heat. I'm certain I remember the old president kept a couple of space heaters up here. I'll take a look."

Ramona set down her wine bottle and began a search of closets. "Aha!" she called back after checking the closet in the hallway, and reemerged carrying a squat silver-colored heater with a dangling cord.

"Let's see, yes, there's an outlet!"

Sure enough, the heater hummed and its bars reddened, and Ramona poured two glasses of wine and came to sit by Diana.

"Now, then."

Where to start. Diana didn't know if she had enough left in her to edit details from what she told Ramona, but she tried. Her mentoring of Cheryl LeTellier, which Ramona knew about. Her interest in Cheryl's story, their cautious friendship.

"And then Jake—"

"Jake."

Diana took a long sip of wine and began. Her ideas about the historical narrative—no, the historical narratives, plural, the threads that made a weave—and how she had longed for someone to discuss them with, and there was Jake, interested in the topic and willing to talk about it.

Ramona listened, sipped her wine, and said nothing.

How Diana had begun to think of Jake as her friend.

"And now I've hurt him. I hurt him once before, *insulted* him, and I apologized to him, and it was all right. It won't be all right this time, and there's nothing I can do about it."

"You're sure about that?"

Diana said nothing.

Ramona swirled the wine in her glass. "Diana. Forget for the moment your historical narrative. Or narratives, however many you think there are. Those old women who raised you. Didn't you, as a teenager, ever want to rebel? To do what other teenagers did?"

Diana wondered about the change of subject. "How could I rebel? I had nowhere else to go. The great-aunts were all I had. And they were stuck with me. They paid for what I needed, they paid my school tuition—I had nothing of my own, still don't, except what I can earn."

"I think marrying Con when I was so young was my rebellion," said Ramona. "I knew my parents wouldn't like it, and they didn't, but they got over it. Better than I did, I think."

"Tatiana and Maria wouldn't have gotten over it."

"You went to the University of Texas for your graduate program, and they didn't like that. You took this job in Versailles, and they didn't like that, but they haven't disowned you, as far as I can see."

"No. They're trying to reel me back in."

"What does that tell you?"

Diana shook her head, and Ramona set down her wine glass and threw up her hands.

"Diana, it's like you were never socialized. You might as well have been raised by wolves, except, I suppose, for having table manners and wearing clothes in public."

Ramona paused and considered. "Sexless wolves, anyway. And highly educated wolves, although it doesn't sound as though they put their educations to much use. A lawyer who never practiced law, a politician who never achieved public office. Just the way they permitted you to get an education but drew the line at your using it.

"But about Jake," she went on. "What you told Abe that day in your office. You didn't answer when I asked if it was true. Was it?"

"It was when I told Abe that."

"I see."

Ramona kept her eyes on Diana, but she took a serious drink of wine before she went on. "I've seen how Jake feels about you, Diana. I've seen it in his face. What I don't know is how you feel about him. You're not—well, some families would object pretty strongly to his Indian blood. My parents would have been horrified. Con says that down in Fort Maginnis they call Jake's people *the breeds*."

Diana couldn't speak. Her head was spinning. Jake. What he had asked her. How might she have answered, if she had answered for herself and not as *a Karnov woman*?

"It's clear you're devastated, but *don't* go back to Seattle in the shape you're in. And don't shut yourself up in this—*barn*—until classes start again. You can come to us for Christmas. We usually go out to the farm, and you can stay as long as you like."

"Thanks," Diana managed. Just as she had undervalued Jake, she had undervalued Ramona for living in her own soap opera. One more mistake to add to her growing list.

Ramona finished her wine and patted Diana's shoulder. "Jake will be all right. He won't let go of what he wants. You eat something tonight and keep warm. And call me if you need me."

24

Diana listened as the sound of Ramona's car faded into the night. She looked down at herself. She was still wearing the suit and white blouse she had worn to campus. She was holding her glass with the wine Ramona had poured for her and she hadn't finished.

What Ramona had said about socialization. Oh, Tatiana and Maria had socialized her, all right. In their own way.

Turn the page, she told herself.

She set down the glass of wine and stood, getting her bearings in the cavernous living room after what seemed like a long sojourn in strange territory. Then she climbed the stairs to her bedroom, where she changed into a robe and carefully hung up her suit and blouse. Back downstairs, barefoot, she turned on a kitchen light and opened the refrigerator.

Two white plastic containers sat side by side on a middle shelf. Her leftovers and Jake's from last night's dinner at the steakhouse.

"No," she said aloud, and then she reconsidered. If dinner last night was supposed to be a celebration of her successful stalls, let the leftovers be a requiem. She forked her steak and french fries on a plate to warm in the microwave oven and poured herself a little more wine. When the microwave pinged, she carried plate and wine into the living room and sat by the radiant space heater to eat.

Her intention was to plan how best to use the evening and coming weekend to be ready for Monday, but she found her mind wandering, inevitably, to the Karnov house in Seattle. She had been so small—but surely she remembered crying for Sister Holman after being dropped off with the great-aunts. Surely she remembered how strange the gray Seattle drizzle had seemed to her after the sun that beat down on Texas. Surely she remembered wandering the corridors of the Karnov house, a little red-haired ghost searching for what she had lost?

Had she ever been held on a lap after Sister Holman dropped her off? Been kissed? Comforted? *Touched*, even, until Annabel decided to seduce her? And she had gone with Annabel as much from curiosity as any other reason—well, trying to fit in was a reason, she supposed.

You're flinchin like a colt that's never felt a human hand.

Think of something else, she instructed herself. Done is done.

But her mind only turned to another unwelcome question. If she looked under *H* in a Rockdale, Texas, phone book, would she find a Holman? As Jake had shown her Victor Wheeler's name in the Versailles phone book?

She remembered a moment—how many years ago? Herself, maybe at thirteen. Her red hair clipped close, hardly longer than a crewcut. Lingering on the sidewalk in front of the Karnov house in thin Seattle sunshine. Playing a skipping game by herself, skipping over cracks in the sidewalk, *step on a crack, break your mother's back*, when the red-haired boy from down the street rode past on his bicycle, saw her, and did a wheelie.

Hey Red!

The door behind Diana opening. Tatiana gripping her by her upper arm and hissing through her bared teeth: *Get in the house! Don't you know you're a Karnov woman?*

Diana finished her wine and unplugged the space heater and carried her plate to the kitchen. She would take a couple of the senior seminar papers to bed with her, she decided, and give them a first reading. Cheryl's, of course. And also the Blackfeet student's. Just to see how they had done. Just to get her mind off the Karnov women.

* * *

Thanks to her new subscription to the Versailles *Daily News*, Diana could follow the police blotter, where she read of lost dogs, bit-ing dogs, cats in trees, fender-benders, neighborly assaults, forged checks, public drunkenness, and shoplifting. Also she could follow the public announcements, which was where she learned that Senator Victor Wheeler would be holding a question-and-answer session the coming Wednesday in a conference room at the Bellevue Lodge, which passed for an upscale motel in Versailles.

She laid the newspaper on the kitchen table, where she'd been drinking her morning coffee, and thought about the Q&A session. She could spare the evening, she was making good progress on the senior seminar papers, and maybe a break from stumbling through the last week of classes would refresh her enough to face finals week and the seniors' oral reports.

Yes, she had vowed to put Victor Wheeler out of her mind, but that was before, well, Jake. Before she left a message for Chris Beaudry canceling her flying lessons. She had laughed at herself when she imagined stalking the senator, but attending one public meeting hardly counted as stalking. And—it was hard to admit to herself, but she yearned to lay eyes on the man who almost certainly was her father. To sit for an hour in the same room with him, even if it was in the company of a hundred strangers.

⁂

Victor Wheeler's audience turned out to be nowhere near a hundred people, closer to forty, Diana estimated, seated on folding chairs in a windowless room with a raised platform and a podium with an attached microphone at the front and a table at the back where leaflets were displayed.

Diana hadn't changed from the navy suit and white blouse she had worn to campus that day. She found herself an aisle seat toward the back of the rows of seating where she could observe the other attendees. Judging from their stockman's suits and hats and boots, many of the men had driven in from farms or ranches with wives in wool coats that trailed whiffs of snow. Most looked to be in late middle age, perhaps close to the age of the senator himself.

Diana, who was curious about the Stillingers' politics, thought Con might come to hear the senator, and she watched for him but didn't see him.

About fifteen minutes after the advertised hour, a stir rippled the audience. A bald man in a brown business suit had gone to the microphone and tapped on it.

"Who is he?" Diana whispered to the man next to her.

"That's Mayor Tollefson."

The mayor glanced nervously around the audience, welcomed everyone, and began his introduction of the senator. Diana hardly listened. She wound her fingers, wondering at her growing anticipation. Already the mayor was finishing his introduction and stepping back from the podium to a little polite applause. Suddenly everyone in the audience rose to their feet, with Diana a little late in rising because she hadn't anticipated the protocol, and the applause was warmer now, because the silver-haired man of the photograph was striding to the podium, flanked by two very young men in dark suits.

Senator Wheeler spoke into the microphone, thanking the mayor and the county Republicans, but Diana was too busy absorbing details to listen. The senator was a lean man who obviously kept himself fit. He spoke in a deep, unhurried tone. His eyes swept his audience with a long-sighted attentiveness that reminded her of the eyes of pilots, always mindful of their perimeters. As in his photograph, she could see no trace of a physical resemblance that might warn an observer that she was the senator's daughter. But she felt an attraction she hadn't expected. To brush it away, she began to concentrate on what he was saying.

The format of the Q&A, she gathered, was that the senator would lead with a few remarks about legislative work and special concerns and pitfalls, and then he would welcome questions—"You got a question, just stand up, and Jeff or Zane, here, will bring you the hand mike."

Five minutes into the senator's remarks, Diana knew what she already suspected, that Victor Wheeler's politics would infuriate Tatiana if she weren't already infuriated with him. Diana herself wouldn't vote for him, supposing she still was living in Versailles when the next election came around. She watched as a burly man in a plaid mackinaw rose, accepted a hand mike from Jeff or Zane to ask the first question, and instead launched into a lengthy jeremiad on the harm done by regulations on agriculture, while the senator nodded and commiserated with him and promised legislation to loosen the regulations. The next questioner was worried about taxes, which the senator promised legislation to lower, and Diana stifled a yawn.

About forty-five minutes into the Q&A, however, the tenor of the meeting took a sudden swerve when an elderly man near the front of the seating spoke into the hand mike.

"Senator, where do you stand on this here Equal Rights Amendment I hear talk about? You wanna see women prison guards? You wanna see little girls on wrestling teams with boys?"

Before the senator could disavow women prison guards or girls on wrestling teams, an uproar in the back row brought every head swiveling to see what was going on.

"E! R! A! E! R! A!" Clap clap clap. "E! R! A! E! R! A!" Clap clap clap. "E! R! A! E! R! A!"

Diana, who had turned to stare with everyone else, recognized one or two faces among the chanting, clapping women whom she had seen on campus, probably students. Most were strangers, and when she chanced a look back over her shoulder, she saw the senator looked unsurprised at the demonstration.

Not so his audience, which rose in rage.

"Shaddup and siddown!"

"Missoula agitators! Go back to Missoula!"

"Go home and tend to your knittin!"

"A woman's place is in the house," screamed one of the demonstrators. "And in the senate, too!"

Now the chanting women were leaving their seats to file up the aisle toward the senator, while Diana, torn between keeping her anonymity and wanting to join the protestors for the sheer hell-raising pleasure of it, stared in disbelief as a man confronted the woman at the head of the demonstration by grabbing her arm and twisting it until she screamed and sank to her knees.

As more scuffling broke out, Diana saw the senator speak an aside to one of his aides. The next moment uniformed Versailles police burst into the conference room to separate the combatants. The man who had twisted the woman's arm made the mistake of throwing a punch at the intervening policeman and found himself under arrest along with two or three of the women and several more men from the audience.

As one of the policemen led a handcuffed woman back down the aisle, he glanced at Diana and paused. It was Jake's friend Saylor. He seemed to struggle for what he wanted to say.

"Jake's real cut up. Hope you ain't—" Then he remembered his prisoner, who was observing him and Diana with stark curiosity, and moved on.

Diana sat down. She felt shaken by the level of anger she had sensed from the Wheeler supporters, and her legs were giving her no other option. Those in the audience who weren't under arrest or arguing with each other were straggling out of their seats and putting their coats back on. It was a thinning group, no more than eight or ten leftover stragglers. From their faces, Diana judged they had thoroughly enjoyed the Q&A's exciting conclusion.

Senator Wheeler, deep in consultation with one of the young aides, walked past Diana on his way to the door, glanced at her, paused, and gave her a longer look before he walked on. A minute or two later the young aide was back.

"Miss? The senator wonders if he can know your name?"

The aide was no older than some of Diana's students. He seemed unsure about his errand, twisting his hands and trying to decide whether to say more. It gave Diana a minute to decide what to tell him.

"Tell him my name is Diana Karnov. That's Karnov with a *K*."

The boy nodded and fled.

Diana's neighbor eyed her, considering. He was a smallish red-cheeked man who cocked his head like a robin on the hunt. "You must have made quite an impression on the senator."

"Does the senator have that kind of reputation?"

"Oh, no. Not that I ever heard. Course he's been single for a long time. He had a wife, years back, some mystery there, but I think she died."

"I see," said Diana. "Well, nice talking to you. I'm glad you didn't get arrested."

"So am I. But we had an exciting evening, didn't we?"

"I had the feeling the senator wasn't surprised."

"Those women follow him from appearance to appearance. Most of them are from Missoula, from the university. The university is a little pink, as they say. Well, good night, then."

"Good night." She buttoned her coat, gathered her handbag and gloves, and thought she remembered a side door from the meeting room to the parking lot where she wouldn't bump into either Saylor or the senator again. On that hope, she wished herself good luck.

25

Diana stayed in the mansion on Thursday, subsisting on coffee and cheese sandwiches and continuing her second round of reading final papers until she could read no longer. On Friday, with her eyes throbbing from weeping and her intensive reading, she crept to campus on icy streets to hold her office hours and get through the final seminar of the quarter.

The Montana university system's ten-week quarter schedule was a hundred-yard dash compared with the leisurely sixteen-week semester schedule of the Texas universities, and Diana wondered how the students stood it. She experienced a weary vision of her life through the upcoming winter and spring quarters, and the year after that and the one after that if by some miracle she was rehired.

She was unlocking her office door when the history department's work-study student hurried out to catch her.

"Dr. Karnov! You've been getting so many phone calls!" The girl thrust a handful of While You Were Out notes at her. "Here! This woman's been calling and calling, and she's very angry. I could hear her shouting at Nelda over the phone."

"Yes," said Nelda, coming out of her own office to join Diana and the work-study student. "What country does that woman think she's the queen of?"

Diana read through the notes. *Call Miss Karnov. Call Miss Karnov. Call Miss Karnov.* At the bottom of the stack, *Senator Wheeler would like to talk with you over coffee. Please call Zane to confirm.*

"Sorry," Diana said. "She's my great-aunt, and she's very elderly, and she's angry that I'm teaching here and not living at home with her in Seattle. She has no business taking her temper out on you. I'll call her."

"One of those, is she," said Nelda, and she and the student rolled their eyes.

Diana turned on the light in her office and dropped her stack of books and papers on her desk. Then she dropped herself into her desk chair and tried to collect her thoughts. All she had to be thankful for was her unlisted phone number at the mansion. But she had to call in return. Tatiana could have been phoning about anything, after all. Maria's heart was iffy. Diana had an awful vision of one of the great-aunts causing her own heart attack in a last-ditch effort to force Diana back to Seattle.

And the senator. What—

Diana's phone rang. She stared at it for a moment before she answered.

It was Nelda. "I have a Zane, here? He's on the line for you. I'll transfer him over to you."

Before she could ask Nelda to say she was out of the office, Diana heard the double pings of the transfer, and then a young man with a tentative voice.

"Dr. Karnov? This is Zane from Senator Wheeler's office? I left a message for you yesterday? The senator would like to talk with you over coffee. Is there a time when you might—"

"I'm sorry," Diana said. "I just now got back to my office and saw your message. We'll be busy with finals this coming week, but—"

Zane sounded distressed. "I think the senator hoped to meet with you today. He's traveling to Helena tomorrow."

"I don't get out of class until five."

Diana heard a muffled discussion on the other end of the line. Then Zane returned. "Five thirty? In the coffee shop at the Bellevue? Shall I meet you on campus and drive you there?"

The Bellevue was the big motel at the west end of Main Street, where the Q&A had been held. She wouldn't risk being trapped there without her own wheels when she had no idea whether the senator had recognized the Karnov name and what his interests were. From his perspective, Diana could be a pretty dolly or a major political embarrassment or both. "No, I don't need a ride. The Bellevue will be fine."

After she hung up, Diana sat with her hand on the phone. She should call Tatiana and get it over with. If only she didn't feel so tired. Where had her energy gone?

One of her survey students knocked on her door, wanting to talk to her about the final exam and look at his grades up to now—was there a chance of a strong final exam nudging that C up to a B? Diana spent a good twenty minutes going over the quarter's readings with him, doing everything but telling him what the questions would be. When he finally left, another student knocked.

"Mark Gervais!" she said, looking up in surprise.

"Dr. Karnov. Can I—"

Diana gestured to the students' chair. "Mark, I haven't seen you in class, in what—a week? This close to finals?"

Mark sat and shifted in the chair, looking more like an embarrassed student than the drunk Diana had seen spoiling for a fight. Sober, he was a good-looking boy, a young man, really, with a shock of dark hair and dark eyes that looked everywhere but at her. His nervous energy overrode his features. Diana glanced down at her grade book. He had been maintaining a C, maybe even a C plus, all term. Bright enough but bored.

Now he chanced a look at her. "I been in jail."

Diana waited.

"Rosalie's mother took out a restraining order against me. But I—" His voice trailed off.

"You violated the restraining order?" Diana suggested, and Mark nodded.

Another long pause. Voices in the corridor, students on their way to classes. Diana tried not to look at her watch.

"I tried studying for your final while I was in jail," Mark said. "It didn't work out so well. Look, I—oh, hell."

He was on the verge of tears. Diana thought of what she knew about him. A student in the back row of the survey class with a vacant look on his face. A combatant in the mindless violence that erupted like spontaneous combustion in the heart of Versailles. Mark's part in the battle at the Stockman's. Mark's losing fight with Con Stillinger at the Palace. Mark's thwarted attack on the hippies in the county park. And here he sat in her office, a shambles of a young man in distress.

"Sounds to me as though you've made some major mistakes," she said.

"Yeah."

"So what are you going to do about it?" Diana thought she could just about scrape up a grade of Incomplete for him, but he was going to have to ask for it. "You've hung on all quarter, maybe by your fingernails—"

"It's Rosalie I gotta do something about," he blurted. "Look, Dr. Karnov, I'll take your class over again if I hafta, but Rosalie, she wants to run away to California, she thinks she can be a star, and I think she's got the voice—"

"Mark, how old is Rosalie?"

His face was a study in misery. "Fifteen."

"And you're how old?"

"Twenty-two."

Diana sighed while he blinked furiously and wiped his nose with his finger until she handed him a tissue from the box on her desk. "Mark, I think I can see why her mother would be concerned."

"Yeah. I can see that. I'm not stupid. Just dumb." He wadded the tissue in his fist. "I know what I need to do. Doin it's another thing. You know what I mean?"

"Actually I do," said Diana and got a startled look from him.

He shook his head. "You're somethin else, Dr. Karnov. We all think so." He studied the tissue in his hand as though he was surprised to see it there, but went on. "Yeah. Quit drinkin. Quit fightin.

Take your class over again and pass it. Stay away from—" his voice wobbled. "Stay away from Rosalie. That's the hard part."

Diana shook her head. "Is there anything you enjoy doing, Mark?" She didn't add, *besides getting into fights and chasing an underage girl.*

Something woke in his face that might have been a dim light. "I play the guitar, some," he said, "and sing. Nothin like Rosalie, a course."

All Diana had to offer him was good advice. "So play your guitar. Don't run away to California. That would be worse than stupid. Worse than dumb."

And he nodded.

* * *

Diana listened to Mark Gervais's receding footsteps and remembered Tatiana. The seminar would start in half an hour. What Mark had said about knowing what to do was one thing, doing it another. Now or never. Diana shut her door, picked up the phone, and dialed.

It was snatched up on the first ring.

"Diana! I *must* know your plans! *When* are you arriving in Seattle?"

"Didn't you get my letter? I'm not planning to come to Seattle for Christmas."

"That letter. Nonsense. You *are* coming for Christmas. You *will.*"

"No," said Diana. "I will not."

The other end of the line erupted in a fury, some of it in English, some in Russian. Diana listened for several minutes until Tatiana either exhausted her wrath or her voice.

"Tatiana," she said, "I will call you again tomorrow. But you must not trouble the department secretary by calling here repeatedly. And in five minutes I have a class to teach."

A silence, and then, in what clearly was a question and not a command, "You *will* call me tomorrow?" A pause, a restart. "And you *will* come for Christmas!"

"Yes, I will call. No, I will not come to Seattle for Christmas."

Silence.

For the time being it was over. Diana hung up the phone, gathered her seminar materials, and left her office for the classroom.

* * *

The coffee shop at the Bellevue was full and noisy at five thirty in the afternoon. A clatter of dishes rang from the kitchen, a matching clatter of voices rose from tables and booths. Waitresses in short black dresses hurried back and forth with order pads and pots of coffee. Diana saw Senator Wheeler's silver head bent over a sheaf of papers in a booth by a window, and she threaded her way to him.

He looked up, saw Diana, and drew a breath as he rose to shake her hand, holding it for just a moment and looking less like an embarrassed man than a stricken man who had to bend toward her to make himself heard over the coffee-goers.

"I don't think this place is going to do. Shall we try the bar across the hall?"

The bar had plenty of Happy Hour customers, but it was dimly lit, with thick carpeting and heavy draperies that absorbed much of the sound. The senator guided Diana to a table at the back and seated her with a careful courtesy.

"I can ask the waitress to bring coffee here. Or—perhaps a glass of wine?"

He studied her face, intently enough to memorize it, with a raw expression on his own face, as though the political mask had been peeled away from a younger, more vulnerable man.

"It was a shock to see you in the conference room that night. I thought I'd seen a ghost. And then the name."

This man's hazel eyes that were her own eyes. The straight lines of brows and mouth that she recognized from the newspaper photograph. The illusion from the screen of the microfilm reader, grown older by thirty years, sitting across the table from her.

"I'm told," Diana said when her voice returned, "that I don't look at all like my mother."

"No. It's my mother you look like. The way she looked when I was a boy."

"Did your mother have red hair?"

He nodded. "And hazel eyes like yours. She was very beautiful. Of course, I was a boy looking at his mother."

The moment stretched. It contained nothing but Diana and this man who continued to gaze at her as though he still wasn't sure she was real. When he spoke again, his voice was husky.

"For me—right now—Dr. Karnov—it's as though you dropped out of nowhere. Zane dug up the newspaper article, that you're a professor at the college, but I don't know anything about you—where you came from—just your face and that name. Lillia's name."

"My name is Diana. I'm twenty-eight now. You must have known that."

"I knew she—we—" he couldn't finish.

The cocktail waitress stopped at their table. "What can I get for you and your friend, Senator?"

Diana watched his face struggle back to the physical space of booth and carpeted bar.

"Dr. Karnov—will you let me buy you a glass of wine?"

Diana thought she had never seen a face as naked as his. It dawned on her that he was in a state of shock, or something close to it, and she remembered her own shaken state when Jake got out his phone book and showed her *Wheeler, Victor*. Since then she had prepared herself through uncounted hours turning the handle of a microfilm reader and scanning years of newspapers in search of the man, and now it was up to her to give him the space of time he needed.

"I'd love a glass of red wine," she said, "and I'm *Diana*."

He spoke the name of a label to the waitress, who nodded and disappeared.

"Senator, when I went to your meeting, I just wanted to see you. That was all. There are questions I have that I think you might be able to answer for me, but I hadn't planned to get in touch with you."

"You just would have walked away?" He shook his head. "I sent Zane and Jeff scouting all over the Bellevue, but you'd vanished."

The cocktail waitress brought two glasses and a bottle, which she uncorked at the table and poured a thimbleful for the senator to taste and approve before she filled both glasses and disappeared again.

"Diana," he said, and again he lingered over her name before he raised his glass to her. Then he was silent for a long time that Diana did not interrupt, but instead sipped wine that contained a deep fragrance and layers she could taste but could not name.

"Diana." He looked up from whatever his reverie and found her face. "What do you want to ask me?"

What indeed. Who was Sister Holman, how had Diana happened to be born in Rockdale, Texas, what had happened to Lillia, and how had five-year-old Diana come to live with Tatiana and Maria in Seattle?

"Tell me about my mother."

"God." He took a deep draught from his glass. "I have to travel to Helena early tomorrow morning, but I may just get drunk tonight."

He set down his glass. "Lillia. She was beautiful. And I fucking loved her. I loved her, and I married her, and she was pregnant with our child. And one day she fucking disappeared." His face wrenched. "That's all. Well, it's not all, but—and I apologize for my language, Diana, I wasn't raised to talk like that in front of a woman, but—"

His face reminded Diana of Mark Gervais's face earlier that day when he told her about Rosalie. Without knowing what she was about to do, Diana reached across the table and touched the senator's hand, and that was when she saw the ring he wore.

* * *

The seniors' oral reports were scheduled for the late afternoons of Monday, Tuesday, Wednesday, and Thursday of finals week; three groups of four and, on Thursday, a group of three to round out the fifteen students in the seminar. The students had drawn straws, and the two whose papers Diana held the highest hopes for,

Cheryl LeTellier and the Blackfeet boy, James Archambault, would give their reports on Thursday, after which the department would meet to discuss the reports and papers and assign their grades. On Friday morning both classes of survey students would meet in Main Hall's auditorium to write their finals, which Diana would carry back to the mansion to read and grade. Once the grades were turned in and finals stacked in a basket on her desk for the handful of students who would show up in January to claim theirs, Diana's quarter was done.

What she would do next, she so far had managed to bury under the day-to-day. She had options, she told herself. Ramona's invitation for Christmas at the Stillinger farm, and now an invitation from the senator.

* * *

She and the senator had talked until past midnight while he finished the bottle of wine and described her mother for Diana. How he'd been working at a loading dock at the train station in Versailles when he saw the girl in the blue dress step off the Pullman car.

"She told me later she left the train for a breath of air and a look at the town and that she intended to reboard, although she didn't know where she was going. As far as she could, she said. But I—all I knew at the time was the way she smiled at me, and that I was going to do every damn thing I could to keep her from getting back on that train."

So the blue dress of Diana's fantasy was true. The detail was unsettling, but a blue-eyed blonde girl might often wear blue.

"We had eight months together, Diana. I loved her and she loved me. We were living on the ranch and she was six months pregnant with our baby—" it took him a minute to go on—"and it was just about this time of year. Snow on the ground. I hitched a team to a sled and drove out with a load of hay to feed cattle, and when I came back to the house she was—she wasn't there. Vanished. I called everybody I could think of. Thing was, not a lot of ranchers had phone service in those days."

Another long pause. "I called the sheriff here in Versailles, and he said he'd send out deputies—and then I pulled myself together and started to look around the house for a note or—but nothing. But the little suitcase she'd brought with her was gone, and some of her clothes and the baby's things we'd been collecting."

He took a deep breath. Diana watched a man on the verge of tears as he relived that long-ago day.

"I went back outside then, and I saw what I'd maybe seen and not registered when I came back from feeding cattle. Tire tracks in front of the house where a car had driven up and turned around."

"And that was all?"

"I never saw Lillia again. Never heard from her again. The sheriff's deputies drove out and checked the borrow pits for wrecks, and they followed the car tracks I'd seen as far as the highway, which had been ploughed and windswept bare, and that was that. Except—except later that day—it wasn't dark enough for headlights yet—and I was half out of my mind, when here came another car, bobbing up to the yard fence and stopped, and it turned out to be the Karnov sisters. They'd hired a taxi in Versailles to drive them all the way out to the ranch."

"Not what you needed to round off that day."

"I was only twenty-three, myself, and I'd had a couple of stiff whiskies to—well, brace myself to go on."

So that was the origin of the *drunken* part of the drunken vagrant. How had the great-aunts come up with *vagrant*?

"I could see why Lillia was petrified of them. There wasn't a damned thing I could tell them, if I'd wanted to. But that timing— Lillia vanishing that morning and the Karnovs turning up that evening—I've wondered about that for the past twenty-eight years."

He drank the last of his wine and looked at his empty glass. "I take it you know the Karnov sisters."

"They raised me."

His eyes shot up. "Does that mean they found Lillia?"

"No—at least not until after she was dead."

"So Lillia is really gone," he said, more to himself than to Diana, and he turned the ring on his finger. "Then how—they had come to Versailles on the train from Seattle—how—so you must have grown up in Seattle."

"Yes. From the time I was five. All I know about my mother is that she's buried in Seattle. But if I still were in school in Austin, I'd be looking for answers in Rockdale, Texas."

"That could be done," he said, again to himself. Then he glanced past Diana, toward the bar. "They're getting ready to close. And I've talked you to death."

When they stood, Diana saw the senator was unsteady, and she caught the eye of the cocktail waitress over his shoulder and got back a nod. He was known here, he'd get assistance if he needed it.

"Are you all right? Will you be all right to drive in the morning?"

"I'm all right." He managed a smile. "Better than all right. And Zane will drive tomorrow. He's a Mormon. But Diana—will we talk when I come back north again? I'd like to show you the ranch. May I call you?"

When Diana told him the phone number at the mansion, he took out a pen and wrote it on his hand, the way one of her students would have.

"All I know about you," she said, "is that you want to cut taxes and ease regulations. I don't even know what to call you. Senator Wheeler? Mr. Wheeler? Victor?"

He laughed then, dissolving years from his face, which lit as Jake's face lit when he smiled and wrung Diana to remember.

"I don't know a lot about you, either, Diana, but I suspect you'd have been clapping and chanting E! R! A!"

"Oh, yes. I would have been."

"Lillia called me Vee," he said.

26

Diana awaited Thursday afternoon with a mixture of anticipation and dread. The sessions earlier in the week went well enough. Her seniors had shown the poise the oral reports were intended to display, their papers were credible and didn't stir much disagreement among the faculty, even from Abe, and no one received a grade below a C or above a B. Friends and family were free to attend the sessions, along with the other seminar students, and each report had drawn a small audience to clap with enthusiasm for it. Diana feared seeing Jake in Cheryl's audience and perversely hoped she would see him.

The stage of the auditorium was arranged as it had been for the previous sessions, with three chairs for the students angled along one side, six chairs for the faculty and the dean angled like a jury along the other side, and a podium in the center. The three seniors already were seated when the faculty filed in: Janet Sorenson, the young woman who had written her final paper on her grandmother's diaries; James Archambault with his paper on the Marias River Massacre; and Cheryl LeTellier. Diana kept her eyes straight ahead, resisting the urge to glance at the audience. She heard Abe Dennison behind her, drawing a deep breath and blowing it out in exasperation. On the way into the auditorium she'd overheard him arguing with Dean Maki, an argument that was cut short when they saw her.

The seniors would devote the next two quarters taking classes to fulfill their graduation requirements, but the oral reports were a rite of passage, and all the students had dressed for it. Whether they had drawn straws again or decided their order among themselves, Janet Sorenson stepped up to the podium after Abe introduced her. She wore a very short skirt and a sweater, and she had taken pains with her hair and make-up.

Diana had read Janet's paper and found it a careful documentation from the historical record of events mentioned in her grandmother's diaries, thorough and exact but unimaginative in its conclusions. Still, a commendable effort by an undergraduate, and Janet was poised during her presentation, describing the content of her paper and underlining her main points. When she finished, to applause from the audience, she flushed and waited for questions.

Abe, predictably, asked her to review her sources—"You say your grandmother went to church on Sunday and heard the news about Lindbergh's flight from a friend. What gives you confidence that your sources about the flight are accurate?"

"I checked more than one newspaper."

"Why do you think it's important to know that your grandmother heard about Lindbergh's flight from a friend in church?"

That stopped her. "I just thought it was interesting."

Dean Maki cut in. "Will you talk a little more about the value of these texts you've inherited?"

"Texts?"

"The diaries."

"Well, I value them because they were my grandmother's. She kinda comes alive when I read them. And I recognize her handwriting. A lot of what she writes can't be documented. When she has a headache, for example."

More questions followed, several from the seniors in the audience who already had delivered their oral reports. Diana usually didn't ask questions, these were her students, after all, but now she asked,

"Do you think your grandmother expected her diaries to be read by anyone else? Was she creating a historical record of her own?"

The young woman bit her lip and considered. "When I write a paper to be handed in," she said, "I look it over and use Wite-Out to correct the typos, and I make sure the typing looks good. Nice and straight and even on the page. My grandmother sometimes used a pen, sometimes a pencil, and sometimes she erased or crossed out, and sometimes she didn't bother. I don't think she expected anyone else to read them."

Not a bad answer. Janet could develop into a close and critical reader if she continued working along those lines, although it was likely she wouldn't. Earning a bachelor's degree was an enormous accomplishment for most of these students.

Abe thanked Janet, and she sat down while James Archambault stepped to the podium and Abe began his introduction, which was when Diana looked up, inadvertently glanced out at the audience, and instantly looked away, because she had seen Jake, and Jake was watching her.

She fixed her eyes on James Archambault and concentrated on her breathing. Slow, even. Slow, even. Damn Jake, damn Jake, all the strength of will she had drawn upon to blank out any thought of him, all undone in that instant. And what she had seen, Abe would have seen. With Abe sitting to her left on stage and Jake to her right in the audience, the only safe place for her eyes was on James Archambault, who could have been talking about Charles Lindbergh for the last ten minutes for all she knew.

He wasn't, of course. He was talking about the relative values in the newspaper coverage in 1870 that was given to eyewitness accounts by Indians of the Marias River Massacre and those given by white soldiers and civilians, and how the historical record was informed by those accounts and coverage. Although Diana doubted he could have articulated it, he was in fact interrogating the historical record, and she wondered how Abe would react to his approach. Always provided, of course, that Abe had been paying attention to James Archambault's report and not to Jake LeTellier's presence in the audience.

James concluded his report, to another patter of applause, and Abe called for questions.

"You argue that white eyewitnesses were given more credibility than Piegan eyewitnesses," said Dean Maki. "To what extent would language barriers and difficulties in translation affect the credibility of the witnesses?"

"Bound to have affected it some," James agreed. "Hard to measure. You'd have had a white investigator taking notes on what a translator said the witness said, when the translator's English might have stretched to how many miles to camp, or how many ponies passed along the trail, but wouldn't be good enough for complicated stories."

"What about Baker's scout? Joe Kipp? He was a half-breed, wasn't he? How was his credibility judged?"

James and Dean Maki kicked around the question of Joe Kipp and his credibility for some time. James thought he was given more credibility than the full bloods, but it also might have been because his English was pretty good. Diana thought the most striking aspect of the discussion was how much James and the dean were enjoying it. Out of the corner of her eye she could see Abe with his arms folded, glowering.

The students asked a few questions, James sat down to applause, and Cheryl walked to the podium. She wore neat black slacks and boots with a red sweater, and she had brushed out her long black hair that fell nearly to her waist. Briefly she summarized her project—reading the accounts of their lives that Métis women in the past had written or told to someone else to write, interviewing living Métis elders, evaluating their stories, and drawing conclusions from them.

"The conclusion that interested me the most," she concluded, "was the difference in the ways that boundaries of all kinds were perceived by the old people and how boundaries came to be perceived after white settlement."

Behind Diana, a chair scraped as it was pushed back. She was hearing an angry exchange between Abe and Dean Maki in whispers that she couldn't make out, but were loud enough to interrupt Cheryl, who paused and looked up from her notes. Dean Maki seemed to be remonstrating with Abe, who snarled some answer. Then rapid footsteps and the door behind Diana opened and closed.

Silence.

"Cheryl, can you continue?" asked Dean Maki, and Cheryl found her place in her notes after a brief pause.

"Boundaries," she said. "None of the elders I interviewed could remember a time when they hadn't lived on a ranch that had been surveyed, or in a house in town that had been platted. But they remembered the old folks telling how they followed the buffalo back and forth across the border, same as the tribes did—the real Indians, as we Métis called them—without worrying whether they were in Canada or the United States. It caused all kinds of problems later, when the buffalo were gone and the Métis had nothing to eat. The Americans didn't want to feed them and decided they were foreigners from Canada, but the Canadians didn't want to feed them, either."

"Or land measurement. Indians didn't measure it, except how far away something was. Or maybe what they considered their hunting grounds—"

But a disturbance was turning heads in the audience from the presentation on stage to the big double doors, which had been thrown open to pour a river of light down the center aisle. There Abe loomed as he scanned the auditorium before plowing his way through a row of seats while onlookers tried to scramble out of his way.

Cheryl and the other students on stage were shading their eyes, trying to see what was happening, but the double doors had swung shut again and the auditorium was too dark to make out much more than a roiling knot, whether of combatants or spectators, in the middle of a row. Behind Diana, Dean Maki pushed out of his chair, said distinctly, "Damnation," and hurried out the door.

Cheryl stood, stranded, at the podium. With the dean gone, with Abe gone, who was in charge? Diana glanced at the professor next to her, the sociologist George Schultz, but George just shrugged, he didn't know, either. Well, damnation indeed. These were her students.

"Cheryl," she said, "won't you take a seat until we find out what seems to be interrupting your presentation?"

And Cheryl nodded and slipped away from the podium.

The confrontation seemed to have subsided. Onlookers were sitting back down as the double doors opened again and someone—Abe?—stumbled out just as Dean Maki appeared in the center aisle. He held up a hand to silence the excited chatter and spoke.

"I apologize, everyone, for the interruption. Please remain in your seats for a brief pause to give Cheryl a moment before she resumes her presentation. Thank you."

All was so quiet now that the proverbial pin could have dropped. No one on stage looked at one another. Then Dean Maki was back with them.

"Cheryl, do you feel you can continue, or do you need more time?"

"I'm okay."

At the podium, she returned to the issue of boundaries. "Everyone I interviewed told me the story they had heard from their elders about the cause of the first Riel Rebellion. They explained that Métis farmers in Saskatchewan had long, narrow farms that ran down to the rivers, so everybody had access to irrigation water and river travel. But when the English-speaking Canadians moved into Saskatchewan, they ruled the land into square sections and acres, which destroyed the Métis system of farming."

"Or identity. I learned that lots of Métis identified themselves with Indian tribes and lived and traveled with them. Others identified more with their French heritage. Nobody cared much, and nobody thought of doing what the white census-takers did, which was to ride around the country, deciding who was white, who was an Indian, and who was a half-breed. I think the Chinese gave them less trouble deciding how to count them."

"Today lots of Métis also are enrolled members of Indian tribes, like the Little Shell Chippewa band. And I can tell you that being an enrolled member matters a lot to the Little Shell band. It matters a lot to the Blackfeet, too. Doesn't it, James!"

James Archambault looked startled and sat up straighter in his chair, then grinned and nodded.

"Still, you never know. Take James, here. He's an enrolled Blackfeet. But his last name is Archambault, which is a common Métis name. My grandmother's maiden name was Evangeline Archambault, and I have scads of Archambault cousins. Hey, James! Are you Blackfeet *and* Métis? Do you think we might be related?"

James was laughing now, and the audience was laughing.

Cheryl sheafed her papers together, bounced them square on the podium, nodded an end to her presentation, and waited through a burst of applause for questions.

Diana couldn't have asked a question if she'd wanted to. She had been awed by Cheryl's demeanor during her presentation, by her ability to keep her concentration through all the disturbances, and by the contrast between this Cheryl and the downcast Cheryl of last fall. She wondered if the bastard husband was in the audience, but she wouldn't know him if she saw him and she didn't dare look. But involuntarily she did look at the audience where Jake had been sitting, and Jake was gone.

The dean asked Cheryl several questions, as he had James, while Diana fought back an uneasy surmise. Finally she heard George Schultz ask if any of the Métis elders had turned down Cheryl's request for an interview.

"No, and they seemed to love talking about the past. Of course they've known me since I was a child."

The dean rose. He thanked the seniors for their presentations and their audience for attending, and then he left for the small conference room with the faculty in a straggling file behind him.

27

Students in excited conversation in the corridor:

"What happened?"

"Nobody knows!"

"Somebody got punched in the auditorium is what I heard."

"I heard it was Dr. Dennison!"

Chatter abruptly ended and students dodged out of Dean Maki's way as he led his faculty to the conference room and opened the door.

"Holy smokes," George Schultz whispered.

Abe Dennison was sitting at the head of the conference table. The overhead fluorescents were switched on, giving his face a greenish tinge that didn't disguise a purple bruise on his cheek.

A silence. Everyone simultaneously staring at Abe and trying not to look at him.

Dean Maki seated himself across the table from Diana with his hands folded. She thought the dean looked deceptively mild-mannered, sitting between Professors Carlin and Brown, who were old enough to have known the dean when he taught in the department. George Schultz had taken the chair beside Diana, and she actually felt grateful to the old lecher, who for weeks had been undressing her with his eyes every time she walked past his office door, for not making her sit alone and ostracized today. Schultz, too, was of an age to have known the dean for years.

Abe immediately opened on her. "What in the name of God were you thinking, Diana? Letting them get away with trivial topics like those? There weren't but two or three decent papers and presentations out of your whole seminar. We've got a wasted class of seniors on our hands, and what the hell are we going to do about it? Tell them they all have to register for another seminar? And who's going to teach it? I can't teach everything around here!"

A pause. Dean Maki cast his gaze around the seated professors and spoke.

"I thought all the projects were remarkable. Especially the three who gave their oral reports this afternoon."

Diana felt a ripple of feeling circulate around the table. Everyone was avoiding eye contact, except Abe, who stared at the dean.

"You can't think that, Maki!"

"I thought they were pretty damned good, myself," said Schultz. "Diana's got them thinking for themselves and interested in what they're digging up. That girl this afternoon with the diaries? She was on the verge of a genuine insight about her texts."

"I'm with you there," said Carlin, and Brown nodded. Something about the expressions on their faces made Diana think of students laying a plot against a teacher and about to pull it off. Both men were longtime associate professors who, because they lacked PhD degrees, never would be promoted to full professorships. How many sneers at their "mere" master's degrees from Abe Dennison, PhD, had they had to endure?

Abe stared from one to another, momentarily at a loss for words. "You're all taken in by these *fads*? Oral histories? Of no more historical veracity than rumors and tall tales?"

"Fads are one thing," observed the dean, "and cutting-edge research techniques are another. True, time tests all theories. There was a time for me, but alas, I've been too long out of graduate school and too far from a research library. We're fortunate to have Dr. Karnov with us. Even with the limited resources of our library, she's taught the historical method to those students, and they're excited about it."

"We're all agreed, aren't we?" said George Schultz. "We may as well tally the grades."

A ripple of satisfaction went around the table, and Diana saw from the men's faces that they knew what they'd pulled off against Abe.

* * *

The early evening was cold when Diana left Main Hall, with a sky full of stars that still surprised her after the fathomless night sky over Seattle's lights. The parking lot had a security light over both ends, but she had left the MG near a low brick utility building that abutted the parking lot, and now its shadow fell over the little car. Diana paused with her key in her hand and listened to silence, which gradually gave way, as it always did, to the faint rumble of traffic on the street, the brush of a bare branch against brick, a gust of wind that drove fingers of snow across the paved lot.

She took another step toward the car and stopped. What was she feeling at the back of her neck? The night in the parking lot behind the Stockman's when she had been startled by the dark figure waiting by the MG—but Jake would not be waiting for her tonight.

No. Put Jake out of mind. Diana gave herself her marching orders, unlocked her car, and got in and was relieved as always when it started without objection. She drove out of the parking lot, glanced in her rear-view mirror, and saw the black pickup truck parked behind the utility building.

* * *

"All three of Thursday's seniors received overall grades of As," Diana told Ramona the next afternoon. "James got five As and a B. Janet got five As and a C. Cheryl got five As and a D."

"A pattern emerging there, do you think?"

Diana laughed. They were drinking wine at the back of the Chinese restaurant, which Diana hadn't known had a beer and wine license, and where, as Ramona pointed out, no one who knew them was likely to find them. The hostess, a tiny Chinese woman who looked to be a hundred years old, left them to themselves with only a glance now and then to see if they needed refills on their wine.

The restaurant was long and narrow, with booths along both sides and high ceilings hung with paper lanterns. Chinese characters in molded red plastic were stuck to the walls above the booths, and a brilliantly painted papier-mâché dragon crouched in the bay window next to the cash register where he could look out at the falling snow. Diana had noted that each booth was furnished with its own bottles of catsup and mustard, a sugar dispenser, and a paper napkin dispenser in uneasy company with bottles of soy sauce. That, as Ramona would say, was Versailles for you.

"The forecast says more snow," Ramona sighed. "Maybe snow means it won't stay quite so cold. The cold is what frightens me. Do you realize it's cold enough tonight to freeze us to death?"

Diana shivered with the memory. She had told no one about the night Jake drove her home half-frozen from the Stockman's.

"Only if we decided to walk home."

"People have frozen to death here. There were times—when I'd be driving out to the farm at night, alone, or maybe with one of the babies with me—I'd look out at the frost crystals in the headlights and think how very little shelter the walls of the truck gave. How fast that metal cab would chill if the engine died. Con always says people don't freeze who don't do anything foolish—"

"Con's right."

"—like run out of gas and then get out and walk."

"You're not going to do that."

"With me it's the idea. The way the intense cold settles in, especially later in the winter after a heavy snowfall, so heavy—don't you feel it out there? Bearing down? I feel it."

"God, Ramona! How did we get on this topic?"

"I don't know if I can last another six months. But if I leave him, then what? Douglas is the most sensitive man I've ever met, but—"

"Does Con know about you and Douglas?"

"No!"

Diana wasn't so sure. She didn't think Douglas was so certain, either. He had asked her to coffee and recited his litany of conflicts: love, desire, and faith. He showed her a poem he had written. Laced through his anxiety was a certain practical edge that was asking for a listener.

Where would they go, how would they live? What would Douglas's mother say, and worse, what would Con do? Diana remembered the night Con had beaten up Mark Gervais in the Palace and humiliated Ramona for the way she was fawning over Douglas. What else Con might do to Douglas and Ramona was a question to take seriously.

Ramona drank the last of her wine. "Have you decided about Christmas?"

"No—well, I think I may have gotten it across to Tatiana that I'm not spending Christmas in Seattle. I've fantasized about driving somewhere, maybe Great Falls, checking into the best hotel, and spending a week in a hot bubble bath."

Ramona laughed. "What a lovely fantasy. And by the way, I love the way you're letting your hair loose from that knot. Shall we have another glass of wine?"

"Why not?"

* * *

Why not, indeed. Sitting beside the space heater in the lonely living room of the mansion, Diana thought about the half-bottle of wine waiting in the refrigerator and reluctantly decided against another glass, which would only make it harder to keep her thoughts from wandering back to a freezing night and a black pickup truck.

She had no reason to think the truck parked by the utility building in the dark was Jake's. There must be plenty of people in Versailles who drove black pickup trucks.

As a distraction, she replayed the meeting in the conference room, lingering on the sense of glee that had emanated from Professors Schultz, Carlin, and Brown over their part in helping their old friend the dean thwart Abe Dennison's agenda. She had seen, she realized, an academic political machine rolling over its opposition. Was a political machine unique to Versailles State College, or were there cabals of allies circling their enemies on all campuses?

Her own words gave her pause—cabals, allies, enemies. She never would have thought to use them about the graduate history faculty at the University of Texas. Those professors had seemed to her to live for the most part in the rarified environs of their own heads. Even her adviser, who came close to choking her by puffing on his pipe whenever she met him in his office, thought his thoughts on an ethereal level above hers. Could he, did he accept an invitation to meet for a drink, say, knowing the conversation within a conversation that might take place?

A conversation within a conversation not unlike hers with Dean Maki?

Ramona Stillinger. Had she—yes, of course Ramona knew what she would set in motion with her quiet word to the dean at his wife's birthday party. Diana shook her head. What yesterday's skirmish between Abe Dennison and the dean and his allies would mean for Abe's future and for her own, she would think about when she'd had less to drink.

* * *

Diana finished reading and grading the papers from the two survey classes, and on Monday afternoon she drove to campus to visit the registrar's office and turn in her grades. She visited Bob at the bookstore and bought a couple of books he pressed on her, and then she made a quick stop at Safeway to pick up a few groceries, mostly bread and cheese and fruit, to get her through a few days while she decided what next to do. She thought of stopping by the liquor store for a bottle of wine, decided not to, then changed her mind and drove around the block and parked for a quick dash in and out.

At the door of the liquor store she met George Schultz coming out. He gave her a sloppy smile—"Hey, Diana, got your grades all turned in? I bet you have. I know you women and your efficiency!" while the paper bag he was carrying gave a *clink* when he held the door for her. He beamed at her and winked and walked away, and Diana stood among shelves and rows of bottles, thinking about male assumptions regarding women and about smiles and winks and the ways the machine worked.

Ramona's word for her. Unsocialized. Diana thought she might be making slow progress toward socialization.

28

The phone at the mansion was ringing as Diana came from the garage with the books and wine and a sack from Safeway in her arms, and she set everything down hastily and snatched up the receiver, cursing herself. No matter how many times she told herself it would not be Jake's voice she heard, she still was letting a ringing phone wake the promise of *maybe*.

"Diana."

It was not him, of course, but Senator Wheeler.

"I know it's short notice, Diana, but I came in from the ranch this afternoon for a meeting, and I wondered if I could persuade you to have dinner with me? Or at least a drink before I go back to the ranch?"

Why not. It would make a change from the bread and cheese sandwiches that were becoming her staple. It might even lift the despondency she felt when maybe turned out to be not. So she agreed, yes, the Bellevue, and no, seven was not too late.

At the Bellevue Diana parked by the side door and followed the carpeted corridor past conference rooms to the bustling coffee shop on one side, the quieter bar and restaurant on the other. She saw the senator's silver head at what apparently was his regular table, bent in conversation with another white-haired man, and she worried that she was early, but the senator looked up and saw her and beckoned to her.

"Our meeting ran over," he explained, "and we're just going over a few loose ends. Diana, this is an old friend, up from Fort Maginnis for the day—"

Both men had risen when Diana approached their table, and now the friend smiled down at Diana with a warmth that reminded her of an afternoon at the bookstore.

"Mr. Adams! Pat Adams! You're a friend of Bob's at the bookstore!"

"Diana! The girl who reads our kind of books! So this is your daughter, Victor!"

The senator was pulling out a chair for Diana, seating her with the careful courtesy she remembered. She was trying to process what she had just heard. That the senator had told Pat Adams he had a daughter. That she was seeing an easy friendship between the two men, who seemed to have known each other for years. Hadn't Bob at the bookstore mentioned that Adams sometimes came to Versailles for some work he did for a state senator?

A cocktail waitress hovered.

"A glass of wine, Diana? Or would you rather have a proper drink?"

Dregs of what looked like bourbon remained in the glasses before the senator and Pat Adams.

"Not a Square Bottle Ditch," Diana blurted, and both men laughed.

"So she's already learning about life on the Highline, Victor!"

"I told you she's talented."

"And you're a damned lucky man. Well—good to see you again, Diana."

"You won't stay and have dinner with us, Pat?"

Pat Adams shook his head. "I'm having dinner with the boy. He's got something eating on him, and maybe he'll tell me and maybe he won't, but I'll give him the chance."

"I hear he's been doing a lot better," said the senator, and Adams nodded.

As Adams left the bar, the waitress brought the bottle of wine the senator had ordered, and he sampled and nodded at the thimbleful she poured for him.

"That grandson of Pat's," he said when he had raised his glass to Diana. "Been a headache to him for years, and he's not even his blood grandson. An honorary grandson, you could call him. He's a young man of promise, but trouble seems to find him somehow."

Trouble there. Diana dragged her thoughts back from their wandering ways when the senator said, "And how have you been, Diana? I hope trouble doesn't seek you out."

"No," she said, and paused. Trouble? Let her count.

"I've had to adjust to life in Versailles," she began. "Winter weather. Winter driving. I keep making mistakes."

The senator nodded and didn't interrupt.

"It's hard for me to understand the people here, whether they're joking, or—" she couldn't speak of her last big blunder. But the senator waited patiently, his hazel eyes were warm, and she felt drawn to him as she had the night of his Q&A.

"A friend says I've never been properly socialized. She says—" Diana had to smile, remembering—"it's as though I was raised by wolves."

The senator swallowed wine the wrong way, coughed, and chuckled. "The Karnov sisters? Maybe. Maybe at that."

"They want me to come back to Seattle. To live in the Karnov house. Tatiana keeps calling and calling. She still won't believe I'm not returning to Seattle for Christmas."

"Diana, do you want to go back to Seattle?"

"No. But I feel guilty. They did everything for me, Vee. Paid my expenses, saw that I got the finest education—and now Tatiana and Maria both are in their eighties—"

The senator touched her hand. "Are they thinking you should take care of them in their old age?"

"Maybe. No. They're not women who would *let* anyone take care of them. It's—I don't know exactly what."

He left his hand on hers. Blunt fingers, as rough from calluses as Jake's were. Probably the senator did ranch work when he could. Square fingernails, unmanicured but neatly clipped. The plain gold wedding band.

"You never knew your great-grandfather, Diana? I didn't think so, he must have died before your time, but Lillia remembered him very well."

The scowling old man in the portrait in his library. He had a growth on his lip that Diana realized as she grew older was a moustache, but as a child had wondered if it was a kind of excretion, like a fungus growing out of a tree trunk.

"He ruled those women, Lillia too, with an iron hand as long as he lived. He lost one daughter—Lillia's mother—and he was not losing another."

Diana thought of a red-haired boy on a bicycle, calling to a red-haired girl, and Tatiana's long-ago words—*Don't you know you're a Karnov woman?* Was that why Tatiana was so determined now to force Diana back to Seattle? To make sure she still was a Karnov woman?

"Maybe in his view, he was protecting his daughters. Doing the best he could by his own lights. Lillia said he'd had them well educated—"

"He did."

"—and I suppose he controlled their money?"

"I think he taught them how to control it."

The senator's smile erased the years from his face. "You see, Diana? We've already thought up some good qualities for him."

Diana laughed. "We'll have to hope he really had them."

* * *

A week dragged by. Diana set up her electric typewriter on the kitchen table, plugged in the space heater, and tried to concentrate on the book about multiple narratives that had been forming in her head. When she lost track of her thoughts, she started the MG, drove to the cramped library at the college, and rummaged through its card indexes for helpful sources. She typed up a list of books the college library didn't possess and took it to the interlibrary loan desk, where the librarian shook her head over it. She'd see what she could do, but there was a limit on interlibrary loans at any one time, and Diana couldn't expect to see a book for six weeks, maybe longer.

As an alternative to the library, Diana visited the bookstore on Main Street and hunted through Bob's back shelves. Bob kept an upholstered chair with a sagging seat in that cramped space where she could curl up and read. Bob himself would be seated at the counter, deep in his own book, and he would leave her to her browsing until he had to throw her out at five when he closed the store. Tonight, however, he had a couple of old paperbacks on the counter, waiting for her.

Today the mansion was dark and echoing when Diana drove into the garage, punched the button to close its door, and carried a sack from Safeway into the kitchen. Ignoring the typewriter, she lit candles in the living room and moved the space heater and wrapped herself in a comforter she had brought down from her bedroom. She ate bread and cheese and drank a mug of cocoa made from heated milk and powder. The evening stretched before her.

She was bracing herself for one inevitable outcome of the meeting in the conference room. Abe would hold the directions and methods of the students' research against her. He almost certainly had given up on seducing her, and his defeat in the battle over grades would infuriate him. She might as well face the probability that he would recommend against offering her a tenure-track contract, a contract she hadn't thought she cared about, except as a way to support herself and avoid the great-aunts' clutches.

But now? What she hadn't expected was the pleasure she felt when her students showed how much they had learned when they gave their oral reports. Cheryl. James. Janet and the others. And she hadn't expected the responsibility she was beginning to feel for her students. Even for Mark Gervais, whom she had not seen again.

Would the machine roll into action for her, would the dean and the other professors continue to support her? It would depend on their personal stakes in the battle, she knew. They might stand by her, and then again she might easily become—what had they called it on the evening news, talking about combat in Vietnam—collateral damage. She was, after all, a young woman giving shocks to the systems of crusty old fossils, to borrow Ramona Stillinger's words.

On the other hand, Dean Maki had seemed genuinely interested in her ideas and her students' methods. Even George Schultz had seemed interested. Before she laid plans to go to work in the Chinese restaurant when the hundred-year-old hostess inevitably keeled over, or better yet, start her own restaurant, she would concentrate on next quarter's classes and on her work. Which was, of course, another way of depending on herself.

Diana yawned. The cocoa and the warmth of the space heater were doing their work. She carried her mug and plate to the kitchen and picked up one of the novels Bob at the bookstore had pressed on her, a battered secondhand copy he charged her fifty cents for. Just what she needed to read, Bob said. The only Pulitzer Prize winner ever to come out of Oregon. It was about pioneers in Oregon. *Honey in the Horn*, by H. L. Davis.

29

The phone rang in Diana's bedroom, shattering the quiet.

Shadowed years in her dream dissolved into the present. The walls returned. The dim oblong of the window showed itself against the night. On the second ring Diana fumbled for the receiver.

"Hello?"

No one spoke, although she was sure someone listened, and she thought of the series of late, voiceless phone calls following her near-freezing. She thought she knew who had been calling her then, checking on her. But he wouldn't be calling her now.

"Hello?" she repeated testily.

"What are you doing?"

Her heart lurched at the sound of his voice, and for a moment she couldn't speak. When she could, she said, "Sleeping."

"You don't sound asleep."

"You sound drunk."

"I am drunk."

The silence dragged on. Diana sat with the telephone held to her ear. Opposite her in the window was the ghost of her own reflection, as pale as though a voyeur, some disassociated part of herself, hovered out there above the twenty-foot drop to the terrace and tapped on the glass. Diana felt as unsubstantial as her reflection. What was happening to her?

"Sure do want to see you," he whispered.

She waited, but he still did not hang up.

"Want to see you."

"It's—" she turned to her bedside clock. "—three in the morning."

"Just for a little while."

"Jake—"

"My grandpa's dead," he whispered.

* * *

Diana's heart raced. Her own face glimmered back at her from the window, like a moon waylaid on its night's progress. The furnace in the cellar switched on, stirring air vents all over the mansion. Under its hum she recognized the sound of Jake's pickup truck shifting gears for the steep private drive. In a moment she would hear the crunch of tires on snow as he parked on the circle by the evergreens. Then the sound of the door of his pickup slamming in the cold, and then another moment of small sounds that she imagined more than heard as Jake waded through the snow on the unshoveled walk. His bad leg and the booze would be slowing him.

I want to see you. She had a good idea what he needed from her. She only hoped she could give it.

He would be at the door now, and the door was locked. She needed to get up and go downstairs to let him in. After a few minutes she swung her legs over the side of the bed.

* * *

She opened the door and found Jake waiting on the doorstep, in the shadows cast by the evergreens against the ornamental lights. His collar was turned up against the cold, his hands jammed in his pockets. Three unsteady steps brought him over the threshold, and in the space of a breath he caught her in a rough grip. She felt the coarse canvas of his coat against her face and smelled whiskey fumes and the snow he had brought in with him.

"You stink of booze," she said. "Shut the door."

"Professor Lady," he whispered.

"Shut the door!"

He seemed to collect himself enough to shake his head to clear it and reach back with one hand to close the door, but he wobbled in her arms, and Diana realized how very drunk he was. She freed an arm to close the door herself and found his hand on the knob under hers when she pulled it shut.

"Jake!"

"Sorry, Professor Lady," he muttered. "I'm in real bad shape."

"Yes, you are. Can you get your coat off? Can you manage the stairs?"

"Think so. Coat, anyway. Don't know bout the stairs."

He fumbled with his coat and finally Diana unbuttoned it for him, helped him shrug out of it, and hung it on the newel post. She thought of getting him to the sofa, but it made an uncomfortable bed for one person, let alone two, and she didn't think he was going to let go of her.

Well. She couldn't carry him, as he once had carried her half-frozen self. She considered the task and thought if she bore as much of his weight as she could with one of his arms over her shoulders and his other hand steadying himself on the bannister rail, they could manage it. On the other hand, if he passed out, she could try Chris Beaudry's thumb trick on him.

He saw what she intended and made the effort, and together, one step at a time, they reached the landing, paused for a breath, and continued up the second flight to the hallway. Once through the bedroom door, he dropped on his hands and knees on the bed, and Diana, fearing he was going to be sick, ran for the bathroom wastebasket. But when she ran back, he was sitting on the side of the bed. He gave her a shame-faced grin when he saw the wastebasket.

"Sorry to be doin this to you, Diana."

"Do you feel any better?"

"No."

He seemed to mull it over, then lifted his eyes to hers. "Will you set that thing down and come sit where I can hug you?"

Diana sat on the bed beside him, and he pulled her close and buried his face in her hair. Then,

"My grandpa. My cousin Henry called me. He saw it. Said—" Jake's voice broke, and he struggled and went on. "Said my grandpa had just hoisted a bale a hay on the sled, and he turned and took two steps to pick up another bale, and he never took another step. My cousin said he pounded on his chest, and then he tried mouth-to-mouth, what do they call it, I learned how in the Navy. Couldn't get a pulse, so he carried him to the car, and he drove and my grandma sat by my grandpa and did mouth-to-mouth all the way to town. Forty miles, Diana."

Jake's grip on her was desperate enough to hurt her, and Diana wondered what she could say to him.

"Maybe not quite so tight, Jake?"

"God. Sorry." He relaxed his arm and his fingers, which had been digging into her shoulder. "Tryin to squeeze you to death after every other fool thing I've done, like startin on the whiskey after Henry called and not stoppin."

"Did you talk to your grandmother?"

"Yeah. Henry left her with his great-aunt, that's my grandma's sister, and he drove back to the ranch to take care of the cattle. And I ought a be there."

"Not till you're sober."

"No." He considered and added, "Eight hours from bottle to throttle. Probly longer for somebody in the shape I'm in."

"You're going to fly home?"

"Yeah. When I'm sober. To Fort Maginnis. When I've got my head straight enough. God. Diana, you ever take care of a drunk before?"

"No. You're my first."

"Diana? Will you come with me to Fort Maginnis?"

"Yes."

She knew she was signing on for more than a cross-country flight to a funeral. One more thing on her list to think about later.

✳ ✳ ✳

Her bedroom window was still dark, although she thought it must be nearly morning when Diana felt Jake stir behind her. His hand searched for her wrist, found it, and began its rhythmical stroking, and she leaned back against him.

The night before—well, no, earlier this morning, because somehow they'd segued into Saturday—she tried to pull Jake's boots off for him, and he said hell no, he had to get himself straightened out, and he managed the boots with only a little fumbling. He unbuckled his belt and dropped his Levi's, unbuttoned his shirt and dropped it while she watched by lamplight. Stripped off his shorts and T-shirt and socks and stood for a moment looking down at her. In the shaded light he was darker than he looked by day. Black hair and crust of beard, dark scarred face. Dark muscled arms and muscled chest unmarked by tan lines. The surgical scar that ran across his belly. The thicket of black pubic hair, the unassuming penis.

The bed creaked under his weight. His hands found her, and he pulled the shift she had been wearing as a nightgown over her head. Pulled her to him, her back to his belly. Bare skin to bare skin. Diana remembered the novel she had been reading, *Honey in the Horn*, sliding off the bed. She remembered closing her eyes. She and Jake both must have gone to sleep, because eventually she woke to what was not quite morning light but a lessening of darkness in the bedroom window.

He was awake, too. She could feel him pushing against her buttocks, and she turned to him, and there was enough light in the window now that she could see his face above hers—one of them must have turned the lamp off, although she couldn't remember doing it—and when he kissed her, his mouth tasted sour, but his hands were touching her in the right places until she cried his name, because—going over the edge was how she thought of it, that moment between pulling the plane into the stall and returning it to altitude with full throttle—and now Jake was on top of her, and he was driving into her at full throttle to bury his anger and grief and loss.

He cried out, thrust once more, and collapsed his weight on her.

Diana held him and watched the bedroom ceiling gradually materialize in the slow midwinter breaking of dawn and listened to Jake's breathing slow and lose its rough edges. After a few minutes he raised himself on his forearms and she saw his face was wet.

"Last time," he said, "I got the cart before my horse with you, damn fool I've been."

"What?" But then she knew what he meant.

"What I should a said. I love you, Diana. Half killed me tryin to stay away from you."

He sat up and peeled off the condom she didn't remember him taking the time to wear. "What did you do with that wastebasket you brought in here for me to puke in? Might a felt better if I had. There it is."

He got rid of the condom and came back to get under the covers with her. The bedroom was chilly and Diana wondered drowsily if another space heater might be tucked away in some closet.

"I love you, Diana."

He was lingering over her name as the senator had.

A pause.

"Diana. You have any feelins for me?"

He sounded so cautious that she smiled to herself. "Ye-es. But I've never been in love before, Jake. I don't know for sure what it feels like."

He made a sound that might almost have been a laugh. "I can live a while on that."

Then he sat up in bed. "Jesus. My truck's been parked in your driveway half the night and all morning. Where anybody can see it." He had a second thought and added, "And I hope the hell everything starts today."

Diana yawned. "I think you'll get everything started all right, Jake," and laughed at the look he gave her.

She might not know what love felt like, but she had seen what it looked like on Senator Wheeler's face when he spoke of Lillia.

30

Diana stood at the living room window, drinking coffee and watching Jake shovel a trail through fresh snow from the garage to his truck with his breath rising in a white cloud around his head. He worked with a grim purpose, which was to get airborne and headed for Fort Maginnis by two, when he thought all the alcohol would have passed through his system. Meanwhile he had to warm up his truck, wait for Diana to gather together her clothes and toiletries and reading material, and stop by his apartment for his Dopp kit, his clothes, including a suit and tie for the funeral, and Tip the dog. Then he had to drive to the airport, fuel his plane, and hope Cheryl met them there on time.

He flung the last scoop of snow into the evergreens, carried the shovel back to the garage, and reappeared, uncoiling an extension cord to plug the headbolt heater on his truck into an outlet in the garage. When he straightened from the front of his truck, he saw Diana at the window and gave her a half-wave.

She thought he was doing pretty well, considering. Never had she seen anyone at the Stockman's or even at the Palace as drunk as Jake had been last night—well, early this morning. After they were up and dressed he made coffee for himself and Diana, and he drank down two cups of it as though it was medicine and told Diana that once he got the truck started and warm, he'd take her somewhere for food that wasn't bread and cheese. No point in wasting time starting the MG, which would be cold again when they got back from Fort Maginnis, unless Diana needed it today. Was her antifreeze in the radiator good? Maybe he'd add some. He was still talking to himself when he went out to shovel snow.

＊ ＊ ＊

The food that wasn't bread and cheese turned out to be choices from a grill in the basement of the Stockman's. Diana ate toast and soft-boiled eggs and watched Jake tear into steak and eggs and hash browns as if bolting the food down would get him to Fort Maginnis sooner. When he looked up and found her eyes on him, he gave her an abashed grin and went on eating while she marveled at what had transformed his body—the angle of his head as he ate, the slant of his shoulders, the grip of his hands on his knife and fork—and imprinted it on hers.

"Hey, Jake."

A young black man in a ruffed parka pulled out a chair and sat at their table and looked from Jake to Diana, and she read his curiosity and wondered if the imprinting showed.

"This is Daryl," said Jake between bites. "Daryl, this is Diana. She's a professor at the college."

Daryl gave Diana an inquiring look, but he said to Jake, "I thought we might put in a few hours on the house this afternoon?"

"Can't," said Jake. He stared at his plate as though he expected it to surprise him with something. When it didn't, he looked off into middle distance and told Daryl, "Got to be out a town for a while. Death in the family."

"Hey man, I'm sorry!"

"Yeah, these things happen."

"How long you gonna be gone?"

"Don't know yet. Depends on what needs taken care of. Daryl, you ought a talk to Saylor. I was thinkin of it, myself. I think he'll give us a hand."

"I'll do that. And I'm sure sorry, man."

Daryl got up and gave Jake a little punch on the shoulder and left the grill. Diana thought about the strange friendships that men in this far northern borderland seemed to form, the examples she'd seen lately, and wondered how many young black men could be wandering around Versailles. There had been something familiar about the face in the ruffed parka. Was Daryl the kid from Philadelphia who was living in a tent in the woods, the hippie Jake had said didn't know anything?

"Got a project goin with Daryl," said Jake, and didn't explain. He cut another bite of steak and chewed grimly.

* * *

Jake drove through the airport gates—"Hell no, I'll do it!" when Diana tried to get out to open and close them for him—and parked by Pete's trailer. Pete peered out a window to see who it was and came out in his coat and cap. Diana thought he must have gotten one of the calls Jake had made from the mansion, because he said,

"Fueled her up for you, Jake. Gimme a call when you're ready to come back, and I'll plug in the truck for you."

"Appreciate it."

Jake already was out of the truck and lifting his and Diana's suitcases and Tip's sack of dog food out of the back and heading toward the Cessna to stow it all with Tip glued to his heels. Tip, sensing as surely as Diana had sensed the relentless energy that was driving Jake.

Pete saw Diana sitting in the cab of the truck and jerked his head at her. "Better come inside and sit by the heater. Gonna cool off real fast out here."

Diana hesitated. An elderly tan Plymouth she knew belonged to Cheryl had pulled up beside Jake's truck, and Diana didn't know if Cheryl expected to see her with Jake. Cheryl got out of the Plymouth in a coat and a knitted cap she'd bundled her hair under and went to pull her suitcase out of the Plymouth's back seat, and then she looked up, and it was clear she had not expected to see Diana, because her mouth fell open.

Pete, oblivious of any tension, took Cheryl's suitcase from her and urged her and Diana to come inside the trailer, where it was warm—"Jake, he'll need a minute or two to do his walk-around, and then he'll likely want to come in for a cup a coffee, so you might as well—"

Jake had finished stowing luggage and was walking back toward them when another vehicle bulleted around the trailer, screeched its brakes, and skidded in a half-circle before it stopped. From the high seat of the cab of Jake's truck, Diana watched a sequence of actions and reactions that each seemed inevitable after the last. Out of the new vehicle barreled a blond man who charged Cheryl and grabbed her by the upper arm.

"No, by God, you're not goin nowhere!"

Tip was barking with all four legs braced and the hair of his neck standing on end as Jake advanced.

"Forget it, Ritchie."

Diana realized she must be watching Cheryl's bastard husband as he let Cheryl go and spun around to confront Jake with his shoulders hunched and his legs braced.

"Whadda you think you're going to do about it?"

Jake never slowed, one purposeful stride after another toward Ritchie, and Diana, reading his face, clamped one hand over her mouth, because Jake had been on the brink of another kind of edge all day and was about to fall over it. In her peripheral vision she caught a glimpse of Cheryl, cowering under Pete's arm.

The blond man, Ritchie, bellowed something incoherent and lunged at Jake as Tip barked his rage. Without a change of expression, Jake executed a kind of dance step to his left and a feint with his right fist that Ritchie mistook and followed, and then in what seemed like slow motion, Ritchie doubled over from Jake's left fist driving into his gut and was propelled backward by Jake's right hook to his chin. His legs windmilled for balance and lost, and he sat down heavily in the snow, looking dazed.

Tip stopped barking. In the still moment a magpie winged down, lit on the fence, and cocked its head, alert for blood.

"Ritchie!"

Cheryl was screaming. Diana would have been screaming, herself, if her hand weren't clamped over her mouth. She watched Ritchie try to get up and make it as far as his hands and knees, where he rocked back and forth a few times before he made it to his feet.

"You son of a bitch, there's felony assault charges in this. Fucking boxer! Your fist's legally a deadly weapon, you know that? And I got witnesses!" He turned to Pete, who had wrapped his heavily bundled arm around the trembling Cheryl.

"I didn't see a goddamn thing," said Pete. "You see anything, Cheryl?"

"No," Cheryl quavered.

Ritchie advanced on Cheryl, teetering a little. "You comin home with me now? Or are you goin with the fucking boxer?"

She raised her chin. "I'm going with my brother."

"Then don't come back."

He limped back to his truck, then turned and glared around at his wife, Pete, his brother-in-law, and a bristling Tip before he took a couple of tries at climbing the high step to the cab. He slammed the door after him and revved his truck in reverse until it fishtailed, righted his traction, and roared around Pete's trailer and out of sight. They all listened to the fading sound of his motor down the airport road.

"Guess I better go look," said Pete. "Don't think he stopped to shut the gate."

"Bum some ice off you?" said Jake.

"Sure."

Pete trudged off, and they stood looking at each other, Jake and Diana and Cheryl with her suitcase sitting in the snow beside her. Tip watched all three, wagging anxiously.

"Come on inside," said Jake. "I got to ice my hand. We got time to get warm."

Inside Pete's familiar trailer, with its humming heater and omnipresent simmering kettle of hot water, its odor of wet wool and men's bodies, Diana was struck by something like homesickness. Maybe if she and Jake really had put things right between them, she could resume her flying lessons. She watched him take an ice cube tray from the miniscule freezing compartment of Pete's antique refrigerator, break out the ice into a handkerchief, and wrap the handkerchief around his hand, and she felt vicariously the sensation of ice on bruised flesh and bone, and she remembered a bruised cheek.

"Diana? Can you give me some help? Real hard to tie a knot with one hand."

Diana took his hand, wrapped the handkerchief a second time, and tied it under his palm in a double knot. When she looked up, he smiled at her.

"Why didn't you tell me Dr. Karnov was coming with us?" said Cheryl.

"Didn't know, myself, until real recently." He hadn't taken his eyes off Diana.

"Jake, what he said, about a boxer's fist being a legal lethal weapon. Is that true?" asked Diana.

"By law? No, though some folks have the idea it is. Probly would weigh against a man in court, though, if he's got training and hurts somebody who doesn't. If he's got reason to defend himself or somebody else, that's another thing. I'm not goin to worry about Ritchie."

"Jake, I thought you told me," Cheryl interrupted, "that you'd learned a real hard lesson about her."

"I'm not what you'd call trained," said Jake. "A Catholic priest taught me to box. He was a friend of my grandpa's." He grinned at Diana. "I was an altar boy."

"Jake! Why the *hell* aren't you telling me what's going on with you and her?"

Pete was opening the trailer door, stamping snow off his boots.

"At least the damn fool didn't try to bust through the gate on his way in here," he remarked.

Jake turned slowly to his sister. He laid his iced hand on Diana's shoulder, winced, and flexed his fingers.

"Think I'm fit to work the stick," he said. "If you're thawed out, Cheryl, we better head for Fort Maginnis."

31

The flight path from Versailles to Fort Maginnis, being direct, cut off nearly half the highway distance, and Jake and Diana were aloft for about an hour, with a glowering Cheryl beside Tip in the rear seats. Jake had borrowed George's telephone to call his cousin and let him know they were running a little late, but daylight still was strong when Diana saw the low mountains that sheltered Fort Maginnis and Jake reached for the radio to identify his aircraft and his approach. The radio crackled back at him, and Diana wondered how he made out his instructions amid the static and how she would ever learn.

A better question was how she was going to make her way through an indeterminate number of days with Jake's extended family, all of whom would be grieving, and at least one, Cheryl, who was radiating hostility. Diana sighed for Cheryl, who had been her friend, and imagined the trickster god, the Coyote, stirring up a storm of a situation while chuckling to himself: *Ah yes! That unsocialized Diana Karnov will be just the woman for the task!*

The Fort Maginnis airport lay on a low plateau. Diana saw the nest of the town's buildings, many of them stone buildings, and snowy streets as Jake made his approach and banked into the airport pattern. Then he was cutting throttle and pulling back on the stick to lose altitude and raise the nose of the plane to set down the rear wheels on tarmac, bleed off speed, and taxi to the end of the runway. The propellers reappeared, wavered, and stopped. They had landed in Fort Maginnis.

A man came out of a door in the terminal and walked toward them. Cheryl uttered her first word since they'd left Versailles—

"Henry!" She unsnapped her seatbelt and leaned forward, but she couldn't get out of the right-side door until Diana got out, so Diana unsnapped herself, opened the door, and jumped down to the pavement. Jake already was out of the plane, chaining the wings and lifting down luggage, but when he saw Cheryl running toward the man named Henry, he walked after her. Tip, who had bounded out of the plane and started to run after Cheryl, glanced back at Jake and followed sedately behind him.

Henry swept Cheryl into an embrace that lifted her off her feet. He set her down when Jake reached them, shook his hand, and punched him on the shoulder. Diana, watching the tight family group, wasn't certain what to do, but thought she probably looked more conspicuous standing by the plane than by joining them, so she picked up her suitcase and Tip's sack of dry food, which was all she could manage, and walked toward the terminal.

"Your grandma's still staying with Aunt Rita," Henry was saying as Diana approached, "but she'll probly want you to drive her back to the ranch. They're talkin about holdin the funeral this Tuesday. Don't know what's gonna happen, other than that."

He saw Diana and looked perplexed.

Jake put his arm around Diana's shoulders. He was still wearing the soggy handkerchief, and she reached up and pulled it off his hand.

"Diana, this is my cousin Henry Archambault. Henry, this is Diana Karnov."

Henry looked to Diana to be younger than Jake, and he was just as dark as Jake, although not quite so tall in cowboy boots and Levi's and a heavy coat. Of course, no scar. He nodded to Diana and studied her and Jake briefly, then puffed out a white breath and clapped his gloved hands together.

"Your plane all right? We best get the rest of your stuff and get somewhere warm. I borrowed Aunt Rita's car and left it runnin out front."

Henry took the dog food and suitcase from Diana and led her and Jake and Cheryl through an empty terminal with a few rows of chairs and out the plate glass front doors to the street, where a large old car with tail fins sat puffing clouds of exhaust.

"You girls get in out a the cold," Henry said, and held open a rear door for Diana and Cheryl. He shut the door behind them, and Diana sat in tense silence beside Cheryl.

Ha-ha! Diana Karnov is just the woman for this task!

"Cheryl," she said. "Let's not go on like this. If you'll tell me what's on your mind, I'll tell you what's on mine."

"Dr. Karnov! Diana—I don't even know what the hell I have to call you now, but—"

She interrupted herself and clamped her mouth shut as Jake opened the front passenger door. He gave her and Diana an uneasy glance, but made no comment.

Henry was getting behind the wheel—"Everybody good?"

* * *

Henry drove along the street near the creek where Diana knew from her reading that the old Métis had built their cottonwood-log cabins. If so, the cabins had been torn down and replaced with single-story clapboard bungalows and the occasional ranch-style house. The day was fading toward twilight, and lights were appearing in windows. Henry pulled into the driveway of one of the larger ranch houses.

The driveway had been shoveled, but at least a foot of snow covered the lawn and big drifts lay over what Diana supposed was shrubbery. They got way more snow down here in Murray County than Versailles did, Jake had told her. Once she was out of the car, the air felt cold, but perhaps cold with a softness. Maybe it was the absence of wind. Not as much wind, either, as Versailles got, Jake said.

She could hear the thousand muted voices of the creek current. So the creek hadn't frozen over.

"Spring Creek?" she asked, and Henry answered, "Yup."

"Not much of a crick," said Cheryl, "in spite of all the Métis romantic stories about it."

"Got some deep holes, though," said Jake. "One night I helped a man pull a girl out a one. Back in my hell-raisin days."

He and Henry lifted luggage out of the trunk of the car while the creek current went on arguing with itself with its thousand busy tongues. Cheryl was silent. The Coyote nipped Diana. *The obvious woman for the task.*

"You can call me Diana. And I'll call you Cheryl. Unless you object. Maybe we can take it from there."

"I just want to know what's going on," said Cheryl.

She sounded close to tears. But Jake and Henry came up from the trunk with suitcases and dog food and Tip, and Henry knocked on his great-aunt Rita's door, then opened it and beckoned them inside without waiting for an answer.

　　＊ ＊ ＊

"Grandma, this is Diana."

Jake walked straight into his grandmother's arms and held her while everyone else looked away in what Diana had come to recognize as Montana reticence in the presence of emotions. When he could let his grandmother go, he turned and caught Diana's hand and drew her up. Jake's touching her in the presence of others was new to her, but she understood his arm around her had been a statement to Henry and now was a statement to his grandmother.

What to say.

"I'm so sorry to meet you under these circumstances, ma'am."

Diana was having to look up at her, because Jake's grandmother was a tall woman, almost as tall as Jake in his cowboy boots, with a crown of thick white hair and dark eyes, and the same marks of grieving in her face as in Jake's, but older and deeper. She startled Diana by sweeping her into an embrace and holding her for a long moment before letting her go.

The embrace also must have sent a message, because Henry and his mother and his great-aunt Rita and several other women in the room relaxed and went back to talking about funeral plans and the weather forecast.

"I'm nobody's ma'am," said Jake's grandmother. "The kids call me Evvie, the ones that don't call me Grandma. My whole name's too much of a mouthful for em. And now I want you and Jake to come sit with me on the couch, and you, too, Cheryl."

Cheryl looked stubborn, but she uncrossed her arms and came to sit by her grandmother. Evvie—Diana wondered if she dared to call her that—pulled Diana to sit on her other side, and Jake sat by Diana with one leg draped over hers to get closer to her and his arm around her shoulders to reach his grandmother's shoulder and stroke it. Diana thought they must look as though they'd been posed to have their picture taken by a drunken photographer.

"I want to go home, Jake," Evvie said after a time.

"Tonight?"

"Need to. Henry fed the cattle this morning, but there's nobody to feed em tonight or in the morning, and I'm not havin them bawlin for hay and goin hungry."

"You got the car here?"

"Henry drove it in with me and—" Her voice quivered for the first time and she didn't finish. "It's been plugged in, and I think Henry filled the tank. I need to remember to pay him back for the gas."

"Better get movin, then. You got enough groceries at the ranch?"

"I think I'm good. I'll send you back to town if I don't. Keep the road hot."

Jake got up and said something to Henry, who nodded, and they both put their coats back on and left.

"Grandma, have you got clothes and stuff here?"

"Folded it all up in a paper sack when I knew you were comin. It's upstairs if you'll run and get it for me, Cheryl."

Cheryl got up and headed for the stairs, but Evvie kept Diana's hand.

"Just sit here with me," she said in a voice that revealed more than she had let Jake or Cheryl hear. "And let me hold your hand."

32

Their headlights swept through more darkness than Diana could have imagined. The ranch was forty miles from Fort Maginnis, she remembered Jake saying. Forty miles of snowbound darkness, tops of fence posts capped with snow, shadows of some sparse shrubs poking bare twigs through the drifts, once in a while a pair of wild eyes caught in flight. How did people live out here?

"Want me to drive?" Henry had asked Jake before they left his great-aunt Rita's house, and he took the wheel when Jake shrugged. Now Diana listened to fragments of low conversation between Jake and Henry in the front seat.

". . . can stay on while he wants me to, but he's not gonna want . . ."

". . . he could decide to sell it . . ."

". . . what'll you do, Jake?"

Diana wondered what Jake would want to do. She thought he might stay with his grandmother on the ranch until its mysterious owner decided whether to sell or hire another manager. Con Stillinger wouldn't have much work for Jake until spring, months from now, so little was keeping him in Versailles, short of coyote-hunting and whatever his project was with Daryl. If Jake decided to stay, Diana would have to return alone to teach during the winter quarter. She'd probably buy a return ticket on the little commuter plane that flew into Versailles twice a day. She'd seen its logo on a sign at the Fort Maginnis airport. The thought was bleak.

"Diana," said Cheryl. "What graveled me the worst. All the times we talked in your office. Questions you asked me about—" she almost spat it—"my Métis *heritage*. I was stupid enough to think you were really interested. Interested in me. You never said anything about Jake. When all the time you were pumping me about him."

"I was interested," said Diana. "In the history and in you. I thought we were becoming friends. And I was proud of how you bloomed. I was proud when the men couldn't stop praising your oral report."

This conversation with Cheryl absolutely had to happen before more time passed, whether or not Cheryl's grandmother was sitting between Diana and Cheryl in the back seat. Evvie seemed not to pay attention, but Diana didn't believe she was missing a thing. She hadn't let go of Diana's hand, and Diana thought she probably was holding Cheryl's hand, too, drawing strength as Jake did from the physical contact.

"He said he made a real bad mistake about you."

"I made the mistake."

"He came by my house that night, and he was in the blackest mood I ever saw him in. I love my brother, Diana."

"Cheryl. I only met him last October. We hadn't—still haven't—spent a lot of time together. I made some bad blunders with him, because of how I was raised, and he's—" she was going to say *touchy*, but said instead, "proud."

A silence continued for several miles, to the hum of the car and the low voices of Henry and Jake in the front seat. At one point something huge lumbered out of the dark and into the headlights, and Henry braked hard.

"Looked like one of the yearling calves. Nother thing to check in the morning."

Silence resumed.

"He was a real badass," said Cheryl.

"He told me that."

"Course, I went and married Ritchie."

Henry slowed and made a sharp turn off the road and over what looked in the headlights like an arrangement of rattling planks above a pit. Silhouettes of ranch buildings materialized out of the dark. Wherever they were, they had arrived.

Once outside the car, everyone stood still for a moment. Diana was aware of a sound like nothing she had ever heard, an unceasing slow ululation that flowed in from beyond the ranch buildings like hundreds of tongues in wordless mourning.

"Oh, God," said Cheryl. She put her hands over her ears, and Evvie put her arm around her.

"Guess that's a first thing," said Jake, and Henry nodded.

* * *

A flurry in the house. Walking through her own door seemed to have given new life to Evvie. She hardly gave herself time to hang up her coat before she headed for the kitchen and began slicing meat for stew while simultaneously directing Cheryl to peel vegetables and set the table.

"The bed in your old room is all made up for you," she told Cheryl, over her shoulder, "but Henry's been usin Jake's room, so you better get out the clean sheets and make up the bed for Diana."

Diana tried to help Evvie and Cheryl in the kitchen and ended up trying not to get in the way.

"You've had a long day. Just go and sit in the front room," Evvie ordered her, and Diana wandered out of the kitchen.

She had to smile at how relieved she'd been to see electric lights that came on when their switches were flipped, a telephone, a kitchen sink with hot and cold running water, a bathroom. Her ideas of ranch life must have been shaped by her childhood reading.

Cheryl had explained the ululation. "It's the cattle bawling because it's late for them to be fed and they're hungry. It'll take Jake and Henry an hour or so with the tractor and sled to spread hay."

"Reason I had to come home," said Evvie. "Would a taken the tractor and sled out myself if the boys weren't here. Never want to hear that sound again."

The living room was spacious, with a river-rock fireplace and paneled walls and a leather-covered sofa and armchairs in carved dark wood. The whole room spoke of affluence, although perhaps a faded one.

On the mantel were framed photographs of Jake and Cheryl that Diana supposed were high school graduation pictures, also a framed photograph of Cheryl posing in a wedding dress with the blond man, Ritchie, in a tuxedo, and another of Jake in Navy dress blues. Diana studied the face of the young Jake, familiar and yet unfamiliar without the scar and without knowledge of what was to come. She wondered if the Navy came before his hell-raisin days, as he put it, or after.

How much she didn't know.

Above the fireplace hung a print of a watercolor painting that captured a cowboy on horseback just as he had roped a steer and shifted his weight in the saddle to offset the impact of the steer hitting the end of his rope. The painter had achieved the immediacy of an action suspended in time. In the lower left-hand corner was the artist's name, C.M. Russell, a tiny steer's skull, and a date, 1919.

Cheryl came to the door of the living room—"Grandma wants to know if you'd like a glass of her chokecherry wine."

She saw Diana had been looking at the painting. "That's my grandpa when he was a young cowboy."

Diana thought again how much she didn't know about Jake, and in that moment knew with a sick certainty she was going to lose him to this place.

When she hadn't even known she wanted him until a few days ago.

"Tell your grandma I'd love to have a glass of her wine," she said.

* * *

It was late when Jake and Henry came in from feeding cattle to brush snow off their coats and stamp it off their boots and sit down to a supper of thick beef stew. Jake sat across the table from Diana and ate with remote interest in anything around him. Diana knew he must be exhausted, drained, even as she felt the pangs of his imprinting being scraped off her. All she could do was tell herself she had a life in Versailles to go back to, even if that life turned out to be waitressing in a Chinese restaurant.

She was carrying a stack of bowls to the sink where Cheryl ran hot water into a dishpan when she saw a picture of herself morphing into the ancient hostess and had to smile.

"So shove that into your craw, Coyote," she said aloud and got a curious look from Henry, who was pouring himself another cup of coffee from the pot on the stove.

"Ma'am," Henry said, "coyotes don't have craws."

"Then he'll have to shove it somewhere else," said Diana, and Henry stared at her, but she heard Jake's involuntary snort of laughter.

So he wasn't entirely withdrawn into himself.

"Jake, Cheryl made up your bed for Diana," Evvie told him, "so you and Henry will have to sleep in the bunkhouse. There's a good stove out there, and a woodbox, and the bed's clean, but you better take a flashlight with you."

Jake nodded, but his face was grim. He got up and put on his coat and stuck Evvie's flashlight in a pocket, and then he looked at Diana.

"Come and tell me good night?"

She followed him to the little entryway. He kissed her and she touched the scar on his face and followed it with her finger.

"Diana, I wish you weren't thinkin you'll have to leave me."

"I wish I weren't, either." She didn't have to ask how he knew.

Out of the corner of her eye she saw Henry in his coat and cap stop in the doorway and take a quick step backward.

"Can you stick it out until after the—" a pause on the word— "funeral? Until I can talk to Pat?"

Pat. Maybe he was the man who owned the ranch?

"Yes. I can stick it out until then."

"I can live on that a while."

He grinned, almost like the Jake she knew, and kissed her again. Then he called back over his shoulder to Henry.

"Let's cut a trail."

＊ ＊ ＊

Two days of falling snow and white light between long dark nights alone in a bedroom with a window that looked out over the road from the barn and the gentle swells of prairie cut with tractor and trailer tracks from the morning and evening rituals of feeding the cattle. At night Diana could see the light in the bunkhouse window, and at first she'd thought Jake might come to her after all was dark and quiet, but she soon sensed he had scruples about his grandmother's house.

Two days of vehicles pulling up to the house, many of them four-wheel-drive trucks, and even a tractor driven by an elderly man with his quilt-wrapped wife clinging behind him.

Neighbors. Coming from miles away to pay their respects and tell stories about the man they called Albert. Everyone brought food. Covered dishes, roasts, pans of homemade bread rolls, cakes, cinnamon rolls, dried-apple pies, green-bean casseroles, potato salads, and platters of stuffed eggs filled the refrigerator, crowded each other for counter space, and took up so much space on the kitchen table that it was hard to set it for meals.

Tip the dog sneaked into the kitchen at every opportunity and sat guiltily sniffing. *Out a here, Tip!* were the kindest words he heard, but when Diana slipped him a crisp-fried strip of bacon, he accepted with a grateful dignity.

Evvie dragged out the three-gallon coffee urn she told Diana she used for calf brandings and such, and she kept it filled, because every visitor had to be served coffee and whatever wedges of pie or slices of cake she could press on them.

Diana and Cheryl were kept busy washing plates and cups and silverware.

"It's what everybody does in the country," Cheryl explained about the visitors and the food. "In town, maybe not so much."

Diana saw Jake when he and Henry came in for breakfast after feeding cattle and sometimes when he came to the house to sit for a while with a visiting neighbor and listen to stories about his grandfather. He was teaching Henry to weld, Cheryl said. A lot of the ranch equipment needed repairs. Grandpa had let things slide. Cheryl thought Jake probably would service the trucks when the weather got warmer. He'd need everything good to go by calving time, which was when ranch work went into full throttle.

On Sunday afternoon Diana came into the kitchen to wash more dishes and found Jake at the window with a tall white-haired man in a wool shirt and Levi's and boots whose hand clasped Jake's shoulder. With their backs turned to the room, they seemed intent on the snowbound view, but occasionally they exchanged a word or two, while Diana felt the emotional bond between them.

"Need to get moving," the older man said after a while. "Don't much like to drive after dark on that road. We can talk about the ranch tomorrow."

Jake turned from the window and saw Diana. He pulled her hands out of her pan of dishwater, buffed her dry with a towel, and led her to the white-haired man.

"Pat, this is Diana Karnov. She's a professor at Versailles State—"

"Pat Adams!" said Diana.

"Diana," Pat Adams said, and smiled at her, and for a moment his blue eyes and his smile made Diana think the white fresh-snow light at the window had turned to sunshine.

"You know her?"

"We've met a couple times," said Pat Adams. "She's the daughter of a friend of mine." He smiled again at Diana, although she could see the lines of grief in his face.

"I'm bringin her with me tomorrow."

"Be glad to see you both." He shook Jake's hand, stepped back and looked at him and then embraced him. When he let Jake go, he hugged Evvie again and told her how real sorry he was, and then he was gone.

"Pat Adams is the owner?" Diana asked.

"Yeah."

Evvie made a small sound, and Diana saw tears on her face for the first time.

33

Diana watched for the light in the bunkhouse that night. When it went out, she settled down between chilly linen sheets and took up *Honey in the Horn*.

The novel engrossed her even as it puzzled her. What to make of the crabbed voice that told of a teenaged love affair while telling a great deal about the history, the culture, and the flora and fauna of a region in eastern Oregon, and meanwhile relating the stories a huge cast of characters told about themselves? As a historian, she wasn't trained in reading fiction, and she feared she was missing the crabbed voice's passions.

She also feared she would finish *Honey in the Horn* before she got back to Versailles and would have nothing to read. Surely Fort Maginnis had a public library, and maybe it had a bookstore. She'd have to ask Jake or Cheryl.

She turned out her light, to save the final chapters for tomorrow night, and lay back thinking about the stories today's visitors had told about the man they called Albert.

There had been stories about Albert's roping—"I set there on the corral fence at the St. Pierre branding and counted sixty-seven calves Albert hind-footed before he missed one," and a time when a ten-year-old Jake was trying to chase a locoed cayuse out of a pasture—"Jake, he rode and he whipped and he rode and he whipped until Albert finally says, *Run him past me one time, Jake*, and Albert roped that ornery cayuse around his neck and took his dallies and set his rope just right and broke that horse's neck for him."

Hind-footing calves. Locoed cayuse. Taking dallies. Diana felt as though she were listening to a conversation in another language.

One of the most dramatic stories, with several elderly men joining in and jostling for their place in the narrative, had been Albert's rodeo story. Their faces had shone with the telling, and even Evvie smiled.

"See, we didn't have a fenced arena in those days, so we useta hold the Murray County Rodeo out in the middle of the high prairie," explained one grizzled old man for Diana's benefit. "Instead of a fence, we'd have three-four guys on horseback, posted out a ways, where they could haze the bronc back in sight if he quit buckin and stampeded. So this one time—"

"Albert, he drawed a doozy that day," chimed in another old man, grinning. "In fact that's what we called that bronc. Doozy. He was a spinnin bucker. To see old Doozy let loose with his spins, man, that was somethin."

"Hadn't ever been a cowboy stick with him the full eight seconds."

"Hell, I tried ridin Doozy myself, and I didn't make it past his first spin," interrupted somebody else. "Pardon my language, ma'am."

"We had a pen we was usin for a chute. That day Albert and Doozy come outa the pen, and Doozy was spinnin and Albert was rakin Doozy hip to shoulder with his spurs. Ma'am, have you ever seen one a them perfessional rodeo cowboys rake a buckin horse with spurs? I tell you, these boys today don't have nothin on Albert. So anyway—"

"Other thing about Doozy, he was faster'n hell," chimed another. "Sorry, ma'am. Once that bronc spun and spun and figured out he weren't gonna unstick Albert, he lit out runnin like you never seen a horse run. Them outriders never stood a chance. Albert and Doozy went past em like a streak a lightning."

"We give em bout half an hour, but no sign of Albert and Doozy—"

"—we're just thinkin we might oughta send out a search party—"

"—when here comes Albert, ridin back to the rodeo grounds. Hell, he had old Doozy bout halfway broke to ride."

"Doozy never was no good as a bucker after that."

"So what does Albert do the next year at the rodeo? He enters Doozy in the mile race! He sets Jake, there, up on Doozy to ride him in the race—what were you, Jake, mebbe twelve?"

"—and damn if he don't beat all them fancy hotbloods by a couple a lengths! Sorry, ma'am!"

The story had broken up at that point as the old men fell to arguing whether Doozy had been a brown bay or a seal bay, a distinction lost on Diana, who was wishing she could have taken notes on what had been a multivoiced performance. Then somebody remembered another story.

"—how Albert had Jake and Cheryl on horseback before they could walk? He'd set one a them little kids in front of him in the saddle and give em the reins to hold. And then he went out and bought em that Shetland pony. You remember that Shetland pony, Jake?"

Jake gave Diana an embarrassed glance. "Yeah, I remember that pony, Gus."

"Mean little devil! And smarter'n any horse. He'd think up tricks faster'n you could unlearn him of em. Remember that time he took you under that cottonwood branch, Jake? You was ridin him bareback, and he took the bit in his teeth, runnin like hell, and you couldn't stop him, and he dived under that branch and scraped you off in the dirt?"

Gus cackled. "Albert, he rode up to ask if you were hurt, and you said, *No, I was kinda wantin off*?"

Jake's face was too dark for Diana to be sure he was blushing. "Thanks a bunch, Gus. When you know damn good and well Cheryl was a better rider than me. She was the apple of Grandpa's eye."

And Cheryl's hands went still over the dishpan of cups and bowls she was washing, and all the old men laughed, and talk turned for a time to Cheryl's exploits as a barrel racer and breakaway roper in the local rodeos, stories they interrupted by correcting each other and disagreeing, but always circling back to their main theme: never, ever lived a cowboy to match their cowboy with the long Dutch name. Albert Vanaartsdalen.

At first Diana supposed the stories were being told to Evvie and Jake and Cheryl, but then she reflected that the family had listened to tales of Albert's exploits again and again, perhaps to tease and embarrass Albert as well as to praise him. The old men's performance itself had been the point, not only as a celebration of Albert's life but of a way of life that valued consummate ability, artistry even, but didn't blink at casual violence like breaking a horse's neck. Diana, as an outsider, had been vital as its audience.

Now, in bed alone in the dark, it occurred to Diana that the stories the old men told about Jake's childhood also carried a message. *Remember where you're from, Jake. Remember you're one of us.*

Was it possible their message also was meant for Diana?

He's ours.

* * *

Jake asked Cheryl if she wanted to ride along with them to town, but Cheryl said no, she thought she'd better stay with Grandma and help her cope with the visitors who would arrive in a steady stream for the rest of the day. Maybe Diana could pick her out a few magazines at the Bon Ton. That's the soda fountain on Main, she added. Did the Bon Ton also sell books, Diana asked, and Cheryl said she thought they did.

Jake drove Evvie's car to fuel it at the ranch's gas barrel, which looked to Diana as if someone had started to sculpt an elephant, using a giant metal barrel set on four tall posts. Fueling accomplished, Jake drove as far as the turn onto the county road, at the arrangement of pit and planks that Diana now understood was a cattle guard, and stopped.

"You holdin up all right?"

"Yes. What about you, Jake?"

"Missin you."

His fingers closed on her hand and then let go, and he made the turn and drove between the banks of snow the county plow had thrown up on either side of the road. Diana watched the endless prairie swell and sink under the weight of snow, all the way to the rim of mountains with their white slopes and caps, and remembered what Ramona had said about deep snow and intense cold and the flimsiness of a vehicle's thin metal skin.

"Jake, tell me about Pat Adams?"

"He's a lawyer," Jake said, which Diana already knew from Bob at the bookstore. "Was the county attorney for Murray County for a lot of years. Opened a private practice in Fort Maginnis after he retired, and he still keeps an office and I think helps a few old clients. Like my grandpa. Anything came up my grandpa worried about, he'd have talked it over with Pat."

"How did he come to own the ranch?"

"Inherited it from his father. It's one of the real old properties in Murray County, goes back to the Homestead Act. But Pat never wanted to ranch, which is why he set up my grandpa to manage it. He and my grandpa are best friends." Jake choked and said, "Try that again. They were best friends all my grandpa's life."

"Pat doesn't have children of his own, or grandchildren?"

"No. But he's been like a grandfather to Cheryl and me."

He drove several miles in silence. Then, "Diana? We could maybe—hell, Versailles is only an hour's flight away. Doesn't take longer to get there than it does to drive to town. Weekends—" he stopped, and Diana could read what he was thinking. Cattle had to be fed twice a day, seven days a week.

She thought of Victor Wheeler on the day Lillia vanished and the Karnov sisters descended on him. He would have had cattle to feed again that evening. He wouldn't have left them hungry and bawling.

"Chris would fly you down here, any time you asked him," Jake said. "Or—" he glanced at her and grinned, almost like himself. "You could go back to takin lessons. Learn to fly yourself down."

They were entering Fort Maginnis with its snow-plowed streets and shoveled sidewalks. Jake drove slowly down Main Street and Diana noted the Bon Ton's sign as they passed it.

Across the street from the courthouse at the south end of Main stood a mansion with wings and turrets. Like many older buildings in Fort Maginnis, it was constructed of dressed blocks of the local sandstone. A curlicued veranda, which had been swept clean of snow, stretched across its front.

"Is this where he lives?"

"No. Just where he keeps his office."

The entry was immaculately kept. Polished hardwood floors, paneled walls, plaster ceilings with elaborately carved cornices. Jake's hand at the small of Diana's back guided her toward a wrought-iron staircase and a door on the second floor with an ancient brass numeral 2 and a small white card in a brass holder. PATRICK ADAMS, ATTORNEY AT LAW.

Jake opened the door and there was Pat, sitting behind a desk with his chair comfortably tipped back and smiling that smile. Bookshelves behind him, bookshelves to both sides of him, filled with even more books than Diana owned. Maybe that was why he still maintained an office, to have somewhere to keep his books.

He stood and welcomed Diana with a courtesy that reminded her of the senator, seated her and Jake, and poured coffee from a pot on a burner behind his desk. A few remarks about the weather, the snowfall, the water table for spring, and he and Jake were into a conversation Diana didn't want to follow.

". . . calf crop this spring, far as you can tell, Jake?"

". . . looks on track, and the hay's holdin up fine . . ."

". . . Henry's a good kid, but he needs experience . . . I know you couldn't fill Albert's shoes, nobody could, but you'd come the closest, Jake."

To keep herself from listening to what was about to happen, Diana began reading the spines of books. Pat Adams' shelves held the rows of law books she would have expected, but also the books of a man who had been reading and collecting for many years. Then she saw a familiar title, *Honey in the Horn*, the same old edition Bob at the bookstore in Versailles had pressed on her, and without thinking she pulled it off its shelf with a finger and opened it to the bookplate.

She looked up and found Pat Adams' blue eyes on her.

"Fine novel," he said. "Not many people remember it."

"I've nearly finished it. Mr. Adams, is there a bookstore in Fort Maginnis?"

"Name's Pat. Yes, the Bon Ton stocks some, but not what you'd want if H. L. Davis is to your taste. I hit the used bookstores in Missoula when I get over there. Once in a while I get down to Albuquerque. Albuquerque's a used-book paradise."

He stood and walked around his desk with the spring in his step that Diana had noticed before and pulled another book from the shelf.

"You might give this a try. *Winds of Morning*. Some folks think it's the best book Davis wrote. I don't, but it's still damn fine."

"Maybe I can get Bob to order me a copy—"

"Take this one. No, I mean it. How many books do you think I'm going to want to reread, at my age, when there's so much I haven't read?"

"Thank you," she said. It didn't seem adequate. But he was seating himself behind his desk again and saying,

"Doesn't all have to fall on your shoulders, Jake. I got to thinking last night. You know Sam St. Pierre? Second cousin of yours, isn't he?"

"Yes, but I can't tell you the connection offhand. Grandma can."

"He's old Jerry St. Pierre's youngest boy. His brother has done well on the old Harrington place, but there's not enough work for Sam there, not to make a living. And Sammy's a good hand. I've known him since he was a kid."

Pat Adams smiled to himself. Another story there, Diana thought.

"Think it over, Jake. Talk it over with your professor, here."

She stood with Jake to leave and for the first time noticed one of the framed photos between bookshelves. Pat Adams. Shaking hands with a tall silver-haired man.

"Victor Wheeler," she said without thinking.

"I've known him for years, Diana. Not my politics, but Wheeler's a straight-up man. And now he's a lucky man."

Jake came out of his deep thought to look from Diana to Pat Adams, but he didn't ask about Senator Wheeler's good fortune. Instead he said, "Already know I'll do whatever I have to do to keep Grandma in that house."

"I'd never do that to Evangeline, Jake. Took care of that years ago."

34

They were halfway back to the ranch with their separate thoughts like a humming wire between them before Jake said, "You know I have to stay here. A while, anyway. Whatever gets decided. Helpin Henry is one thing. Grandma won't ever say it, but she needs me here, and I'll stay as long as she needs me."

Diana nodded.

"I can fly you back to Versailles, maybe Wednesday after the funeral, and fly back. Or I can get you a ticket on Big Scare."

"On *what*?"

"Big Sky Airlines. Big Scare is I guess a kinda pet name for em. They're safe enough."

"The Big Scare ticket sounds the simplest. I can call somebody to meet me and drive me to the mansion, hopefully somebody who can get the MG started for me."

"I'll call the airline when we get home to save a seat for you. And I'll call Saylor and ask him to meet you."

A few more miles while Diana wondered where home was for her until Jake said,

"Don't know what Cheryl wants to do. Hope to hell she goes back for the winter quarter and finds somewhere to live that's not with that bastard Ritchie."

"There's plenty of room at the mansion. She can stay with me if she likes."

"Decent of you."

The wire hummed. Filled the space in the car.

"*Hell!*"

A screech of brakes. Diana caught herself on the dashboard and tried to see what was accounting for their sudden change of course, but she bumped up and down on the seat as Jake turned off the highway on a narrow road that led to a wire gate behind a stand of pines where snow had drifted. He pulled into a small space behind the pines that their branches had protected from the snow and slammed the gearshift into park.

He turned to her—"I can't take any more a this—" and pulled her into an embrace made awkward by the bulk of coats and the placement of the gearshift. "Where's your mouth?"

"Christ," he gasped when he came up for breath. "I can't—can't—don't have what I need with me."

"We can take the chance."

That sobered him. He stroked her hair. "You mean that? You'd—what I might be getting you into?"

"I need you too."

"No. Won't do that to you." He kissed her again, more gently, but his hands were under her coat and making their way inside her sweater. "Maybe just sit here like this for a little while?"

"I want to feel skin too."

He laughed and took his hands away to shrug back his coat and unbutton his shirt for her, and she squirmed around the gearshift to get her arms around him and bury her face in him, while his hands went back to their work of exploration and found a nipple.

"Diana. Professor Lady. Maybe it won't always be like this for us. Maybe we can be us. Unless you don't want to be."

"I do want to."

"Maybe we can both live off that."

* * *

The graveside service in the Catholic cemetery in Fort Maginnis was mercifully short. Even the priest wore overshoes and a black overcoat with the collar turned up. The church had been filled to the point of overflowing, but fewer stood and bowed their heads in the cold. Several of the nuns from the school and the hospital were there, including an elderly nun who still wore the full black habit under a black cloak and who hugged Evvie again and again.

Patrick Adams and his wife, their bereavement written in their faces. Evvie, wearing her stoical face and holding Cheryl's and Diana's hands. A few other old neighbors.

Jake and Henry with the other pallbearers. Getting Henry into a suit and tie had been a last-minute panic. When she learned he didn't own a suit, Evvie had given him one of Jake's grandfather's, and Henry hadn't wanted to put it on. "I'll feel like Albert's ridin on my shoulder for the rest of the day," Henry complained, "and he'll be givin me hell for borrowin his clothes without even askin!"

"May his soul and the souls of all the faithful departed through the mercy of God rest in peace."

It was over.

* * *

The reception in the parish hall, predictably laden with food. Faces that were suitably glum, lightening into considerable laughter as the afternoon waned and the punch circulated. Jake steered Diana around the hall, introducing her to LeTelliers and LaPierres and Broussards and Archambaults and Charbonneaus. Most, perhaps all, were related in ways only the old women kept track of. They were polite, shy or perhaps reserved, and they looked from her to Jake with some wonder. Jake, himself strange in dark suit and necktie. He wore his cowboy boots, though, and so did most of the men present, and Diana remembered the wedding photo of Lillia Karnov and Victor Wheeler and how she had tried to find clues in the boots Wheeler wore with his suit.

As the afternoon darkened into early evening, Diana set down the cup of punch someone had pressed on her and slipped along a corridor and into the women's room and found an empty cubicle. She sat, thankful for the few minutes of privacy as much as for the relief to her bladder, smelling her own stream, hearing a toilet in another cubicle flush, hearing quick footsteps on tile as someone left, then a door opening again on giggles.

A voice—"Who is she?"

"Big-city white bitch, I forget her name. What she's doing is easy to see. Making Jake LeTellier choose between her and his own folks."

A faucet running into a sink drowned the voices while Diana sat rigid with her skirt rucked around her hips and her toilet unflushed under her. Then the faucet was turned off—the voices resumed—

"I could go for Jake."

"Who wouldn't? He's for sure got the eyes and the Levi's."

Giggles, retreating footsteps, opening and closing of the door. Diana took several breaths. Flushed. Pulled up her underpants and tights, straightened her skirt. Rinsed her hands. Saw her own face, pale and tight in the clouded mirror. Set her chin and left the women's room.

Back in the parish hall she tried not to look for the young women she had overheard. *The eyes and the Levi's.* She saw Jake glance at the darkened windows. He caught Henry's eye and jerked his head toward the door, and Henry, from the midst of a flock of cousins and looking to have gotten over his anxiety at wearing a dead man's suit, nodded his agreement. Cattle needed to be fed. Time to cut a trail.

* * *

Evvie stopped Diana before she went upstairs to bed and sat her down in the kitchen, where the supper dishes had been washed and put away and counters wiped and the big coffee urn shut off and waiting to be put back in storage until when, branding time, Diana supposed. Whenever that was.

Except for purpose, Evvie's face was unreadable, but her dark eyes were fixed on Diana. "I'm glad you came with Jake. And I want to tell you some things."

Diana nodded, waited.

"My Jake. I think time and the Navy got most of the hell-raisin out of him, thank the Lord, but not all of it."

Evvie's electric kitchen clock hung above the sink. Its second hand was starting its slow sweep around another minute, and Diana watched it as she had watched a clock's second hand in the kitchen of the mansion in Versailles when she was sure she had lost Jake forever. The overheard conversation in the women's room at the parish hall burned into her. Was Evvie about to scold her for making Jake choose?

"He's got it better controlled now. But it's there, Diana."

Diana had a flash of Ritchie on his hands and knees, rocking back and forth. And a bruise on Abe Dennison's cheek.

Evvie's eyes turned inward for a moment. "Diana. Couple more things. First, you've been good for Jake. I wouldn't be lettin him stay with me now if I could make him leave."

Diana met the dark eyes that were so intent on her and knew she was going to hear more. Evvie smiled at her, a smile so much like Jake's that Diana's heart lurched.

"You kids. You're all alike. You've got the notion you're the first ones in the world to discover the sweetness of the flesh. You'll know better when you're a little older. And you're not the first one I've had to tell this to, that when the priest tells you you're now one flesh, it's true. You and Jake would a better waited for the priest. But that's the way of things today."

After a moment Evvie went on. "Your family, Diana? Have you got folks that are going to fret over you takin up with a breed?"

Diana felt the word *breed* like a slap. To hear it coming from Evvie's mouth was worse than Abe Dennison's *buck Indian*. And what to tell Evvie? That Diana's only living relatives would—well, *fret* wasn't a strong enough word for what Tatiana and Maria would say about anyone she *took up with*.

"It nearly killed Albert's mother when he married me, Diana. She forced herself to come to our wedding, but she said she wouldn't have a breed girl in her house. And she never did."

"I don't have much family left," Diana said, and then she thought of the senator. Would he see Jake as a breed? As a buck Indian? Or as Pat Adams's honorary grandson? Too many questions to ask, let alone answer, and so she fell back on what she knew. "I couldn't live here on the ranch, Evvie."

"No. Life out here is another thing you have to have the heart for. I had the chance to talk to Pat a little, Diana. A course Jake is his first pick to manage the ranch. But Jake's got a choice, because Pat's good and I'm good with Sam St. Pierre. Pat and Sammy and I go way back."

Evvie's smile lit her face with a dazzle of memory. "Way, way back! Sam the Substitute, and how that boy could run! Maybe he'll have his chance to substitute all over again."

She took Diana's hand and held it for a moment. "I think Jake plans to drive you into town for the morning flight before he feeds cattle. I'll be up and fixing breakfast for you. And I'll say good-bye to you then."

35

The midweek morning commuter flight from Fort Maginnis to Versailles carried only a handful of passengers. From her window seat Diana looked down on the streets and miniaturized buildings, and yes, there was Main Hall on campus, as the pilots turned on final approach. She picked out the presidential mansion on its hill above town, and then the plane set down in a bumpier landing than Jake or Chris would have executed and everyone around her reached for coats and belongings and was told through the intercom not to get in a hurry about unsnapping seatbelts.

She waited to pick up her suitcase from the cart and walk to the familiar terminal, where, sure enough, Saylor waited for her, out of uniform in Levi's and a sheepskin coat—"Good to see you, ma'am. Jake doin okay? Sure sorry to hear about his grandpa."

He took her suitcase and helped her into his truck and drove her to the mansion and got her MG started for her and left it running.

"Should do okay for you, ma'am. You happen to talk to Jake, tell him me and Daryl are makin progress."

And that was that.

* * *

The mansion echoed around her. Diana made herself coffee she didn't want and drifted through the living room. The sofa where she and Jake had loved each other. She drifted upstairs and unpacked her suitcase. The bed where she and Jake had loved each other. She thought of Evvie's words. The sweetness of the flesh.

She carried the novel Pat Adams had given her, *Winds of Morning*, back downstairs with her. *Honey in the Horn* she had thrust at

Jake in their last minutes at the Fort Maginnis airport. "Have you read this? No? Read it so we can talk about it next time."

Jake had taken the book, kissed her briefly, and turned and walked out of the little Fort Maginnis terminal without a word. Diana had watched the plate glass doors close behind him. He had not looked back.

Now the phone rang, and Diana looked at it for a moment and answered.

"Dr. Karnov?" It was the work-study student in the history department office. "That Miss Karnov keeps calling. Nelda wants to know if you can satisfy her somehow."

Satisfy Tatiana? Diana shook her head.

"I'll call her," she promised the work-study student, and hung up and went back to her mansion-drifting. At the living room window she looked out at snow-capped evergreens, the fresh tracks of Saylor's truck in the drive, and the circle of ornamental lights between her and what once had seemed endless prairie and now felt familiar after the isolation of the ranch in Murray County. A stray thought—a few months ago she would have been longing for a cigarette, to buy her time before she dialed. Could it be she really had quit smoking?

She sensed the Coyote waiting to see what she would do, and she dropped the edge of the curtain she had been holding and dialed Chris Beaudry's number.

"Sure," he said, when she asked him if she could start her flying lessons again. "I was disappointed when you quit. Saturday afternoon good for you?"

They agreed on an hour. "By the way," Chris said as Diana was about to hang up. "That student of yours? Mark the jerk Gervais? He's got himself in a world of hurt this time."

"Oh?" Diana was thinking she seldom had heard Mark's name without its being glossed as *the jerk*.

"He run off with a fifteen-year-old to California. They got most of the way to Los Angeles before the California Highway Patrol

234

caught em. We got em now—at least we got Gervais. Her mother's got the girl. She's *fifteen*."

"What's going to happen to Mark?"

She could almost hear Chris's shrug on the end of the line. "Dunno yet. Up to the county prosecutor. There's talk of filing kidnapping and statutory rape charges on him. Was up to me, I'd hang him up by his balls."

Diana thought of the boy who had wept in her office. His words. *I'm not stupid. I'm just dumb.*

She set down the receiver, sighed, picked it up again, and dialed another number. As she expected, the phone on the other end was snatched up on the first ring on an explosion in Russian and English.

"Tatiana, stop!" Diana shouted into the receiver and heard an incredulous gasp on the other end.

Never mind. "Tatiana. I have several things to tell you. First, I've had a long talk with Victor Wheeler. He's a Montana state senator now—"

"No! No! You can't mean what you're saying—"

"Let me finish. I plan to spend Christmas with him."

She didn't know if that was quite true. The senator might have called any number of times while she was in Murray County, or he might not have called at all. Never mind.

"Second. I've fallen in love with a man who services diesel trucks for a living."

She had to pause for a moment. To speak that last sentence had wrung something in her. Maybe it had wrung something in Tatiana, for Tatiana was silent.

"While I don't know whether my temporary position will be renewed, I plan to stay in Versailles and find out. And finally, Tatiana, you *must* stop badgering the history department secretary. I will call you once a week, but that's all I will do."

What she heard on the other end unnerved her. Tatiana was weeping. A thousand guilty memories flooded her. The great-aunts had taken her in. They had put their own lives on hold for her, they had fed and clothed her, they had seen to her education. They had let her curl up in the armchair in their library and read and read. Those books on those shelves. Their marks of use were histories of lives she could never read. The least she should do for Tatiana and Maria and the poor battered books left without a reader.

No. Tatiana and Maria should just be thankful they never had a fifteen-year-old Rosalie Pence on their hands. "Tatiana," she said, "enjoy your Christmas, and give my love to Maria."

* * *

"*Diana*! I've been calling and calling! *What* is going on? I've been so worried about you, so afraid you might have given in and gone back to Seattle—"

"Ramona! I'm all right."

A pause.

"Are you just not answering your phone? Why?"

"I flew to Fort Maginnis with Jake and got back this morning. I should have called you, but I was sure Jake called Con—"

"Con! The *bastard*! He never told me! Why did Jake fly to Fort Maginnis? Is he back in Versailles now?"

"No."

"Will you meet me for lunch at the Chinese restaurant?"

* * *

For the second time that morning she answered the phone.

"Diana." The senator drew out her name. "It's good to catch up with you at last. I've tried to call several times, but—"

"Vee. I was out of town, an unexpected trip to Fort Maginnis—" she caught her breath, why was she telling the senator more than she had told Ramona? "For a funeral."

A pause.

"A funeral in Fort Maginnis? Not by any chance the Albert Vanaartsdalen funeral?"

Diana was surprised, but of course Fort Maginnis was a small town, and the senator was a reader of newspapers and canvasser of voters.

"I should have gone myself," the senator went on, "but so much had come up right then. I spoke with Evangeline on the phone, of course, and I'll make a detour through Fort Maginnis and visit her the next time I travel to Helena—but Diana, Albert Vanaartsdalen, how in the world—wait. Maybe I know the answer to that."

"Tell me you haven't been making inquiries about me!"

He sounded tired. "Certainly not. Other inquiries, but not about you. But I did have dinner with Emil Maki shortly after you and I met, and he brought up your name, and of course that got my attention. He was talking about some departmental battle, apparently these things go on as often in academics as they do in politics, and I can't say I listened all that closely until he mentioned Dr. Karnov. You've got a chairman who's after your scalp, Diana?"

"He wants to fire me, if that's what you mean." Diana was scrambling to find a detour around the reasons why her chairman wanted to fire her—or, colorful image, why he *wanted her scalp*—but the senator continued.

"You mentored Albert's granddaughter? Cheryl LeTellier? And your chairman was angered at the way you went about it?"

For the second time in her life Diana was thankful to be talking about Cheryl LeTellier and not Cheryl's brother.

"He disapproved of Cheryl's approach to historical research, and he disapproved of my encouraging her. As you say in politics, battles in academe happen all the time."

"Emil said Cheryl did very well. Hmm. Diana, I don't suppose by any chance you ran into Pat Adams in Fort Maginnis?"

"Yes, I did! He gave me a book."

"He would. Pat and Albert. Two grand old men. Friends their whole lives. It's hard to watch that generation fade away. They fought in the war before mine, Diana."

A pause.

"Back to the reason I called, Diana." A long pause. "Yes, I made some inquiries, or made some calls to start inquiries, not about you, but about some people in Rockdale, Texas, twenty-eight years ago, and I've learned a few things. Maybe—well, it's taking me some time to work through what I've learned. Don't know if I ever will. Would you care to come out to the ranch for dinner one night so we can talk? I can send Zane into Versailles for you, and he'll drive you home again."

"Yes," she said, "I'd like that."

Another hesitation.

"Emil says you're friends with Albert's grandson. Jake."

Damn the dean.

* * *

"Diana, do you love him?"

The temperature in downtown Versailles was somewhere around thirty degrees below zero, but the sun shone on the papier-mâché dragon in the front window of the Chinese restaurant. Since Diana's last visit a rope of artificial greenery spangled with Christmas ornaments had been hung around the window and the dragon tilted to look up at the ornaments, as though surprised at the holiday he was celebrating. The ancient hostess tottered up to pour wine, and Diana had to smile. No job opening here for herself yet.

Ramona's question. A thought teased Diana—she'd told Tatiana she loved him, but she hadn't told Jake. And in her heart she knew as surely as Jake was making a choice, she had made hers. She might be clinging to her position at Versailles State College by her fingernails, but she wasn't letting go.

"I care about him," she said.

"And this ranch of his?"

"Not exactly his. He doesn't own it. It's more like the ranch owns him. And it's forty miles from town—from Fort Maginnis. It's not as cold there as Versailles, but it has a lot more snow. And nothing but prairie in every direction."

Ramona shook her head. "I think I told you once before. I honestly don't know if I would have married Con if I'd had the first idea what northern Montana would be like. When I was nineteen, Con was—" she sighed. "I didn't know anything. It was as though Con had blown into our suburb from a western movie. In those days he rolled his own cigarettes, which I thought was so romantic. And he was oh so handsome a young man."

She sipped her wine. "So I married him. And here I am. Diana, will you come out to the farm with us for Christmas?"

"I don't believe so. No, no, I'm not going back to Seattle. But Ramona—" What to explain to Ramona. "Do you and Con know Victor Wheeler?"

Ramona stared. "Senator Wheeler? Well, yes, but why?"

Without giving Diana a chance to answer, she went on. "He's an interesting man. There's an old tragedy in his background, a missing wife. And like a lot of politicians, I suppose, he knows almost everybody but he's close to hardly any. Although I think he and Emil Maki are friends. That's another oddity, because Emil is as liberal as they come, and Senator Wheeler, well. Though I don't think he's as reactionary as some of the people who vote for him, and I do think he's represented our district fairly. I know that when—"

Diana stopped listening to Ramona's analysis of Montana's internal politics. She had realized too late that she could not say more about the senator, could not explain her interest in him to Ramona or anyone else. The senator was a senator, after all. Did he really plan to introduce a long-lost daughter to his constituents? A decision best made by the senator himself and not by some chance words of hers.

"—but now there's a rumor going around town about Wheeler. He's never had a reputation as a skirt-chaser, but apparently he's been seen out at the Bellevue Lodge, lately, meeting a young woman.

I actually heard it from Con. I suppose he heard it from his floozy barmaid. Why did you ask?"

"Oh, I was just curious," Diana said, keeping her eyes on her glass of wine. "I saw the ERA women demonstrating against him."

Ramona shook her head. "They've tried hard, but there's been too much backlash. The Equal Rights Amendment's never going to be ratified."

36

After a vigorous discussion with Zane, who wanted to seat her by herself in the back seat while he drove her, Diana settled in the comfortable front seat of the senator's Lincoln where she could look out over the prairie north of the Milk River until the light faded. It was a harsh and broken landscape of cliffs and eroded gullies, exposed boulders and windblown snow against occasional drifts of evergreens that Zane, when pressed, explained were cedars. Cottonwoods grew along the river, he added, and willows. It was good deer-hunting country. Senator Wheeler bagged his whitetail buck every fall.

The road to the senator's ranch was well maintained, perhaps a perquisite of his office, and the drive only about ten miles. Diana hardly had time to reflect on traveling the miles driven first by Sister Holman and later by the Karnov sisters on the same frantic day twenty-eight years ago, when Zane pulled into the driveway of a substantial log house and nearly broke his neck getting around to open Diana's door for her before she could do it herself.

Zane shepherded her along a neatly shoveled walkway to an ample doorstep lighted by an overhead globe while Diana remembered Ramona's rumors, wondered how much Zane had been told about the senator's young guest, and whether that was making him so jumpy. Then the door was opened by a gray-haired woman in a dark dress and a white apron—the housekeeper the senator had spoken of—

"Welcome," the woman began, with a rigid smile, but she took a step back and stared, open-mouthed, when the light from the globe fell on Diana's face.

Senator Wheeler appeared behind her in the foyer. He looked as tired as he had sounded on the phone, and it seemed to Diana that he had aged since she had seen him, but he managed a smile for her. "Thanks, Myrna. Diana, my dear—"

Then he looked from Diana to Myrna and to Zane, who had flattened himself against a paneled wall. Meanwhile the front door stood open to freezing December until Diana reached back and shut it and found herself the focus of an audience of three.

Had to be the Coyote again, up to his old tricks.

"Senator, who is this girl?" cried Myrna. "Where is she from? How, when I thought—I mean, she's—"

"Myrna, I beg your pardon." The senator reached for Diana's hand. "I'm so sorry. It never occurred to me that you'd see what I did. I thought I'd seen a ghost."

Zane, who had been sent to inquire the ghost's identity, opened his mouth and shut it again. The anxiety he and Myrna both exuded was for the senator, Diana realized. They were worried about him.

Myrna's face was a study in questions quarreling with each other to be asked first. "Senator! What are you going to *do*?"

Excellent question, Senator. Diana watched him consider the consequences that had occurred to her. Was it possible a seasoned politician had reached blindly to acknowledge her, when every man or woman of Myrna's age who remembered his mother would see what Myrna saw and draw the same conclusions?

"What I'm going to *do*," said the senator, "is introduce my daughter to my constituents."

"Senator!"

"What do you take me for, Myrna? She's Lillia's daughter and mine."

"Oh—oh, Senator." Myrna's face crumpled. "Zane said you'd met a girl—and there are rumors floating around Versailles—and I thought—I've set the little table in the front room for you and her—"

"Nonsense." He put his arm around Myrna's shoulders. "After all the years you've known me? Zane, you should have known better, too. Thinking I'd taken to chasing women half my age."

Zane had gone scarlet.

Diana wondered if the Coyote still thought she was unsocialized. She thought she was sorting out the various threads of this storm of a situation almost as well as Ramona would have. But she wished she knew what was troubling the senator.

"Bud's staying over in Great Falls tonight, isn't he?" the senator said. "I thought so. You've cooked enough for yourself and Zane, haven't you, Myrna? So set the table in the kitchen like you always do, only set it for four. It'll give you and Zane a chance to get acquainted with Diana. She and I can have our talk over wine after dinner."

* * *

The senator poured wine while he and Diana sat in leather armchairs by a crackling fire. Diana thought the senator's ranch house looked much as the Vanaartsdalen—*Adams*—ranch house must have looked in its glory days. Pat Adams hadn't done much for his house beyond basic modernizing of plumbing and electricity, or maybe Evvie had loved her home so much that she liked watching its furnishings age with her. But here were polished wood floors, rugs, plenty of books in bookshelves. The sweet odor of potpourri rising from a bowl on the low table before the fire, evidence of Myrna, the careful housekeeper. And over the fireplace behind the senator, the portrait of the red-haired woman in a dark green silk dress.

Myrna and her husband had worked for him for years, the senator had explained. Ranch manager and housekeeper. Of course they'd known his mother. And they'd known the girl in the blue dress who stepped off a train in Versailles, Montana, and married the young rancher and then vanished.

"The right thing to do," the senator answered the question Myrna had asked. "Only thing to do, Diana, unless you'd rather go to live in Seattle and never come back. We'll be a nine-day's wonder in the newspapers. Folks that want to believe the worst about me will go on believing it. The ones that care about me will be happy for me.

You might get a little more attention than you want, but it won't last. Something else always comes along. Where trouble would come would be trying to hide it."

Diana watched his face. He was hiding something now. Was it his Texas investigator's report?

"I hope you've decided to spend Christmas with me, Diana. I always have some friends, some staff, for Christmas dinner. I'll introduce you as my daughter, and we can get on with living."

Over dinner the senator also had spun out time, reminiscing about Pat Adams and Albert Vanaartsdalen. He'd worked for Pat a couple of summers when he was in high school, and Pat had taught him to ride. "Pat Adams on a horse. Something to remember. Do you ride, Diana? Would you like to ride with me when winter's over?"

"I've never ridden a horse."

"You were more a little girl on a bicycle on Seattle sidewalks?"

"Not that, either." Diana told him a little about her great-aunts' house where the draperies were always closed to shut out the sunlight, where other children never ventured, and where her main companions were the scarred and lonely books on shelves that were never dusted.

The senator nodded. "Lillia told me about her life there. What she was running from."

"And yet she named me for them. Diana Maria."

"Diana with a difference. We talked about it—if the baby was a girl, Lillia wanted her to have Tatiana's backbone, but with a difference."

Their conversation dwindled. Diana felt the Coyote nip at her ear and knew what she had to do. She cleared her throat. "Vee, I don't understand. Lillia got as far as Versailles and she married you. It wasn't as though Tatiana and Maria could drag her back physically to Seattle. Or legally drag her back. Why would she run away again?"

"I've asked myself that, often enough, since my investigator in Rockdale called." The senator scoured his face with his hand. "She'd been under her aunts' thumbs from babyhood. The only life she knew. She didn't even know how to drive a car until I taught her. And then she met the Holman woman."

"So there was a Sister Holman."

"Damned right there was. Still is. My man in Rockdale talked to her and took notes, and he's going to send me a transcript, but I got the gist of it from him over the phone. And everything I ever felt sure of—" he tilted his wine glass and watched the legs sink down into the wine—"is in the dregs."

A pause. "What the Holman woman told him. She'd driven all the way to Versailles from Texas to visit a cousin. Lillia was in town, doing some shopping, and the Holman woman met her on the street and thought she looked unhappy. Took it as her mission in life to befriend her. They started meeting when Lillia came to town to shop, and apparently Holman drove out here a number of times, though I never saw her."

He stood, tended the fire, and watched the flames for a moment. Diana saw his face in the flickering light as it might look in ten or twenty years.

"I'm not clear how Holman found out the Karnov sisters were in Versailles. Maybe from the hotel clerk. Or maybe she recognized them from Lillia's description. Woman should have gone into investigative work herself. She called Lillia to warn her, and Lillia was terrified—I wasn't there, I was feeding cattle—and Holman jumped in her car and tore out here to save her. Once they got back to town, Holman packed up her own things in a hurry and headed with Lillia to Texas."

"So that's why Tatiana and Maria never were able to trace Lillia from Versailles." Diana pieced the story together, wondering which part of it had devastated the senator. "No train tickets, no bus tickets. Nobody else knew she and Sister Holman were friends. And maybe the cousin saw her license plates, but had no reason to connect Sister Holman and her car with a ranch woman gone missing north of town. Otherwise, nothing but tire tracks in the snow."

"Yes. I think I was a suspect for a while. Man kills wife for some reason, says he's as baffled by her disappearance as anybody. Oh, hell."

Long pause. "What else he told me, Diana. What Holman's pastor told him. Do you know what a Boston marriage was, or maybe is?"

A Boston marriage. Fragments from an undergraduate class on Henry James. A novel he had written, although Diana couldn't recall the title, about two women in a romantic friendship. "Ye-es, I think so," she ventured.

The senator stared at his wine glass. "Had to have it explained to me. I never heard of such a thing, myself. I have to say it shook me. What Holman told her pastor. Pastor was still shocked by it, my man said, even though Lillia was years dead."

Another long silence. Diana waited. Sooner or later the senator's story was going to sink in, but for now she only felt blank.

"I could see why Lillia might have run away, but why didn't she write to me?" the senator went on. "Why didn't she let me know where she was? I would have come for her, no matter what. And our baby—" his voice broke.

A burning log broke and fell into the flames.

"I loved Lillia, and I always thought she loved me. Now I have to think I was nothing but a convenience. Did she love Holman? My investigator thinks Holman loved her."

Flitting at the dark edges of Diana's thoughts, helping to fill in blanks, was silvery-haired Annabel, who had loved Diana. Would Annabel have run away with Diana, driven her as far from Texas as Montana, as Sister Holman apparently had driven Lillia in reverse?

"I never even knew two women—men, hell yes, I was in the Marines, and even here in Montana, you'll find two old bachelors setting up housekeeping together, not that it's talked about openly, but I never dreamed, never supposed that *women*—"

What Diana could tell the senator about women's liaisons with women. About herself and Annabel. Would he feel better or worse? She decided not to chance it. "How did Lillia die?"

"My man in Rockdale looked up her death certificate. Took him a while, she was calling herself Lillia Holman."

Father unknown on Diana's birth certificate. Tatiana and Maria, knowing full well the name of Diana's father, must have substituted *Karnov* when they petitioned for legal custody of her.

"Seems the drive down from Montana was long and difficult. Camping out at night, cooking over campfires, jouncing in Holman's old car during the day—and the roads twenty-eight years ago would have been considerably worse than they are today. Lillia barely made it to Rockdale. Long and short of it, she went into labor a few weeks early. She died bringing you into the world, Diana."

She left behind that little bit of a baby. Words that had haunted Diana over the years, now filling in more blank spaces and making her hands tremble on the stem of her wineglass.

"Holman kept you until you were five before she wrote to the Karnov women—don't know why she wrote, maybe her Christian duty, but my man in Rockdale says she got real cagey when he asked her about that, and he doesn't know, but he thinks money changed hands."

Diana winced. "So I was bought and paid for."

A swirl of wine in his glass, a long moment of consideration. "At any rate, the Karnovs sent for you. And Holman said they paid to have Lillia dug up and shipped to Seattle. My man in Rockdale thinks Holman's been on her uppers for years. Still lives in a little old house on the outskirts of Rockdale, next to a defunct filling station."

Tall grass, the odor of gasoline and road tar.

"Diana, I've had plenty of time to think about Lillia. She was only eighteen. You're twenty-eight. You had five years of more or less normal childhood, running around in the sun and the weeds with other kids. When you were older, you doubled down and finished your education, even if you had to fight the Karnovs for it, which meant you could depend on yourself. You were Diana with a difference."

Yes, Diana had learned to depend on herself, even if the lesson the great-aunts had tried to drill into her was *depend only on us*. But Lillia. As immature as fifteen-year-old Rosalie Pence and just as set on following her star, perhaps what Lillia had learned was how to be devious.

She stole from us, Maria had raged. *She skimmed off the housekeeping money. We thought the housekeeper was stealing it, even though Juana worked for us for years. We fired Juana for it!*

Diana imagined the fair-haired girl stealing into the kitchen of the Karnov house, knowing in which cabinet drawer Juana kept the housekeeping money, slipping out a dollar or two each week until her hidden stash grew large enough to buy her ticket on the train. The housekeeper—*she'd worked for us for years!*—must have known money was missing. Had the housekeeper covered for Lillia and lost her job as a result, while Lillia skipped off to the train station, bought her ticket and traveled as far as Versailles, where she attracted the attention of the young Victor Wheeler and took shelter on his ranch? And had Lillia then attracted the attention of a young Sister Holman, who eloped to Texas with her?

A small red-haired girl in the library of the Karnov house, looking up from her book to the darkened window where the ghost of an even smaller fair-haired girl hovered—Diana was struck by a thought. The senator's bookshelves held well-worn volumes whose titles she hoped to scan—"Vee, did Lillia like to read?"

"I've never thought about it," he said, surprised. "But I don't recall her ever opening a book. Does it matter?"

"No." But Diana's mind was filling with images that crowded images. Her small self, reading her way through the Karnov library, reading books that must have been far above her understanding. How had the little fair-haired girl spent her days in the rambling, silent Karnov mansion? And when she was eighteen, marrying Victor Wheeler and hiding here on the ranch, how had she spent her days surrounded by a landscape of river cliffs and eroded gullies, wind-twisted cedars and miles of snow? How long had the ten-mile drive from Versailles seemed to her? Diana shivered, recalling miles of high prairie and snow in Murray County.

Lillia must have had a way of drawing people to her, people who wanted to protect her. Victor Wheeler. Sister Holman. The shadowy Juana. Diana herself when she imagined the little fair-haired girl, not as her mother, but like a fragile younger sister.

The senator turned from the fire, which he had been tending, and the anguish on his face rent Diana. He touched his wedding ring. "I never thought I'd take it off."

"I hope you don't, Vee," she said, and saw him try to smile. "Lillia's buried in the old Russian cemetery in Seattle," she added. "Maybe we can visit it one day."

"I'd like that."

"Vee? I'd love to learn to ride. If Pat Adams taught you, you must be good enough to teach me," she said, and saw something lighten in the senator's face.

"That's a promise," he said.

"What those old harpies must have done to her."

He shook his head. "Diana. Think of two educated women who are in their eighties now. Fifty or so years ago, they were a hopeful politician and a hopeful young lawyer coming up against a man's world. They had reasons to be bitter. Reasons to protect Lillia from that world, the best way they knew. And to protect you. You may not believe it, Diana, but I know those ERA women have reasons to shout and chant."

Then he surprised her again. "Diana. Jake LeTellier had his wilder days, but he's Albert's grandson and Pat's grandson of the heart, and he's a good man."

"I'm afraid he's married to a ranch in Murray County."

"It does get in your blood," he said gently.

37

A few days before the winter quarter began, Diana glanced out and saw an old tan Plymouth pull around the circular drive and stop in front of the mansion. She ran out the front door as Cheryl stepped from her car.

"You came back!"

To Diana's surprise, Cheryl dropped her shoulder bag into the snow and embraced her.

"If you had let me know, I'd have had a bedroom ready for you."

"I couldn't make up my mind. Grandma told me last night, 'Just do it, girl,' and I knew she was right. Jake called old Pete, and he had my car plugged in and warmed up and ready for me when Big Scare landed this morning. Jake said you told him you had room for me, but I can find somewhere else if you'd rather not."

"Of course I want you to stay with me! Let me help with your things."

"Only if you put a coat on! Look at you!"

Diana looked down at herself. Thin sweater, blue jeans, bedroom slippers. She hadn't taken time this morning to do more than finger-comb her hair and braid it. With only these few days of grace before classes started, she hoarded every minute for her writing. Even as she greeted Cheryl, even as questions flooded her that she wanted to ask Cheryl and wouldn't ask—*why hasn't Jake at least called me?*—the electric typewriter hummed in her head.

She ran for a coat and came back and saw Cheryl had set down her suitcase and was lifting out a cardboard box that looked heavy.

"Grandma sent us some frozen beef," she explained, and at Diana's blank look, "from last fall's butchering. Grandma has plenty for herself in the locker at the creamery. If you don't have freezer space, we can maybe keep it outside, somewhere it doesn't attract coyotes." She looked up at the little balcony over the formal entryway. "Up there, maybe."

"Wouldn't the garage be easier?"

Cheryl grinned. "Getting it up on that balcony would be more fun!"

"Okay. Have you had breakfast?"

"You think Grandma would let me leave without cooking breakfast for me? But I'd drink a cup of coffee."

Diana made a fresh pot of coffee while Cheryl chattered.

"Hope I can run an extension cord from the garage and plug in my car at night. I can hardly wait for classes to start. Wish you were teaching something besides surveys. Professor Schultz is teaching sociological theory, and he said I could sign up for it. I'd have loved to take European history, but Dennison—no way. So instead I signed up for a creative writing class in the English department. Ever since I did my project on oral history with you, I've been thinking about stories and how to write them."

Diana thought if she were writing stories instead of collecting and studying them, she might write a novel about Lillia. The girl in *Honey in the Horn* had run away, she remembered, and been found again. Maybe writing a novel would be a way of exploring why Lillia had run away from Victor Wheeler.

"This will be the first quarter, Diana, I can stay on campus, in the library as long as I want, and study at home, and write, as late as I need to, without—"

Cheryl interrupted herself. Stared into her coffee cup.

"Without Ritchie?" Diana ventured, and Cheryl nodded.

"I'm Catholic, Diana. I've had to choose."

"I see. So you can't divorce and remarry."

"No. And Ritchie—Diana, I didn't *know* anything. And oh, Diana, he was astride his motorcycle, and when he smiled at me with the sun in his hair, and his cigarette pack rolled in the sleeve of his T-shirt—"

Handsome Con Stillinger, blown out of a movie into Versailles, Montana. Handsome blond Ritchie, riding into Versailles on a motorcycle. Mark the jerk Gervais and his dumb love. Quite a lesson in romance Diana was getting. The Coyote was laughing at her.

"Now I can't go near him—"

Diana didn't know if Cheryl couldn't go near Ritchie out of fear or from regret. "What about things in your apartment? You must have clothes there, at least—"

"He won't let me have any of them. Jake told me to ask Chris Beaudry to help me get my stuff back, but I don't want to. I want to get by with what I've got, and I want to start classes, and I want to live in my head for a while."

"That's what I've been doing," said Diana. "It works pretty well for a while."

* * *

Diana's current absorption with the nature of narrative reminded her of her graduate school days, when an electric typewriter had been her gift to herself when she began to write the final draft of her dissertation. After years of hammering the keys of her old Smith-Corona, she was taken aback by the discreet hum of her new Coronamatic and its instant response to the touch of a fingertip. At first the keyboard seemed to race ahead of her fingers, but with practice she caught up to it. She had the spooky sensation that her thoughts were being transported directly to the page, but that too faded as she surrendered to the warm heart and the hum of the Coronamatic.

During that dissertation-writing year, with the electric typewriter as the outward manifestation of living in her head, Diana had torn through the minimal grooming necessary to be presentable in class, rinsed a dish when she needed it, and stuffed down food without tasting it, forgot to set out her trash, and let dust balls take over her apartment. Skipped all the graduate parties, turned down invitations to coffee dates, slept only when she couldn't help it.

Later, when she looked back on the year she spent writing and polishing her dissertation, it seemed the most serene period in her life, because after she finished her dissertation and passed her orals, she returned to the great-aunts' house in Seattle, chafed, and found the advertisement that touched off their explosion—the ad in the Seattle *Times* for a temporary assistant professor of history at Versailles State College, in Montana—and set in motion everything that had happened since.

In time she would finish writing this book about multiple narratives. Then what.

* * *

Diana woke in the night from a dream she couldn't remember and propped herself up in bed. The darkness was peaceful for the time being. A branch tapped against the window. Below the window, along the invisible river, the lights of Versailles lay far-flung and scattered, sparse along the edges of the night that reached for Canada and denser around the few blocks of downtown. From here she imagined she could see the leaping colors of the bars. The Montana Club, the Hackamore, the Jubilee, the Palace, the Silver Dollar, the Stockman's, the Alibi, and more. She had counted the bars of Versailles once, and there were twenty-four, in a town with a population of ten thousand. By now, just before dawn, the bars would be closed, their parking lots empty. Even the stacks of railroad ties by the Palace, where in daylight the drunks sat with their bottles in paper sacks, would be empty now.

Where did the drunks go when it was thirty degrees below zero and dark?

Jake and the black kid from Philadelphia had been renovating a house north of the river that Con owned, Ramona told her. Putting up insulation and installing a decent oil heater. Then they're going to move those hippies, the ones with the kids, into it for the winter, Ramona said. At least, the black kid and Saylor are going to move them in. Saylor started helping the black kid when Jake left.

Diana had to smile, recalling her last conversation with Ramona.

"Senator Wheeler! He was seen having dinner with *you*! Diana, you never told me!"

"It was complicated."

Diana clicked off her bedside lamp and saw her own reflection appear in the dark window and heard, far away, the hum of a motorcycle. No, an airplane at high altitude and outward bound over unconscious Versailles. And she still had not remembered what she needed to remember, but her reflection looked back at her, and then yes, she did.

The sweetness of the flesh. The groove along his spine where his lateral muscles met. The smell of semen, the smell of her own fluids. Oh Jake. The weeks she'd wasted when she didn't know she wanted him, the short time they'd had. A few nights in Versailles and a frantic few moments in the cab of a truck in the shadows of pines.

"Why haven't you called me, Jake?" she whispered into the dark.

The Coyote snorted. *The telephone rings both ways. Why haven't you called him?*

Because it would hurt too much, and it wouldn't change anything. *There's your answer.*

* * *

A few days before the start of the winter quarter Douglas also returned to Versailles from Portland, where he'd been visiting his mother. He called and asked Diana to meet him for a drink at the bar in the Bellevue, where, Diana reflected, Ramona was unlikely to risk the knowing eyes of those in her social circle.

"It's easy to forget how cold it is here," Douglas sighed over his martini. "Once you're over the Cascades and down to the Columbia River, everything is mild and green. If I don't get tenure, at least there will be that."

"You'd go back to Portland?"

"Oh, I'll apply for jobs, but yes—my mother's not well, you know, and she'd like to have me closer. I can always substitute-teach in one of the Portland high schools. At least it'll be better than teaching high school in North Dakota."

"Teaching isn't the only work in the world," Diana said, thinking of her own daydream of waitressing in a wine bar. Not something she would ever do. Or would she.

"I love teaching. I think I was born for it. What I hate is the uncertainty. Hoping for tenure. You've got the drive to get ahead, Diana, I've seen it in you, but I just don't. I could be so happy teaching my classes, maybe getting a class in the Romantic period to teach—friends—a quiet lounge to have a drink at the end of the day. A few of us are trying to get a couple tables of bridge organized. Do you play bridge, Diana?"

"No."

"Somehow I didn't think so."

Douglas rambled on about his hopes and fears while Diana freed her mind to reach the obvious. Oregon. Douglas. A scholar trained in the critical reading of literary texts.

"Douglas," she interrupted, "have you read a novel by H. L. Davis called *Honey in the Horn*?"

"In high school," he said, surprised. "It used to get passed around as a dirty book. It's set in Oregon, you know. Why do you ask? I didn't think historians read novels."

"We usually don't. Especially all that modernist uncertainty. We like certainties." Diana paused, thinking of the uncertainties in her own life. "Except I'm starting to believe that certainty—about what happened—is more complex than we were taught. I'm beginning to *see what happened* as less a single narrative and more of a weave."

Douglas thought about that. "It sounds like some of the new literary theory coming out of France, which I don't understand, but maybe you'd be interested. And I'll see if I've still got my copy of *Honey in the Horn* and refresh my memory."

He finished his martini and fiddled with the plastic spear that had been stuck through the olive. "Diana, have you seen Ramona?"

"We had lunch the other day."

"She—I—" he raised stricken eyes to Diana's, then looked away. "I did a lot of thinking while I was in Portland. I don't think she'll ever leave Con for me. And I—I just can't."

Diana watched a single tear roll down his cheek and felt an unexpected sympathy for the kind, foolish, conflicted man he was. She reached across the table and took the plastic spear away from him, and he clutched her fingers for a few moments before he let her go.

"Well. Must run!" He laughed his annoying laugh. "I haven't unpacked from Portland yet." But he hesitated. "Diana, um, thanks."

38

On campus the winter quarter was set for its sprint toward the spring quarter, and January skidded on its way toward February, and the presidential mansion became a different place with Cheryl in it. Diana thought more than once what a bad choice Ritchie the Bastard made when he threw her out. Cheryl shook her head over Diana's bread and cheese and empty refrigerator, went grocery shopping, came back with sacks of root vegetables and salad greens, and thawed a slab of round steak to cube for stew. She rummaged the kitchen cabinets for a kettle and skillet and muttered dark things about the bastard Ritchie's keeping her out of her own kitchen, where she had just the right knives and knew where to find them. Nonetheless a rich aroma soon arose from the stewpot she dug out from under the sink and which she judged by its dents to be the property of Versailles State College.

Like her brother, Cheryl thought a fireplace in the winter was a place to build a fire. When the firewood stored behind the paneled door next to the fireplace began to run short, she called someone she knew and ordered a cord to be delivered, grumbling that she and Diana might have to move out when the new college president arrived, but meanwhile they might as well be warm. And the living room indeed became warm with the comfort of a hearth with flickering flames. Diana had to smile. Would Sister Holman's pastor think she and Cheryl were in a Boston marriage?

Cheryl appropriated an overstuffed chair and ottoman in a corner near the fireplace, where she curled like a cat and spread out her books and notes and drafts of last quarter's assigned papers. Her clutter drifted to the carpet. Paper clips spilled, pens and pencils rolled into corners, and the mansion seemed to wake from a long nap. Diana brought her electric typewriter into the living room and plugged it in amid stacks of books. Remembering Pat Adams and his fondness for used bookstores, she consulted Bob at the Versailles bookstore and discovered that oh, yes, Bob had catalogs, no need to travel to Missoula or Albuquerque. She continued her slow quest to put her thoughts about stories—narratives—the history, the histories—the weave—into words.

* * *

One evening when Diana and Cheryl had settled in for quiet hours with books and typewriters, the wind, which had almost died down, came back to life with an angry vengeance and hit the eaves of the mansion with a howl and a blast that brought them running to the window. In the glow of the ornamental lights, the evergreens around the driveway thrashed and flailed in an agony of resistance, as though they were fighting not to be pulled out by their roots.

"What on earth?" said Diana. "A hurricane?"

Cheryl's eyes shone. "It's a chinook!"

"What's a chinook?"

"Did you see the temperature on the bank's thermometer today? Wasn't it like minus thirty-five?"

"I think so."

"You just watch. That wind came over the mountains from the Pacific coast and sank, because it's warm and it's dry, and it's hit us with all it's got. We could be fifty degrees above zero in an hour or two!"

"This snow will melt?"

"Yes! We wait for chinooks all winter. Sometimes we get two or three. They give us a little break when we need it. My grandpa used to be so happy when a chinook wind blew, on account of his cattle. That artist that painted the picture of my grandpa? Charlie Russell? He also painted a picture of a cow starving in the snow and titled it *Waiting for a Chinook*."

They stood at the window, watching the battle between the wind and the evergreens. Diana could feel Cheryl's exuberance. She too was finding something exhilarating in the struggling trees and the howl and force of the wind, like the surge of life and hope itself.

"Won't last, of course. A day or two and winter'll be back."

* * *

Winter did come back, as did Diana's routine of starting the MG and warming its motor and easing over slippery streets to campus. Main Hall looked unnaturally clean and smelled of wax and polish after the time the janitors had had the building to themselves. Diana felt almost happy to be back as she found her office key and opened the door. She had come to campus early to sort through materials before her morning survey class, and she liked the feeling of the academic seasonal shift, a new beginning with the beginning of a term and the illusion of getting everything right with her classes this time around and getting over a diesel man who was owned by a patch of land.

She was jerked from her thoughts and back into the freshly waxed corridor outside her office door by a prickling sensation at the back of her neck that ran down between her shoulder blades.

"*You bitch!*"

Diana turned. Abe Dennison stood within a couple of feet of her, close enough for her to smell his acrid odor and feel the rage he exuded. He'd cast off his suit jacket somewhere, and his shirt under his armpits was soaked with sweat.

"Happy New Year, Abe," she said.

For a moment she thought he was going to hit her. His fists were clenched, his arms rigid, and an ugly vein throbbed above his shirt collar.

"One of these days you're going to get exactly what's coming to you, *Diana*! Exactly what you get for the ball-breaking bitch you are!—Indian-loving *bitch*—I'll have you fired for indecency, and I'll have that son of a bitch in court! He's a *boxer*!"

His voice was so loud and furious that a pair of passing students turned and stared, and across the corridor George Schultz peered around his office door to see what was going on. Abe seemed to remember where he was and collected himself. He glared at the students and strode off.

George Schultz looked an astonished question at Diana, but she shrugged and walked into her office and laid her books and files on her desk and asked herself why she didn't feel more rattled. Abe's behavior had been so unexpected and bizarre that, except for George and the students, she couldn't quite believe it had happened.

Worse than his sulking during the departmental calculation of senior seminar grades. Worse, even, than his tantrum in front of Ramona. And now her first survey class would be waiting for her in a few minutes, and she had to drag her mind back to the state of industrialism after the Civil War.

Her telephone rang, and she wondered what next, but she picked it up and answered.

"Dr. Karnov? I'm calling for Dean Maki. The dean wonders if you could drop by his office?"

"I have a class in ten minutes. Maybe after class?"

"About nine thirty, then? Thanks!"

* * *

The college recently had purchased one of the new Xerox machines and installed it in the administrative wing of Main Hall, but the lines to use the photocopying were endless, so Nelda dug out her old ditto machine and set it back up in her office. This morning Diana called roll and passed out the copies of her winter-quarter syllabus that Nelda had run off for her. Some of the students held the sheets to their noses, like children, to sniff the ditto fluid, and Diana had to smile.

Many of the students' faces in the lecture room were familiar from last quarter's survey classes, and their names were coming back to her. No Mark the Jerk, of course. His legal troubles were just beginning. Diana spared him a sigh for being dumb and in love. She explained all the requirements and expectations for the class, which were spelled out in the syllabus but which many students wouldn't bother to read, and then she launched into an outline of the changing industrial landscape of America after the Civil War, which she would start to fill in on Wednesday.

Sometimes the seventy minutes of a class period could seem to evaporate, sometimes they seemed endless. Diana had expected her upcoming meeting with the dean to drag this one into slow motion. But the pale winter sunlight fell through the tall east-facing windows, and the students scribbled dutifully, and the hands of the clock at the front of the room turned behind her back, and the period concluded with a noisy scraping of desks and stacking of books and chatter of young voices as some of the students hurried out while others with familiar faces stopped to visit with her.

She considered returning to her office to drop off her books and files, but Dean Maki's office was at the other end of Main Hall and up a floor, and it was nearly nine thirty by the time the last returning student had wished her a happy New Year. With her arms full, she dodged her way through the jangle of students leaving classes and sprinting for other classes, climbed a flight of stairs to the third floor, and found the secretary's door open.

The dean's secretary, a white-haired woman whose name Diana couldn't remember, looked up from her typing—an IBM Selectric, Diana couldn't help noticing, with the rotating golf ball of font that was IBM's innovation and everybody's envy—and smiled at her.

"The dean is expecting you."

Dean Maki stood as Diana entered and reached across his desk to shake her hand. Winter light fell on his thatch of thick white hair and deepened the etchings of his face. He guided her to a chair and spoke the pleasantries that she supposed were obligatory—"You had a pleasant holiday, I hope? Surviving this long stretch of cold weather? Looking forward to your classes this quarter?"

"Yes," Diana said. She'd seen Dean Maki and his wife at the senator's Christmas dinner party, had said hello and wished them a merry Christmas when they wished her one, but she didn't suppose he would mention that meeting this morning.

The dean's face had changed, and he steepled his hands on his desk. "Dr. Karnov."

A pause. The dean gazed out the window, as though expecting a revelation, and Diana thought she could write the script for the rest of this unexpected—well, not an unexpected meeting.

So good of you to help us out on short notice. We know you tried hard. But our feeling is—

The dean gave up on receiving a revelation from the snowy hill and bare trees below Main Hall and returned to Diana.

"Dr. Karnov. I'll be calling the history department to a meeting in the conference room this afternoon. Mrs. Murray is scheduling it as we speak, although I haven't yet spoken to any of the faculty, except, well, when John Bowman—our chief academic officer, I mean our acting president—when John and I spoke to Dr. Dennison earlier this morning, and now to you."

He took a deep breath and let it out. "You'll understand there are certain legal procedures to observe, and I'll ask you not to discuss our meeting until I can bring the full history faculty together."

Diana nodded. Just as she hadn't known how much she wanted Jake until she lost him, she hadn't let herself know with certainty that the teaching position, even more than the isolation of the Murray County ranch, was why she had chosen to return to Versailles. Her students—the book she was writing—living her own life.

"John and I had several long discussions during the past quarter and they ran over into the Christmas break."

Another deep breath. Diana watched as a black-capped bird perched on the window sill, peered through the glass at her and the dean, and winged off on its own business.

"We felt so fortunate to recruit Dr. Dennison. To bring a man with a PhD from Brown University to Versailles State College. But now—"

Diana was trying to focus, trying to collect her impressions of the dean's words and fit them into meaning, but they skittered off into the dust on the edge of a bookshelf, found a forgotten ballpoint pen under the dean's desk, and lit on a collection of diplomas and awards framed in black and hanging on the wall behind him.

Dean Maki was looking squarely at her. "I've never seen a department chairman with worse judgment. Insisting on impossible curriculum changes, quarreling with the food service director, quarreling with the book store manager, insulting students—and believe me, Dr. Karnov, it's common knowledge that he's been mistreating you. John and I knew we had to face the situation. We can't fire him because we made the mistake—*I* made the mistake—of hiring him with tenure. We were so eager to recruit him. But he will no longer be the chairman of the history department."

Astonishment brought Diana's impressions skittering back. "Dean Maki, are you going to take over the department?"

"No. We're going to ask you to accept the chairmanship."

He looked wildly at the ceiling. "Dr. Karnov, we've got accreditation coming up. The chairs of departments must have the appropriate terminal degrees. In the case of the history department, the PhD degree."

Herself and Abe. The only two of the history faculty with the requisite degrees. And she didn't have to ask if Abe had been told. "So that leaves me?"

"We know you're competent, and your student evaluations are strong for a first-year professor. We'll promote you as appropriate, and you'll be eligible for tenure."

He managed a half-smile. "Not tenure right away. Not a mistake I'll be repeating. And I know chairing a department that includes Dr. Dennison may be difficult."

Diana wondered how long it would take George Schultz to reach the dean's ear with the scene he'd witnessed outside the history offices that morning. She had a vision of George's story spreading wings of its own and swooping up and down the corridors of Main Hall.

"How long do I have to decide, Dean Maki?"

The smile turned rueful. "Until I can schedule the meeting with the history faculty."

* * *

Diana wandered back downstairs to her office. Nelda waved at her when she looked in for coffee—"Haven't had one of those phone calls in a week!"

"Good."

She had made the promised weekly call to Tatiana and sensed her mix of simmering anger and desperation, but Tatiana hadn't made any threats or ordered Diana back to Seattle. Even Maria had spoken shakily into the phone for a few minutes. What else, after all, could they do?

"So there's going to be a department meeting this afternoon?" remarked Nelda. "Came up in a hurry, didn't it? Wonder what's going on."

Diana wondered what she was going to tell the dean, while the Coyote threw back his head and howled his glee: *Just the woman for the job!*

Another voice, superimposed on the Coyote's: *One thing I have learned about you, Professor Lady. Dare you to do something, and you'll do it.*

39

Friday night grew late. Cheryl thawed and browned a package of her grandmother's hamburger, and she chopped onions and green peppers, and she started a simmering pot with beans and chili powder. As the kitchen grew fragrant she sliced the bread she had found time to bake, and she and Diana ate buttered bread and chili and sipped homemade chokecherry wine in the luxury of the weekend waiting ahead. Now Diana looked up from her sentence she was retyping and saw Cheryl dozing over her textbook in her armchair while the fire burned low. Nearly midnight, too late now to build up the fire, time to let it burn out.

Did a small fair-haired girl tap at the window? Was that child Lillia? Or was her hair red-gold and was she Diana with a difference? What had become of that Diana?

She had become a work in progress, Diana thought. Allowing herself to plan for chairing the history department. Scheduling classes. Working with students. Considering the curriculum, seeing if the crusty old fossils in the department were willing to consider changes. Asking Dean Maki to reprise his class in cultural history—

Headlights turned on the road from the highway. Disappeared when the road dipped. Reappeared. Approached the mansion, growing stronger. They swung around the circle drive. Went dark.

A knock came at the door, progressively louder and more insistent. Cheryl roused, and she and Diana looked at each other—at this hour?—and Diana went into the foyer to open the door to the full arctic blast.

Backlit by the glow of the ornamental lights, the figure on the doorstep was a dark silhouette in a glitter of frost crystals. Outline of hat, shape of shoulders in a heavy coat. Diana stared at the illusion until it spoke.

"My grandma told me Sam and Henry were doin just fine, and she said she didn't like to see me hangin around lookin sad, and then she asked me what I wanted most."

The black-and-white dog burst from behind his heels, wagging and joyous—

"Oh, Tip!"

"You won't leave me standin out here alone in the cold, will you, Professor Lady?"

Lightning Source UK Ltd.
Milton Keynes UK
UKHW012128280719
346921UK00012B/189/P